I0780954

RETRIBUTE

VENGEANCE AND VAMPIRES BOOK FOUR

ALICIA RADES

Copyright © 2019 Alicia Rades

All rights reserved. No part of this book may be used or reproduced in any matter whatsoever without written permission from the author except in brief quotations used in articles and reviews.

This is a work of fiction. Names, characters, places, and incidents are either the product of the author's imagination or are used fictitiously, and any resemblance to actual persons, living or dead, business establishments, events or locales is entirely coincidental.

Published by Crystallite Publishing LLC.
Produced in the United States of America.
Edited by Megan Linski.
Cover design by KnesArt.

To my fans, who make writing possible.

When you've been stripped of everything, the only thing left to hold on to is your free will. Matias Vayne was trying pretty damn hard to rip that away from us, too. No one should have that kind of power.

Even Valkas, the most ruthless vampire in history, hadn't stooped that low. When he'd imprisoned blood slaves on his island, he gave them time to do as they pleased. Valkas knew how valuable free will was—and that even slaves needed a bit of it to comply to bigger demands.

Matias thought this was the only way to cleanse the world. He thought he was the only one who could handle free will, that everyone else would only use it against each other. But when you take it away from someone, you strip them of their humanity—of what makes them unique.

Everyone had a choice, and Matias was making the wrong one.

I paced back and forth in Genevieve's living room, my hands fisting at my sides. The room was just as lavish as the rest of the house, with dark walls, velvety red couches, and a black chandelier hanging over the coffee table. The news played on the big-screen TV across the room, but I could hardly process what the newscasters were saying.

"He's holding our magic hostage!" I growled under my breath.

With The Wise Owl in his hands, Matias had the power to block magic from every witch and shifter on the planet. I wasn't sure what I was madder about—the fact that the heartless bastard had done it, or the fact that I'd let him.

I didn't know, I kept telling myself—but I couldn't shake the guilt settling like heavy rocks in the pit of my stomach.

"Rachel," Jenna sighed. She turned to me from where she sat on one of the dark red couches. "Take a breath and sit down."

How could I breathe at a time like this?

It'd only been a day since we escaped Gregor Island, freed the blood slaves trapped there, and returned to Genevieve's. We left the Soulless up to the Department of Magical Regulation after calling in an anonymous tip. The vampire curse was broken now, which was exactly what Matias had wanted all along. He used to be a vampire, unable to perform magic. Now without the curse holding him back, he had access to his witch magic again, and he was using it to manipulate a powerful artifact that severed any supernaturals' connection to Synchrony at his command. He was now the most powerful man alive.

Jenna's eyes pleaded with me, causing me to pause. Words she'd spoken to me on Gregor Island came rushing back. I could wallow in my regret all day, but it didn't change what Matias had done. The only thing we could do was decide how to handle it going forward.

I inhaled a deep breath and sank into the empty spot beside Venn. He reached out and curled his warm fingers around mine. I felt that weight in my stomach ease slightly.

Venn didn't look good. We all looked like crap, but he looked particularly rough. I guess that was what nearly being turned into a vampire did to you. His eyes looked hollow, and his lips were dry and cracked.

He almost looked as bad as Sondra, who sat curled beneath a blanket on the couch opposite us. She'd been beat unconscious on Gregor Island and still had the bruises across her face to prove it. I'd managed to administer a healing spell on myself before Matias struck. But by the time I got to Sondra, I could no longer access my magic to help her—and she hadn't been conscious enough to do the spell herself.

Everyone else was here: Jenna, Fiona, Ryland, Teagan, Ronark, and Genevieve. Even Genevieve's husband, Richard, was here. They'd come to help as soon as we got back to the mainland and found a phone. Genevieve had been helping us locate Matias, and we didn't know who else to call. Too late to locate him now, I suppose.

"A number of theories have surfaced for the unexplained events," the newscaster was saying. *"As of now, we are still waiting to hear from the Department of Magical Regulation to confirm exactly why vampires have mysteriously reverted to their healthy human state. Is this a trick from the magical community to lure us into a false sense of security, or have we finally found a cure for the magical plague that swept across our nation eight years ago?"*

"What are we going to do?" I asked. My eyes scanned each of theirs, waiting for someone to give the answer, as if they were all holding back a secret.

"What *can* we do?" Fiona replied, chewing her bottom lip.

"I mean, we can't exactly go up against Matias without magic of our own."

She was right. It was hopeless. But if I'd learned anything in the last few days, it was that anything was possible. I'd killed Valkas when I thought for sure I'd failed. I watched my boyfriend undergo the transition from human to vampire—something I once thought was irreversible. Yet here he was, sitting right next to me with blood pumping through his veins and life flourishing in the clear brown eyes I'd come to cherish.

Anything was possible. We just had to find our loophole—but I had no idea what that might possibly be.

I glanced from Sondra to Genevieve. If anyone knew a loophole, it'd be one of them. Sondra stared forward blankly, like she wasn't really with us. I'd never seen her like that before.

Genevieve, on the other hand, looked well rested and alert. She sat at the edge of the chasse and kept her eyes on the TV, like she was trying to absorb everything the newscasters were saying. She ran a manicured index finger along her lower lip, as though she was concentrating hard.

"I don't know, Fiona," I finally said. I couldn't stand to let the statement hang without a response. "All I know is that the longer we wait, the more powerful he'll become."

"He can't actually use the Artifact to take more power, can he?" Teagan asked. Even she looked pale beneath her normally tan skin. "He can only block magic, right?"

Genevieve nodded, though she didn't speak.

"True," I said. "But if he's the only one with magic, he can use it against everyone else. No one will be able to defend themselves anymore. He'll build an army and ensure only his followers have access to magic."

"Okay, but if magic is illegal anyway, he can't get away with it, right?" Jenna offered.

I frowned at her. "We'll have an army of guys with guns up against an army with magic. Which are you gonna bet on to win?"

My money was on the magic.

"Besides," I said before she could answer, "magic shouldn't be illegal to use in the first place. It's people like Matias that give it a bad name. If the government wasn't so scared of it, then maybe we could use it for good on a large scale. I mean, think of all the people I could heal! Matias has stolen that from me—from all of us—and it's not okay."

Ronark shot to his feet, like he couldn't take it anymore. "This is bullshit. I didn't spend eight years on that island to come back to a world where I couldn't shift anymore. It's part of who I am, and I'll be damned if someone keeps me prisoner any longer. I say we go after the bastard!"

"I agree." Ryland stood beside Ronark and crossed his huge arms. "I've spent years using my shifter magic to protect people. I'm not letting that go without a fight."

Genevieve finally tore her gaze from the TV. "I think we can all agree this is wrong. If Matias builds the army he's planning, he could force anyone to comply or die. Innocent lives are on the line. But we're going to need time."

"We don't have much," I said. "He's no doubt already started building an army."

Venn's fingers tightened around mine, and his jaw clenched. His eyes glossed over, like he was thinking of something else entirely.

"You know," I said, feeling that anger bubble up inside me again, "the vampire curse might be gone, but we're still fighting a vampire. He's sucked our magic dry just as he used to suck his victims dry!"

"We don't know if he ever actually killed anyone," Fiona pointed out.

"No, but I wouldn't put it past him," I replied. "He told me himself he would kill to get the world he wants—a place where he decides who lives and dies so that peace can reign. His idea of peace, anyway. According to him, the rest of us can't handle free will. I can't see a world where stripping people of that leads to peace."

Just thinking about it made my blood boil. Matias might've thought he was doing the right thing, but he was going about it in all the wrong ways. His plan would only lead to bitter anger and resentment—because that was exactly what his plan was built on. Synchrony didn't work that way. It would backfire just as it had in his past life.

It'd been nearly two centuries ago when a group of witches teamed up to imprison Valkas. Matias and his followers had planned to double cross them and twist the spell in their favor. They wanted to steal other witches' powers, but it didn't work. Their spell backfired so hard that magic was wiped out for over a century, until Matias freed Valkas in this life and broke the curse holding magic back. On his search for power, he lost it.

Why couldn't he see he was making the same mistake all over again?

Fiona tucked a strand of red hair behind her ear. "Vampire or not, Matias seriously needs to get his ass kicked."

Ryland nudged his sister and chuckled. "You gonna do the honors?"

She punched him in the arm playfully. "If I have to."

"Not without me, you won't," Ryland argued. "If we're going after him, we're going together."

Venn let go of my hand and knotted his fingers together in his lap. His breathing increased, like he was agitated. His gaze locked across the room, but it didn't look like he was focusing on anything in particular.

"You okay?" I asked. It was a stupid question. Something was obviously bothering him, and it went far beyond the current conversation.

Venn snapped out of it and looked at me. Emotions I couldn't quite place—perhaps sadness and sorrow—swam in his eyes. He shook his head, then promptly stood and left the room.

The room fell silent, apart from the TV. Teagan and Fiona both shot me confused expressions, like I could explain his sudden disappearance. I gave them an equally shocked look back.

"What's wrong?" Jenna asked.

"I don't know," I said in a rush before jumping to my feet and following Venn down the hall.

"Venn," I called, but he didn't slow.

By the time I caught up with him, he'd already made it to the guest room we shared. Genevieve's house looked modest from the outside, but it was laid out like a maze, with endless rooms I hadn't even realized were there. I'd probably only explored half of the house.

I found Venn sitting on the dark black comforter with his head in his hands. My stomach sank. Quietly, I shut the door behind myself and tiptoed across the carpet to sit beside him. He didn't move, as if I weren't even there.

"You don't have to say anything," I whispered, "but I want you to know that I'm here. Whatever it is."

Venn nodded, though he didn't speak. When he pulled his hands away from his face, I saw that his eyes were bloodshot, like he was struggling to hold back tears. Which only made me want to cry. I couldn't bear to see him like this.

Testing his limits, I reached out to place a hand on his shoulder. When he let me, I wrapped the arm all the way around his body and held him in an embrace. He melted into me, then shifted until his arms were around me, too. He leaned back and pulled me onto the bed with him.

For the next several minutes, we lay there in silence, staring up at the ceiling. As I waited for him to speak at his own pace, I listened to the sound of his heart. It was the only thing keeping out the deafening silence and the worrying ache entering my chest. What could've caused him to walk out of the room like that? What was bothering him so much?

Finally, after several agonizing minutes and at least a hundred scenarios rushing through my mind, Venn spoke. "I can't stop thinking about him, Rae."

I lifted my head off his chest to look him in the eyes. Water brimmed across his lower lids.

"Your brother?" I asked softly. I understood the feeling all too well.

Venn nodded. "After Tyson was changed, I couldn't save him. He was already gone. But now…"

"He's cured," I finished for him.

Venn nodded solemnly. "I need to find him."

A gaping hole opened up in my chest. It reminded me all too much of what it felt like to lose Jenna. A silent beat passed between us before I swallowed down the lump in my throat and spoke again. "You said he was attacked by a vampire and changed. Do you know where he ended up after the attack?"

Venn shook his head without meeting my gaze.

"Do you have an idea of where to start?" I asked.

"I might know some people I can talk to," he admitted.

Before I could ask him about that, quick footsteps sounded outside the door, then a heavy knock came.

"Come in," I called.

Fiona whipped the door open, and her wide eyes connected with mine. "It's Matias. You need to come see this."

2

Venn and I jumped off the bed and rushed down the hall behind Fiona. I came to a dead stop in the doorway as I caught sight of Matias's eyes on the screen. Everyone in the room had gone silent, but they were more alert than ever. Sondra had snapped out of her daze and sat at the edge of her seat. She leaned forward with her gaze locked on the TV. *Breaking News!* scrolled across the bottom of the screen.

My heart hammered as the camera zoomed out to show Matias hovering above the streets of Chicago, showing off his magic. Dark clouds rushed by above him, and lightning crackled out of his hands, connecting with the sky scrapers. Violent winds whipped through the street, though not a hair on his head moved.

All around him, onlookers were trying to keep hold of their belongings. Couples clung to each other, and people crouched behind cars to protect themselves from the violent winds. Newspapers and litter tumbled down the street. The traffic had come to a complete stop as Matias floated casually above each vehicle.

Behind him, a group of half a dozen men followed like soldiers flying behind their captain. They all wore the same black tailored suit and shiny shoes. They each had a look of anger fixed to their faces, though they held their heads up high in confidence. One guy even smirked to the crowd, like he thought being at Matias's side automatically made him better than anyone else—as if the rest of them were mere dirt on his shoe. Each of them showed off a different type of magic. One guy made flames shoot up from his palms, and another used his telekinesis to manipulate a deck of cards in his hands—like a real magician.

"I have full control of magic!" Matias shouted to the crowd below him. "Join me, and you will see your magic restored. You can be a part of something better—a powerful force stronger than any that has ever lived before. Together, we can overthrow the government and establish a world built on peace."

Several people stepped forward.

"No!" I cried. "You idiots!"

Couldn't they see how flawed Matias's plan for power was? Couldn't they see they were volunteering as his pawns? Matias didn't even *look* peaceful. Everything about him screamed *evil*!

Matias shouted above the strong winds. "Join, or surrender!"

The camera switched back to the newsroom, where an old man with a white mustache sat beside a younger woman with dark brown hair and a red pantsuit.

The man faltered with his words. "This confession is... quite shocking."

"Yes, it is," the woman agreed. "We are currently waiting on the Department of Magical Regulation to comment on this turn of events. We'll be back at nine o'clock with an update on these details—"

The sound instantly cut off, and the screen went black. All eyes turned to Genevieve, who was holding the remote.

"I can't stand to watch any more," she snarled. "Something needs to be done straight away."

"Who were those guys with him?" Fiona asked.

Genevieve's lips pursed tightly. "His first followers, I suppose. My guess is they're all witches he gathered before he ever used the Artifact."

"Did you recognize any of them?" Sondra asked.

The magical community wasn't very large, and Genevieve had all kinds of connections.

"Just one," she said. "The man directly behind him on his right, the one who was playing with the cards. His name is Tobias Ellwood. We've crossed paths a few times, but I refused to work with him."

Ellwood... Where had I heard that name before? I repeated the name several times in my mind, flipping through my memory for where I could've possibly heard of him. Maybe it was just one of those names...

Suddenly, it struck. Maliya had mentioned him to Cowen when I'd been locked up in her dungeon, right before she'd tried to carve me up like a Thanksgiving turkey. *This shouldn't take long, Cowen. You'll have plenty of time to make your flight to Seattle. You can tell Ellwood all about the raven bitch once you get there.*

"I heard Maliya talk about a guy named Ellwood when I was in her mansion," I blurted. "Cowen was planning to meet up with him in Seattle for something. Do you think it's the same guy?"

Genevieve thought about it for a moment. "Very possible.

Ellwood is a witch who's heavily invested in the blood slave trade. His work specifically specializes in shifter slaves. Cowen was probably headed to do some consulting with him. I suppose that business is no longer viable. If I know anything about the man, he ran straight to Matias's side the second he mentioned magic. He's only a mid-witch, and he probably thought Matias could give him more power."

"But he can't give him more power," Teagan said. "Only as much power as he had before."

Genevieve nodded.

"What are Matias's chances of rounding up enough high witches to go through with his plan?" Ryland asked.

Genevieve shook her head. "I don't know. High witches are rare, but there are enough of us that he could very well build an army, even if only a fraction join."

Ronark frowned. "He makes his cause sound noble, too, so I bet a handful of them *will* join."

"And it doesn't matter how many we get on our side," Jenna pointed out. "Since we can't use magic to fight against him."

"No," Sondra agreed, "but at least we can try to *keep* them from his side. If we talk to people, get the word out about what he really wants to do, then maybe we can keep him from getting too strong. He *is* giving people a choice, after all. We just need to get people to reject his offer."

"How are we going to do that?" Ryland asked. "Get up on national TV and announce he can't be trusted?"

"No," Richard spoke for the first time. "That's a good way to spark the spread of misinformation. We need to go directly to the community."

"You need to go to the Department of Magical Regulation," Venn suggested.

All eyes turned toward him.

"Magic like this, so public… the Department of Magical Regulation is going to be all over it and ready to stop it by any means necessary," he explained. "But they don't know what they're up against. We should tell them what we know, so they can use their resources to stop him before this gets out of hand."

"It's already out of hand," Fiona mumbled. "But I get what you mean."

"I think Venn makes a good point," I said. "Like Jenna pointed out, we don't have the magic to fight him. The DMR at least has resources we don't. If we tell them about the Artifact, they can target it and stop this."

"What happens when they get their hands on it, though?" Ryland asked. "What if they start using it?"

Fiona cocked an eyebrow at him. "Really? The DMR hates magic more than any other person or agency alive. You think they're going to use the Artifact?"

"Yes," Ryland said. "*Because* they hate magic. It's the lesser of two evils for them. Use magic once to stop it forever."

"And the Department of Magical Regulation is the lesser of two evils for us," Venn pointed out. "Matias is going to kill people for this. The DMR won't."

My mouth felt like sandpaper, even though I'd chugged a liter of water an hour ago. I was so torn. Everyone was making good points here, but I was leaning toward Venn's side. If we lost magic for good, we might as well go with the option where fewer people died.

Unless… there was a loophole.

"We could offer them a trade," I said.

Genevieve leaned forward, looking interested.

"We offer to destroy the Owl for them once it's in their possession," I proposed.

"So they can throw you in jail?" Jenna argued. "Won't admitting you're witches capable of destroying this get you in trouble?"

"You can't get in trouble for what you are," I pointed out. "Only for what you do—just as it was with vampires. We negotiate immunity on this act of magic. Once it's destroyed, our magic will return, and we can show them that magic can be used for good. It could be the first step in making better laws for the magical community by forming an alliance with them."

My gaze flickered to Sondra, who looked deep in thought. I hoped she would agree with me. Just the prospect of getting the chance at forming an alliance with the DMR made my stomach flutter in excitement. I couldn't believe we hadn't thought of it sooner.

"I think it's worth a shot," Sondra finally said. "We're all registered as witches, so it's not like we're telling them anything they don't already know. I think Venn's right that this is the lesser of two evils."

Genevieve stood. "I will schedule us a meeting. I want Rae and Venn to accompany me."

Ryland dropped his shoulders. "I miss out on all the fun?"

Genevieve frowned at him. "Rae was the one who spoke to Matias about his plan, and frankly, I trust Venn and Sondra the most. But Sondra needs to rest."

"How come you're in charge?" Ryland complained.

Genevieve crossed her arms. "If you'd like to sleep out on the street tonight, you're welcome to. Otherwise, you're just going to have to trust me."

Ryland sank down into his seat, looking totally defeated.

Genevieve breezed out into the hall, and the room broke out into chatter.

I turned to Venn. "What about Tyson?"

"I don't want to delay going after him—"

"Then don't," I said. "Someone else can go to the DMR instead of us."

Venn's gaze fell, and he looked deep in thought. "No, we should go. It will take me a few days to track down some people to talk to so I can get a lead on my brother. And I don't want you going to the Department without me. They're on high-alert, so we don't know how they'll react. This meeting has the potential to be very good for us—or very bad."

I wrapped Venn in a hug. "I don't like the sound of that. I really hope it goes well."

3

The Department of Magical Regulation was like any fancy office building—reception desks, waiting rooms, long hallways with endless doors... except it was insanely busy today. It'd been less than twenty-four hours since Matias made his big announcement, and the department was in a total uproar. Phones were ringing off the hook, and people were running this way and that, trying to deal with all of it. And this was only a branch of the department, a relatively small building that only reached five stories. I hated to see what the headquarters in Washington, D.C. looked like today.

The drive to the Chicago office took forever, and we'd been sitting in the waiting room for three hours past our scheduled appointment. I basically spent the whole time twiddling my thumbs and staring at a large picture hung on the wall that showed the department heads from D.C. I knew the face of Matthew Robertson, the president of the department. He'd been in the news a lot when the department opened a few years ago. But I couldn't place the blonde who stood beside him. She was much younger than him, probably in her forties, but there was something about her that tugged at a memory I couldn't place. Had I seen her on TV before? Or had I met her in a past life?

Finally, a woman in a navy-blue pantsuit stepped through the door. "Genevieve Morgan? Mr. Cavanaugh will see you now."

Genevieve stood, and Venn and I followed. I smoothed out my black dress and kept close to Venn. Pantsuit Lady opened the door and gestured for us to enter. A man of at least fifty sat behind a large mahogany desk opposite the doorway. He was conventionally attractive, with dark brown hair, bright blue eyes, and a strong jaw, but he didn't look up from his computer when we walked in the room.

Such a warm, welcome greeting.

His assistant quietly slipped out of the room. The sound of ringing phones and chatter died as the door closed behind her.

Genevieve cleared her throat, and Leon Cavanaugh finally lifted his head. He gave the four of us a smile that didn't quite reach his eyes, then gestured to the chairs in front of him. I sat in the middle, and Genevieve and Venn claimed either end.

"Mrs. Morgan," Cavanaugh said. "My secretary tells me she had quite the interesting phone call with you yesterday and that this meeting couldn't wait."

"No, it couldn't," Genevieve said with a friendly smile, "but that didn't keep us from sitting in your waiting room for the last three hours."

Oh, snap! Genevieve was throwing some serious shade. She was *so* not having it with this guy.

"I apologize," Cavanaugh said, though it didn't sound like he meant it. "As you can see, we're quite busy today. Recent events have given the Department a lot to handle."

"Yes, and we're here to help," Genevieve said.

Cavanaugh straightened in his chair.

Genevieve continued. "We have information about Matias Vayne that could help you stop him."

Cavanaugh tilted his head to the side, but he didn't blink an eye. "Stop him?"

I gaped at him. "Aren't you the least bit concerned? Haven't you seen the news reports? Don't you know what he's up to? He's in your jurisdiction!"

Cavanaugh shot me a cold smile. "I'm well aware, and I have the best team on the case. But the Vayne case is simple. I'm merely wondering what information you might possibly bring to the table. In the meantime, we have endless unsolved cases that are finally getting some light shed upon them now that magic has been contained."

Cavanaugh's meaning was clear. No new information was coming out about these cases. They were simply prosecuting magic users in full force now that they couldn't defend themselves.

"Contained?" I asked in disbelief. I quickly adjusted my tone and spoke in a more professional manner. "Sir, I don't think you understand the gravity of the situation. Matias Vayne isn't doing you any favors."

Cavanaugh shifted in his seat, looking amused. "That may be true, but I also know that in the last two days, we've freed twice as many blood slaves as we did in the last quarter."

"That's great," Venn said genuinely, though I could hear the irritation in his tone. "But Matias has nothing to do with the vampires. You can take him out and rescue blood slaves all at the same time."

Cavanaugh shrugged. "We can't know that for sure. All we know is that he somehow gained control of magic at the very time vampires returned to human. He could very well be controlling the vampire virus."

His unspoken words were clear in his tone. *And we need it to stay that way.*

He *did* think Matias was doing him a favor! He was *so* wrong.

"That's what we're here to discuss with you," I said firmly. "Aren't you at least curious what we have to say?"

Cavanaugh suddenly seemed more interested, but he quickly relaxed. "I've met with at least a dozen people just today who have offered up their own theories on recent events. What makes your theory more credible than the others?"

I leaned forward and leveled my gaze with his, making sure he knew I wasn't screwing around. "Because Matias Vayne told me himself."

Cavanaugh raised his eyebrows, looking impressed. "I'm listening."

"Matias Vayne is in possession of a magical artifact called The Wise Owl," Genevieve explained. "It was created centuries ago by a powerful group of witches. They infused magic into it that allowed the owner to block anyone's connection to Synchrony."

Cavanaugh narrowed his eyes, like he wasn't quite following. "Synchrony? Never heard of it."

"It's the powerful force most witches believe fuels their magic," Genevieve said. "With this artifact, Matias can flip the switch on any witch or shifter's magic so they can no longer access it. That's why magic has disappeared, and why he's offering to restore it to anyone who joins him."

Cavanaugh nodded slowly, like he was absorbing the

information. "So, how does that explain the vampires? He just flipped off the switch to their magic, too?"

"No," Venn said. His gaze flickered over to mine and Genevieve's. "The vampire curse was broken through other means. It was only after that happened that he was able to use the Artifact. Otherwise, he was unable to use his magic in vampire form."

Cavanaugh took a deep breath and finally straightened in his chair. "Okay, say this is all true. What exactly is it that you're proposing?"

Genevieve held her head high. "We're telling you this information so that you can retrieve the Artifact. Once it's out of Matias's hands, we'd like to offer to destroy it for you."

Cavanaugh nearly choked on his own saliva. "Destroy it how?"

"An object like this can only be destroyed through magic," Genevieve said. "It'd have to be powerful magic, more powerful than the witches who created it."

Cavanaugh smirked. "I supposed that means you, Mrs. Morgan? I'm aware you're registered as a high witch. You haven't been dabbling in any magic on the side, have you?"

"I would never!" Genevieve lied, rather convincingly. "But this issue is bigger than that. We don't have the means to retrieve the Artifact, which is why we need your help. But you need a group of witches strong enough to get rid of it, and that's where we come in. We can gather a team and destroy it, in exchange for full immunity on this magical task, of course."

I held my breath, waiting for his response.

Cavanaugh nodded. "A reasonable trade, for sure. But if the Department managed to retrieve such an object, why would we want to destroy it? Our procedures require us to catalogue and save all magical objects we come across."

"Have you ever come across an object powerful enough for a single person to build a magical army?" Genevieve cocked an eyebrow. "The Wise Owl is very dangerous in the wrong hands. It was created for noble purposes, but only to prevent people from Matias Vayne from rising to power. Now that he has it, everyone is at risk. You wouldn't want to repeat that, would you?"

"No, certainly not," Cavanaugh said, like the mere suggestion was preposterous. "So, this Wise Owl. What is it, exactly?"

"It's an ancient owl skull," I said. "I've seen it myself, even felt its magic. I can personally attest to how dangerous it is."

"Felt its magic?" Cavanaugh sounded intrigued. "How did you come across it?"

I swallowed. Perhaps I'd said too much. "Like I said, Matias showed me. I'm a low witch. I can't control when I feel magic. I didn't use it, if that's what you're implying."

"I'm not," Cavanaugh said. "What exactly is your relationship with Mr. Vayne, Miss…?"

"Collins. Rachel Collins." I shot Venn a quick glance. It was time to come up with a quick lie. I'd broken at least two dozen magical laws getting into that cave to find the Artifact, then following through with killing Valkas on Gregor Island. Cavanaugh didn't need to know about any of that. "Matias offered me a spot in his army. I didn't take it."

Cavanaugh looked like he believed me, so I relaxed.

"Thank you very much for this information," Cavanaugh said as he stood. "I will be sure to pass it on to my team. Unfortunately, I have many more meetings to get to today, so our time is up. We will contact you if there are any developments with retrieving this artifact."

Cavanaugh rounded his desk and opened the door to escort us out of his office. Or more accurately, *force us out.*

In that moment, one thing became very clear. Cavanaugh didn't see Matias Vayne as the threat he was. He was choosing to ignore it to fit how he wanted to see the world, rather than to see it as it was. He would hold off his men as long as he could so that his department kept the upper hand in the other cases they were pursuing. They would only strike at the last minute—and by then, it would be too late.

The three of us exchanged a wary glance, then stood. There was clearly nothing more we could do to convince him.

Cavanaugh reached for Genevieve's hand as she left the room. She shook his hand firmly, but she wore a scowl on her face. "I fear you're making a serious mistake, Mr. Cavanaugh."

He pursed his lips. "As I said, Mrs. Morgan, we'll contact you if anything comes of this situation." He was totally skirting around her statement.

Cavanaugh took my hand next, but the handshake was anything but the kind gesture it was meant to be. His hand was cold and uninviting. As he began to let go, I grabbed on tighter and leaned closer.

"You can't change that this world has magic, Mr. Cavanaugh," I said. "You can only change what you do about it."

The blood drained from Cavanaugh's face. He stared at me with such shock that he didn't seem to notice Venn shake his hand on his way out the door. Venn placed a gentle, protective hand on my shoulder and guided me down the hall until I could no longer see Cavanaugh's eyes on mine anymore.

"Just keep walking," Venn whispered under his breath. "We don't need to piss off the guy who has full authority to throw all of us in jail."

"He's completely ignoring us," I snarled under my breath. "He knows our story has merit, and he's choosing not to see it."

Genevieve pressed the button on the elevator at the end of the hall, and the doors slid open. We stepped inside the privacy of the empty lift.

Genevieve's lips pressed into a thin line as the elevator began its descent. She was *pissed*. "Cavanaugh is a fool. And that's exactly why from here on out, we'll be taking matters into our own hands."

"How?" Venn asked. "We don't have magic."

Genevieve stared straight ahead and took several shallow breaths, as if contemplating the question.

Finally, she turned to us. "Maybe we don't need it."

4

Several hours later, we were back at Genevieve's, breaking the news of our useless meeting with Leon Cavanaugh.

"It's almost like he *wants* Matias to take over," Fiona fumed.

We sat in Genevieve's sitting room, the one with the Victorian-style furniture, piano, and grandfather clock. Fiona was too agitated to sit.

"I don't think that's the case," Venn said. He leaned against the armrest of the couch with his fingers to his chin, like he was thinking hard. "I think he's milking the situation while he can."

"That's exactly what I thought!" I chimed in.

"Milking the situation?" Teagan asked from beside me on the couch. "What do you mean?"

"The DMR is using the situation to their advantage," I snarled in disgust. "They're cracking down on magical misuse while they can. Which is great for the blood slave trade. I'm glad they're helping people out of those situations, but it's not going to take him any extra resources to stop Matias. He already has a team allocated to the case."

Sondra scoffed and rolled her eyes. She rested an elbow against the armrest of her chair. She looked better than she had in days, though her bruises were still healing. "Sounds like typical political nonsense."

"Which means we're screwed," Fiona said. "If we don't get their help, we're not going to stand a chance against Matias and his Magical Merry Men."

Jenna placed her hands on her hips and sighed. "So, what happens now?"

"Maybe we should just take a step back," Ryland suggested from the piano bench. "The DMR will handle it eventually."

My jaw dropped. How could he suggest such a thing?

Ryland exchanged a glance with Teagan that I couldn't quite read. "I mean, why does it have to be us?"

"Seriously?" I snapped. "You're always up for a fight, but as soon as you're not the big bad bear anymore, you're backing down? Wow."

"It's not like that—"

"The better question is why *not* us?" I said. "We gave Matias the locket and led him to the Artifact. It's kind of our fault."

Ryland scoffed. "Finally you admit something's your fault."

The room burst into a chorus of voices coming to my defense. I couldn't even make out what each of them said.

Fiona slapped her brother hard in the shoulder. "I thought we agreed you were over that."

Ryland rubbed his shoulder and scowled at her. "Yeah, well…"

"What are you suggesting?" Jenna demanded of him. "We

just give in? Let Matias take over and kill anyone who opposes him?"

Ronark shook his head. "We can't do that."

Ryland opened his mouth to respond, but Venn stood to face him before he could. "Rae's right. We've been a part of this from the start, and we're not backing down now. The fact is, no one else is going to step up."

"Agreed." I got to my feet beside Venn. "Magic or not, we have to do something about this. This isn't about a personal vengeance anymore. This is about speaking up for those without a voice, for saving the people he's hurt and the ones he will hurt. I believe we're here for a reason, that we've all survived for a reason. Synchrony has chosen us to restore the balance. We will retribute just punishment for Matias's crimes."

Ryland held his hands up in surrender. "Okay, but what's your plan? Because right now, it doesn't look like we stand a chance."

"It didn't look like we stood a chance against Valkas, either," I shot back. "We beat him against all odds. We can do the same with Matias."

Ryland looked to Teagan again. This time, I caught a softness in his expression, like he was worried. "We could get ourselves killed. Is it worth it?"

"Hell yeah, it is!" I replied. "What kind of a question is that?"

"Look, Ryland," Venn said sympathetically. "If you don't want to do this, you don't have to."

"It's not that I don't want to fight," Ryland insisted. "I believe in this cause as much as the rest of you. I'm just trying to think realistically here. If we're willing to put our lives on the line, fine, I'm all for it. Just as long as we all understand the risks. Because right now, I just don't see how we stand a chance against Matias."

Genevieve took a long, deep breath. "I think there's a way to level the playing field a bit."

Sondra immediately perked up. "How?"

Genevieve stepped forward and stopped behind Sondra's chair. "If you don't mind, I'd like to give a quick demonstration—an experiment, if you will. Do you trust me?"

Sondra hesitated. I knew the two of them had a long history together. Genevieve had been Sondra's mentor years ago as she learned magic. When Sondra went out on her own, Genevieve had loaned her money that she'd been struggling to pay off—until we forfeited the Leora Locket to Matias in exchange for Sondra's safety. He'd paid her enough to repay her debts. Even though the debt was resolved, I could still feel the tension between them.

"Y-yes," Sondra said. She cleared her throat and spoke more clearly. "Yes, I trust you."

Genevieve pulled a small vial of purple liquid from the folds of her black dress and held it out to Sondra. "I'd like you to drink it."

Sondra took the vial and eyed it curiously. "What is it?"

"It's a healing potion I whipped up months ago," Genevieve explained. "It's as good of a potion as any to see if my theory is correct."

"You think… potions could still work?" Sondra asked.

Genevieve nodded. "I don't think The Wise Owl is capable of removing all magic, only from allowing another person to access new magic. Anything we've created in the past should still hold its magical properties—potions, magical artifacts, that sort of thing."

Sondra pulled the cork out of the vial. "I guess we should test that theory, then."

Sondra put the vial to her lips and tilted her head back. The purple liquid slid down her throat. It felt as if the whole room was holding a collective breath.

Several seconds passed, and nothing happened. No one even made a sound. Then suddenly, the potion took effect. The swelling on Sondra's eye shrank to normal, and the bruises slowly faded. The cut above her eyebrow knitted itself back together right in front of our eyes. I'd never seen any sort of healing spell work so quickly.

"Wow," Jenna whispered, breaking the silence.

Sondra brought her fingers to her face and pressed on the areas that'd been affected only moments ago. A look of amazement crossed her eyes, then she turned her gaze up to Genevieve. "That was a really powerful potion. It must've been really complicated. You didn't have to waste it on me."

Genevieve smirked. "Yes, well, unless you wanted me to give you fear-inducing hallucinations for the next five hours, I figured this was the safest bet for testing the theory. Now that we know potions will work, we can use them against Matias."

"What do we have available to us?" Sondra asked.

"Not much," Genevieve replied. "I have guns and a few magical weapons, potions that will act like bombs when poured out of their container."

Sondra shot her a questioning glance, as if to ask why she would keep such a thing around. Genevieve didn't seem to notice.

"But I'm hoping to gather more," Genevieve said. "If we can get other witches on our side, we can bring in more potions and artifacts so we stand a better chance against Matias."

"So we build a magical army of our own," I said, thrilled with the idea.

Genevieve nodded. "Precisely. It will take time, but I think we can do it."

Sondra stood, looking hopeful. "I think it's a brilliant idea."

"What happens after we have our army, though?" Venn asked. "We can't just walk straight up to Vayne Tower and steal the Artifact back."

"We lure him out," Genevieve said simply.

"We're forgetting something," Fiona pointed out. All eyes turned to her. "The Leora Locket. He still has it. He'll be able to anticipate our moves."

"You let me work out those details," Genevieve said. "I'm trained in mind manipulation. I can misguide him. When the time comes, we will take any and all measures to retrieve that artifact. I don't care if we have to kill Matias and his men to do it. He's not going to win."

I stepped forward. "Let's do it."

A chorus of agreement traveled around the room, before all eyes finally turned to Ryland and Teagan for their answer. Teagan chewed on her lower lip and looked to Ryland. It was so unlike her. She'd never had any magic, and she'd always been willing to go up against supernaturals with five times her strength and speed. What was holding her back now?

Finally, Ryland breathed a sigh. "We're in."

Just then, the doorbell rang.

Sondra furrowed her brow. "You already called in some favors, didn't you?"

I already knew the answer. Genevieve had called them in the car, and I'd heard most of their conversation.

Genevieve smiled. "Yes. Though we haven't gotten along in the past, we've agreed to put our differences aside for now."

"Who?" Sondra asked.

Genevieve turned to the doorway. "Friends of yours. I believe you're familiar with Clarita White and Amalia Taylor."

5

I followed Genevieve out into the hall. She opened the door to two familiar women. Clarita wore a baby blue 1950s style dress that showed off her curves. Her dark bangs were clipped back, but she had on the same cat-eye glasses as when I first met her. Amalia had long blonde curls and wore high-heeled boots over skinny jeans. They both carried luggage bags with them.

"Thank you for coming," Genevieve said before the other two could get in a word. She swung the door open wider to invite them inside.

"Thank you for calling us," Clarita said as she stepped into the hall.

Genevieve bent down several inches, and the two exchanged kisses on both cheeks. It was meant to be a friendly gesture, but it felt stoic, like neither of them felt comfortable in each other's presence.

I didn't get why no one liked Genevieve. Yeah, she looked kind of scary with the dark hair, pointed look, and black lace, but she'd been helping us this whole time without asking anything in return. I didn't know where we'd be without her.

Clarita's eyes met mine as Genevieve moved on to greet Amalia. "Rachel!"

Clarita dropped her bags and rushed to me with her arms out. She pulled me into a hug, and I squeezed her back. I'd only met Clarita once, but I already felt like I knew her.

"How'd the island go?" she asked.

My shoulders fell. "Well, it's kind of the reason we're in this mess now."

"Nonsense. It's not your fault."

"I killed Valkas, so it kind of is." I bit my lower lip.

Clarita frowned. "Did everyone make it off okay? Your sister?"

I smiled. "Yeah, I found her. She made it."

My eyes turned back to the sitting room, and I spotted Jenna, Venn, and Sondra in the doorway watching us.

"This is my sister, Jenna," I told Clarita, gesturing to her.

Jenna stepped forward and shook Clarita's hand.

"Jenna, this is Clarita. She helped me find you."

"It's nice to meet you," Jenna said. "Thank you for your help."

Clarita waved her hand like it was no big deal. "My pleasure. Sondra, how have you been? It's been awhile."

Clarita moved on to greet Sondra, while Amalia approached me.

I gave her a hug and said, "Thank you, by the way. For helping Venn when that guy cursed him."

"That's what I'm here for." Amalia smiled and turned to Venn. "You're looking great."

"Thanks to you." Venn hugged her.

Suddenly, it felt a little claustrophobic in the hall as more and more people stepped out of the sitting room and into the hallway. Venn and I slipped into the door behind us to make room for everyone else. The room we entered was dark and quiet, with black curtains covering the windows. Bookshelves lined the walls, with all sorts of tomes and potion vials everywhere. The leather-bound book that had been lain across one of the tables last time I was in here was nowhere to be found.

Venn took a deep breath and began pacing around the room slowly. He reached out his fingers to touch the spines of the books as he passed.

"Are you okay?" I came up behind him and slipped my fingers into his. "You look deep in thought."

Venn dropped his hand and turned his gaze to mine. "Yeah. I'm just thinking about what Genevieve said, how we can use different types of magic against Matias. I'm wondering if maybe there's an artifact out there that can counteract The Wise Owl's effects."

I scanned the old books in front of us, but none of them had words on the spines. "Genevieve has so many books. Maybe there's something in one of them."

I glanced toward the hallway, but no one was watching us. "Do you think she'll be okay with us looking through them?"

I reached for the book closest to me and pulled it off the shelf. It was a thick hardback, at least five-hundred pages. When I opened it, the smell of old pages hit my nose. I thumbed through the pages to find endless words and diagrams on different types of spells. The whole book seemed to be about how to summon spirits.

"Mm..." I mused. "I've never done a séance before. You?"

Venn gently took my hands and closed the book. "No, and you don't want to try. Séances are dangerous. You never know what kind of spirit you might accidentally summon. It's not exactly considered a form of white magic."

I returned the book to its spot, feeling a little disappointed. It'd be cool to talk to the dead. My mind instantly went to my parents, but I quickly pushed the thought away. It would only tempt me.

"Hey, guys!" Fiona practically danced into the room, looking chipper as always. "What are you up to?"

"Making out," I teased.

"Oh, no. I wouldn't want to interrupt that," she replied, playing along.

Venn chuckled. "Relax. We're just talking about magic. Maybe there's something in one of Genevieve's books that can help us with Matias—like information on an artifact or something."

"Good idea. Mind if I help?" Fiona reached around us to grab a book off the shelf and began flipping through it. "Oh, cool! Necromancy."

"Not cool." Venn grabbed the book out of her hand before she could read anything out of it. He slammed it shut and grabbed another book. He quickly flipped through it, then handed it to her. "Try tarot card reading. A lot less dangerous."

"Come on," Fiona complained. "You don't want to have a little fun raising the dead?"

"A little fun could get you killed," Venn said. "You know that falls into the realm of black magic."

Maybe that's what we need, I thought.

"Okay." Fiona gave in. "No raising zombies. Not like I could even if I tried."

"Who's raising zombies?" Genevieve breezed into the room.

Fiona threw her book back on the shelf, like she was a kid who'd got caught with their hand in the cookie jar.

"No one," Venn said sternly.

"Shame." Genevieve frowned. "I always wanted to try that spell."

"Hey, Genevieve," I said. "Is it cool if we look through your books to see if there are any potions or artifacts that might help us against Matias?"

She shrugged. "Have at it. You'll do best to start at the bottom. The top two shelves cover rituals and spells, which won't be very useful now that our magic is gone."

"Cool." I bent and pulled a pile of books off the shelf, then plopped them on the table in the middle of the room. "Well, Venn, Fiona. I hope you guys like reading."

Venn smirked and sat in the chair beside me. "I was born for this."

"I'll grab some sticky notes to bookmark pages," Fiona said. "And maybe some popcorn?"

I sat beside Venn and opened the first book off the pile. "Definitely some popcorn. It's going to be a long night."

***

I didn't know how late it was, but I knew we'd been sitting here for hours. Venn had taken a phone call at least an hour ago and hadn't returned since. I wasn't sure if he was still on the phone or had fallen asleep. Since he left, the room had been pretty quiet as both Fiona and I dove into the endless books. I'd been reading so long that my eyes were starting to water. Which was weird, because I was parched and didn't feel like I had an ounce of water left in my body.

I closed my book and looked up at her with heavy eyes.

She'd tied her hair up in a messy bun and looked about ready to pass out from exhaustion.

"Maybe we should call it a night," I suggested. I ran my finger over the sticky notes sticking out of the book I'd been flipping through. "I've bookmarked over half a dozen spells that sound interesting, but none of them are going to help us. You find anything yet?"

"I found a piece of popcorn in my cleavage," she replied with a hopeless sigh.

"Not really the kind of thing we're looking for."

"Oh." She sounded both tired and disappointed. "I was just reading about these types of artifacts. They're just called trinkets in the book, but they can suppress a person's magic if they're a threat."

Fiona turned her book to me. All across the page were pictures of various trinkets, like jewelry, keys, and broaches. These artifacts could be anything.

"I think we sold trinkets when I worked at Bloodstone," I said thoughtfully as I scanned the page. "Devin never called them that, though. We just called them protection charms. This could work..."

I looked farther down the page. "Never mind. It says here they don't work on other artifacts."

"But if we got one close enough to Matias, it might affect his ability to use the Owl," Fiona pointed out.

I pressed my lips together. "Good point. Do you think we can get our hands on one?"

Fiona shrugged. "The book makes it sound like they're pretty common. Creating them doesn't take a lot of magic, but it also means they're not super powerful. Witches used to use them as sort of protection charms. If they wore a trinket, it kept other witches from casting curses on them. But it wouldn't completely suppress another witch's powers. Only weaken them a bit."

"Maybe weakening Matias is all we need," I said. "Let's talk to Genevieve and Sondra in the morning and see if they know anything about trinkets. In the meantime—"

I was cut off by the sound of a door slamming down the hall, followed by a string of curse words. First came a woman's voice, then the muffled sound of a man's.

"Screw you, Ronark!" Jenna yelled. "You don't know shit about me."

"You think I don't know how it feels?" he shouted back.

I left my books on the table and rushed out of the room. I turned down the hall to the guest rooms and stopped in my tracks.

Jenna stood outside Ronark's door, looking like a total wreck. Her short dark hair was in disarray, and her face was red and blotchy.

"Jenna?" I stepped toward her cautiously. "Are you okay?"

Her bottom lip quivered, like she was trying to hold her emotions back. Suddenly, she cracked, and tears began streaming down her face. "No, Rachel. I'm not okay."

6

I wrapped Jenna in my arms as worry for her knotted in my gut. "What happened?"

Jenna drew away from me and shook her head. She wiped the tears from her eyes, but they only kept coming. "I don't want to talk about it."

The door beside us opened, and Venn poked his head out. He looked to Jenna, then to me, as if to ask if she was all right. Jenna buried her face back in my shoulder as she sobbed. I just looked back at Venn hopelessly. I had no idea what was wrong, and it killed me that I couldn't fix it.

"How'd the phone call go?" I asked him.

"I'm closer to finding out where Tyson might be," Venn said softly. "Do you two want some privacy?"

Venn opened the door wider and stepped out of the way. "I'll go help Fiona."

"Thanks," I told him.

Venn placed a kiss on my forehead as he passed, then continued on down the hall. He threw back several worried glances before he finally disappeared.

"Jenna," I whispered, "let's go sit down in my room."

She didn't move until I began guiding her. I closed the door behind us and led her across the room to the bed. We both sat, but she wouldn't lift her gaze. She buried her face in her hands and continued crying.

"Are you sure you don't want to talk about it?" I asked softly.

She sniffled, but otherwise didn't respond. My guts twisted, and I was on the verge of crying myself. I hated seeing her like this.

I put my arm back around her. "Jenna Bean, I can't help you unless you tell me what's wrong."

She finally lifted her head and dashed the tears away. "It's nothing."

"It's not nothing," I insisted. "Did Ronark hurt you?"

"What? No!" She sounded shocked. "No, he'd never touch me. It's not like that."

I frowned. "There are other ways to hurt a person."

"No, look." Jenna's voice came out stronger. "We just had a fight. It wasn't his fault."

"What did you two fight about?" I asked, hoping she'd open up to me.

Jenna bit her lower lip. "I'm thirsty."

I reached for my plastic water bottle on the nightstand and handed it to her.

"Thanks." She opened the cap and threw her head back. I stared wide-eyed as she chugged the whole thing. She handed me back the empty bottle and sighed.

"Do you ever feel so thirsty it seems like you're going to shrivel up and die?" she asked.

The question almost sounded rhetorical, but I considered her words. The last few days, I'd felt parched beyond belief, no matter how much water I drank. Most of the time, I tried to ignore it. It was probably just from stress or something. But now that she pointed it out, I couldn't take my mind off how dry my throat felt.

Jenna looked at me with sad eyes. "You've been feeling it, haven't you?"

"A little," I admitted.

"Now imagine that, only a hundred times worse," she said. "It feels like I've spent a year crawling through the desert with nothing but sand to satiate me. It won't be as bad for you since you were only fed on a few times. But for me... for Ronark... it's unbearable."

Jenna ran her fingers over her neck as it dawned on me what she was saying.

"This is what the addiction feels like?" I asked, though I already knew the answer.

Vampire feedings were addictive, far beyond that of most street drugs. After just a few seconds of being fed on the first time, I already wanted more. But it wasn't enough for withdrawals to set in. But now, after being fed on several times while I was held prisoner on Gregor Island, I was starting to feel it. That was how fast the addiction set in. I couldn't imagine what Jenna and Ronark were feeling right now, not after being fed on night after night for years.

It was a cruel side effect of the vampire curse. If their victims left, they'd feel just how the vampires felt without blood. It created a dependency between the two of them and ensured the vampires would always have a fresh supply of blood.

It didn't matter that they didn't exist anymore. The effects of their feedings lived on. If we'd destroyed all the drugs in the world, addicts would still come looking for more. It was just like that.

"I used to think being fed on was one of the worst things that could happen to me," Jenna said without meeting my gaze. She looked so out of it that it was like she wasn't even talking to me. "Now I know that there are worse things out there."

"Jenna…" I didn't know what I could possibly say to her. My heart broke into a million pieces to watch her break apart like this. My throat began to close up, as if someone was squeezing my neck with a rope. The invisible force tightened with each passing second. "That's not true. You *hated* being fed on. I saw it in your eyes every night you returned from a feeding."

"I did," she admitted. "But it was better than this. At least with Silas I felt like I controlled myself in my own skin. Now there's just this… this *thirst*. I can't stop thinking of my master. I just want him to bite me again, to take this agony away from me."

It would be nice. Just one more wave of euphoria to take away the cravings. The sight of Valkas's fangs flashed through my mind.

What the hell was I thinking?

"Look at me." I grabbed Jenna's face and forced her gaze to mine. "People have gotten through this before. You can, too."

Jenna shied away from me, and tears began to fall down her face again. "I don't know that I can, Rachel. You don't actually know anyone who's overcome it."

"I do," I told her sternly.

Her eyebrows shot up, but her expression quickly fell. "I guess they were stronger than I am."

"Don't say that, Jenna." I reached out for her, but she shrugged me off.

"You don't understand. The one person who would understand—who I *thought* I could talk to about this—is being an asshole!" Jenna shouted the last few words to make sure Ronark would hear through the wall.

"Please calm down," I begged. "This isn't you talking."

She raked her fingers through her hair, making it stick up at all angles. "Sure it is. The withdrawals are just giving me the courage to say it."

"Look, you and Ronark are both irritable because of this, but you can break through it," I assured her. "What happened to positive Jenna from the island? Don't you remember what you told me? You can't change your circumstances, only what you do about them. You can get through this."

Jenna curled her knees to her chest and turned away from me on the bed. Hopelessness sank in my gut. What could I possibly say to help her at a time like this?

"That's not helping, Rachel," Jenna mumbled. "You must've forgotten the other thing I said to you."

I scooted closer to her. "What was that?"

"It only takes one thing to set us back ten paces. But this… this is like a hundred steps back." Jenna threw herself onto the mattress and buried her face in the pillow. "I don't think I have another hundred paces left in me."

Her shoulders began to shake, and in that moment, I knew there was nothing I could possibly say to her. The only thing I *could* do was show her that I was here for her, that she didn't have to go through this alone.

I lay down and wrapped an arm around her. She curled into me as tears began to soak my shirt. I didn't know how long we lay there like that, but it didn't matter. I'd sit beside

Jenna until the end of time if I thought it would help make her feel better.

Jenna went still, and I thought she'd fallen asleep. I continued to brush my fingers through her hair because I couldn't bring myself to fall asleep, in case she needed me. Eventually, she stirred, and she drew away from me.

"Feeling any better?" I asked.

Jenna shook her head. "Not really."

"Maybe you need to take your mind off it," I suggested. "Do something to make you forget."

She frowned. "Like what?"

I shrugged. "I don't know. What's something fun we used to do as kids?"

Jenna thought about it for a moment. "I don't know. Tell scary stories?"

I bit the inside of my lower lip. "That's a little too real right now."

She frowned. "You're right. Honestly, it's late. Everyone's asleep. We should probably get to bed, too."

My eyes scanned the room, searching for ideas on how to get her mind off the cravings. I sat upright in bed when my gaze hit the nightstand and I remembered the flashlight I'd found in the top drawer. I reached over and threw the drawer open, then held up the flashlight for her to see.

"You sure it's too late for some fun?" I grinned.

Jenna's lips turned up into a half-smile, which I found encouraging.

"Come on," I pressed when she didn't answer. "It'll be fun."

"Okay," she caved. "Hold on."

Jenna jumped out of bed and hurried out the door. I followed. She entered her guest room beside mine and flipped the light on. Ronark rolled over in bed and threw his arm over his eyes.

"I thought you were mad at me," he complained in a tired voice.

"Get up, sleepyhead." She tugged at his feet under the covers. "We're going outside to have some fun, and I'm not going without you."

"What are you talking about?" he groaned.

"You. Me. Right now. Under the stars."

Ronark glanced to me, as if searching for an explanation.

I beamed at him. "We're going star-tipping!"

7

A few minutes later, Ronark was dressed, and the three of us were headed toward the back door. I caught sight of Fiona and Venn still flipping through books in the room off the main hall.

"Hey." I popped my head in the room. "You two up for a little adventure?"

Fiona shot a quick glance to Venn, suddenly looking more awake. "What kind of adventure?"

"Just a little game Jenna and I used to play as kids," I said. "You up for it?"

Fiona shrugged and stood. "I'm up for anything."

Venn looked tired, but he joined her. "What are we doing?"

I smiled. "Star-tipping."

Fiona hopped. "Ooh, sounds like fun! I'm going to see if Ryland and Teagan want to join us."

Venn followed me out the back door. "What's star-tipping?"

"It's simple," I explained. "One person looks up at the sky. You focus on a star, then spin around in a circle in the dark.

After a few seconds, another person will shine the flashlight at you. That's your cue to stop spinning and start running toward the light. You get so disoriented that you can't help but fall over. It's hilarious."

We stepped out into Genevieve's back yard. It was dark, with only a soft glow from the city illuminating shadows around the yard. There was a high fence around the perimeter, which met up with a thick line of trees. Various trees and flowerbeds dotted the landscaped yard. In the farthest back corner was a brick fire pit with patio chairs all around it. The rest of the yard was wide open.

"I'll go first!" Jenna offered, looking excited.

She turned her head to the sky and spread her arms out wide, then spun around as fast as she could. I clicked on the flashlight and shone it in her eyes. She didn't make it another step before she stumbled to the side and fell to the ground, laughing hysterically.

"Oh my God!" she cried between laughs. "I forgot how fun that was. Ronark, you go!"

Ronark looked reluctant, but he uncrossed his arms and took Jenna's place. He spun around, then came the light. Ronark tried to stay upright as he moved toward it, but he stumbled with each step. It was like watching him fall to the side in slow motion.

"Oh, fuuu—!" he shouted.

When he landed on the ground, Jenna rushed over to him to try to drag him to his feet, but he was laughing too hard to stand.

"Okay," he said through laughs. "I get it now. I've never felt that dizzy in my life. It's a bit of a rush. Venn, you should try it."

Venn glanced to me.

"Go ahead," I encouraged. "It doesn't hurt to have a little fun."

Venn sighed and stepped forward to the middle of the open lawn. "Okay, here goes nothing."

He spun faster than Jenna or Ronark did, and I let him go a little longer than the other two. When I clicked the flashlight on, his arms went still out on either side of him, like he was trying to stay balanced, but it didn't work. As the world spun around him, he tried to correct it with his footing, which only sent him tumbling to the ground. His laughter filled the yard.

I shoved the flashlight in Jenna's hands and ran over to Venn. Before he could get to his feet, I threw myself on top of him and held him down with a kiss. His laughter instantly died, and he relaxed into it. For the first time in what felt like weeks, the tension melted out of my body. For just tonight, I wanted to forget about Matias—about magic, vampires, all of it. For just one moment, I wanted to act like a normal girl with normal friends and without any cares in the world.

"Get a room!" Teagan's voice called from toward the house.

I drew away from Venn, blushing. He smiled back at me.

"Forget her," he said as he dragged me back to him. I wanted to kiss him back, but I could hardly manage it through the giggles.

"See?" I said when we finally parted. "It's fun, isn't it?"

Venn nodded as he gazed at me with soft eyes that melted my heart.

"My turn!" Fiona hurried across the lawn to Ronark and Jenna, who had moved to another area of lawn to star tip.

I lifted my head to see that she'd rounded up Ryland, Teagan, and Sondra. The three were already gathered around the fire pit, and Ryland was starting a fire. Sondra sat in one of the patio chairs and pulled out her sketch pad.

"Hey, Tea!" Venn called over to her. "You should try star-tipping. You'll love it."

"Nah," she replied as she snuggled up beneath a long cardigan beside Sondra. "I'm good. You go have fun."

"Her loss," I said as I got to my feet. I reached out my hand and helped Venn up. "Want to go again?"

He shrugged. "Sure."

Venn and I joined the others. Fiona had managed to stay upright for a few steps before she fell onto all fours and tried to stand up again. This time, she totally fell on her ass. She blinked a few times to get the world to focus again. I clutched my stomach as I burst into laughter.

"Whoa!" She shook her head. "That was not what I expected at all. That was fun."

It was my turn next. I turned my chin toward the sky and focused on the brightest star I could see. I held my arms out and spun… and spun… and spun. I was already laughing. It felt so carefree, like being a kid again.

Suddenly, a bright light cut through the darkness, and the whole world flipped upside down. I couldn't tell where my friends were standing, only that my feet felt as if they were no longer on the ground. The ground flew up to meet me, and though my body had stopped moving, it still felt as if the world was spinning around me. Only a moment later did I realize that I'd fallen over, as if some invisible force had taken over my body for a moment.

Fiona barked in laughter, and I started laughing so hard that I couldn't hear anyone else. Venn tried to drag me to my feet, but I was still a little dizzy that I stumbled against him.

"My turn again!" Jenna volunteered, shoving the flashlight into Ronark's hands.

This went on for what felt like another half hour. Eventually, I went so many times that it started to lose its effectiveness. Venn and I agreed we were done and went to sit by the other three near the fire. The fire was warm and inviting, but not as inviting as Venn's arm around me.

"What's going on over here?" I asked as we sat.

"Telling embarrassing stories," Teagan said. "And trying not to fall asleep."

"You can go to bed if you're tired," Venn offered.

Teagan shook her head. "No, you guys are all having fun. I want to be out here by you. It's been a long time since I heard you all laugh."

"Hey," Ryland said. "I laugh all the time."

Teagan rolled her eyes. "Yeah, babe. At other people's expense."

Ryland propped his feet up on the chair beside him. "Not my fault if other people's misfortunes make me laugh."

Teagan shook her head at him. "Why do you have to be such an ass all the time?"

"You didn't think I was being an ass earlier when we were—"

"Oh, God!" Teagan threw her hands over her ears. "People do *not* need to know what we were doing."

Venn scoffed. "Because we don't have *any* idea what you two do in your alone time."

"Well, you certainly don't need the details!" Teagan cried.

Venn shot Ryland a glance. "Trust me, Tea. I already know more than I care to admit."

Teagan's jaw dropped, and she widened her eyes at Ryland. "What did you tell him?"

Ryland rolled his eyes. "Relax. It's not like the tattoo on your ass is a secret. I personally find it sexy."

"You have a tattoo?" I asked.

Teagan looked embarrassed. "I got it when I was sixteen. It's just a heart on my right hip. It's nothing. Can we drop it?"

Respecting her privacy, I leaned over to Sondra beside me. "What are you sketching?"

Sondra snapped out of her daze to look at me. She quickly flipped the sketchpad shut before I could catch a glimpse of the picture inside. "Oh, it's nothing. I thought I'd draw you guys having fun, but…"

She didn't finish her sentence. I had no idea what she was about to say, but she never got the chance to finish.

Teagan quickly came to her rescue. "So, have you ever thought of getting a tattoo, Rae?"

I shrugged. "I used to think about getting a raven tattooed on my wrist, but then I realized it was a little conceited and obvious. I mean, I didn't want to be walking around advertising I was the Ravenite. The government still doesn't know I'm a shifter, so it's probably best if it stayed that way."

"Good call," Ryland said.

Venn leaned over to me and whispered, "I think a tattoo would look kind of sexy on you."

I looked to him in surprise. "You think?"

He eyed me up and down, like he was hungry for me. Butterflies danced in my stomach.

"Not a raven, though. Maybe a wolf…" I said. "For you."

Venn smiled, and it sent my heart hammering against my rib cage. I wanted to kiss him to make it slow. Suddenly, I felt very hot, and it definitely wasn't from the fire.

"I'd like that," he whispered.

The way he stared into my eyes was unlike anything else. I

wanted him—right here, right now. Images from the first time we'd shared together flashed through my mind. I'd been dying to do it again, but with everything happening, we hadn't had the chance. Now…

Every nerve in my body came alive just at the thought. What were we waiting for? If he was waiting for a signal, he was sure as hell going to get one.

"Maybe we should go get that room," I said in a voice so low only Venn could hear.

He shot out of his seat like a bullet. He took my hand and started leading me away from the fire pit. Teagan's and Ryland's laughter followed behind us.

"You two have fun!" Ryland called.

"We will!" I shot back.

I was so excited about what was about to happen that I practically raced through the hall and to our room. Venn chased behind me, snickering. I'd never seen him act so carefree before. I loved it.

I locked the door behind us. By the time I turned around, Venn already had his shirt off and was tossing it to the side. I stood on my toes to kiss him, and a warmth spread all throughout my body. My heart felt as if it was trying to beat its way out of my chest.

Venn backed up until his knees hit the edge of the bed. I pressed on his shoulders, and we tumbled back onto the mattress together.

"Tonight… was… fun…" he said between my kisses.

I pulled away from him to place my index finger to his lips. "Shh…"

Venn ran his hands over the fabric of my jeans. "I just wanted you to know before we did this that I really appreciate what you did tonight. We all need to let go sometimes. I needed to laugh."

I smiled. "You're acting like that was the best part of the night."

He smirked. "So far. We still have time to change that."

Hell yeah, we would! I wasn't sure where my confidence came from, but I knew with certainty I was going to make it a night he wouldn't forget.

I ran my hands up his chest and over his shoulders. He shivered beneath my touch.

"What's wrong?" I asked as I kissed the sensitive skin beneath his ear.

His hands roamed over my back, pushing my fabric out of the way. My pulse quickened beneath his touch.

"Nothing," he said with a blissful sigh.

I couldn't take the suspense anymore. I placed another gentle kiss on his lips, then drew away and held my arms above my head. Venn bit his lower lip as he took my invitation and pulled my shirt up over my head. Cool air brushed my skin, but my insides felt like fire. My hands shivered as I took his in mine and guided them to my breasts. Venn beamed as he gently slipped a finger beneath the fabric and ran it across my skin, teasing me.

If he wasn't going to take initiative, I would. I reached behind myself and undid the clasp, then let the fabric fall away. Venn couldn't take his eyes off me as my breasts came out in the open. Warmth rippled across my skin. I felt so exposed, like showing him my body was akin to opening my heart.

And damn it. It felt amazing. I never thought I'd find someone I could share myself with wholeheartedly, but every touch, every moment with Venn, made me question why I'd ever thought that way in the first place. It was clear to me now that there'd always been someone out there waiting for me. I needed him. Without him, I was the bitter, lonely girl with a death wish. Now I was loved, with a purpose.

"Rae," Venn said breathlessly. "You're so beautiful."

I blushed and gazed down at his muscular chest. "You are, too."

A thought suddenly struck. "Oh, shit. Do we have protection?"

Venn smirked and reached over toward the nightstand. He opened the top drawer and pulled out a condom. "Ryland gave it to me as a joke. Look who's laughing now."

Venn gave it to me, then placed his hands on my breasts and squeezed gently. My nipples hardened beneath his palms. I closed my eyes and relished in the glowing feel of his hands exploring my body. They slipped beneath my jeans as he dragged me closer to him. Heat pooled between my thighs as he cupped my butt.

I couldn't get my pants off fast enough. My fingers shook as I undid the button, and my legs quaked as I kicked the jeans off and onto the floor.

Venn took one look at my bare legs and tossed me onto my back. I beamed as he knelt over me and pulled my panties down my legs. For a split second, I lay there fully exposed as his eyes drank me in. Instinct told me to shy away, but I mentally threw my instinct aside. I was his now. He could look at me all he wanted.

"Your turn," I whispered.

I reached for Venn's waistband and undid his belt, then the button. My skin heated as I pulled down the fabric to expose all of him. Venn gasped as my fingers curled around his erection.

Damn! Venn and I had only been intimate a few times before and had only gone all the way once. Touching him there felt like the first time. I still wasn't prepared for the shot of adrenaline and pulse of heat passing over my body.

I helped Venn get the condom on, then dragged him back on top of me. His lips connected with mine, and they didn't stop moving. He kissed me with such a passion that I never thought possible. Emotions I'd never felt before swept through me with such force that I wanted to cry just to let them out.

"I love you," I whispered breathlessly beneath his kiss.

"I love you, too," he said before returning his lips to mine.

His hand traveled down between our legs, making me shiver. He positioned himself and gently pressed down. I gasped as he moved inside of me. My legs wrapped tight around his hips. I wanted to drag him closer to me, as if we could melt into one being, one soul. We fit together like two pieces of a puzzle. He completed me, and I him.

Venn's hands ran over my hips, then down to the sensitive area between my legs. I fisted my hands in his hair as his fingers gently roamed over me.

Gentle. He was always so gentle. He treated me like a queen, always making sure I was comfortable and that I felt the pleasure of these moments as much as he did.

But I wasn't a gentle kind of girl. I wanted him unlike I ever wanted anything in my life. And I was going to have him. All of him.

I pressed my heels into the mattress and lifted my hips, forcing Venn to roll over. He looked up at me with shock as I took the lead. It only lasted for a moment before the shock melted off his face and he grinned at me. I laced my fingers through his and pinned them to the mattress above his head as I experimented with the movement of my hips. With every movement, Venn's body hit something inside of me that sent a wave of pleasure over my entire body. I increased my speed until I couldn't go any faster.

"I should've known you'd want to take control," Venn said in amusement.

"You know me so well," I replied with a smile.

"Yeah, I do." Venn's demeanor instantly changed. It was like watching him shift into wolf form. He went from the gentle, caring guy he started out as when we entered the room into a predator who'd just caught his prey.

It was. So. Freaking. Hot.

Venn flipped me over again, taking control. He looped his arm beneath my leg and pressed into me faster and faster. That pleasurable sensation I'd felt on top of him with each thrust was ten times stronger when he was on top of me like this.

"Oh God, Venn," I cried.

"Good?" he asked.

"Yes," I moaned. "Venn, I—"

I cut off as a strong sensation took over my body. I could no longer find the words. Pressure built up inside of me. I bit into his shoulder to keep the moans from escaping. Like an explosion, the pressure released in a glorious array of sparkling light, sweeping through my body like the blinding sun on a warm summer day. Venn's body tensed above mine as he reached his peak with me.

The room spun around me as we melted side-by-side on the bed. I closed my eyes and tried to hold on to the wonderful blissfulness before it drifted away. Venn had made me feel amazing things before, but never like that. That was… there were no words.

"That was even more fun than the first time," I told him when I finally caught my breath.

"It was," he panted.

I opened my eyes to see his beautiful face hovering over me, a hopeful look in his eyes. My heart melted. I didn't think I'd ever seen anything more wonderful in my life. I reached my hand up to caress the side of his face. "I never want this to end, Venn."

"It won't," he whispered. He bent to place a warm kiss on the top of my head. If possible, I relaxed even more.

"Venn?"

"Mm?" He pushed my hair out of my face and gazed down at me like I was a goddess he was seeing for the first time. There was such warmth and love in his eyes.

"I want to try everything with you."

Venn clicked his tongue. "Not so fast. We have plenty of time for that."

I bit my lower lip. "Well, the night's not over. Maybe we could try… one more thing?"

His eyes lit up. I grinned and rolled over so that my back-side pressed against his front. He curled an arm around me and pulled me close to him. I tilted my head back to look him in the eyes. I felt so safe and secure in his embrace.

"Can we try it like this?" I asked.

Venn put his fingers in my hair and tugged back slightly to expose my neck. He trailed kisses down it and to my shoulder, then pressed his lips against my skin as he spoke. "For you, Rae, I'd do anything."

I woke the next morning to warm sunlight brushing across my eyelids. The normally dull colors of Genevieve's house seemed brighter today than normal. I lifted my head from Venn's chest and gazed at him. His eyes were closed, and his chest rose and fell softly. He looked so peaceful, and I didn't want to wake him. I quietly dressed and grabbed a fresh pair of clothes Jenna had loaned me, then tiptoed to the bathroom to shower.

The water was warm and refreshing. It felt like I could finally breathe, and I kept replaying the night over and over again in my mind. I wanted more nights like that, where I could laugh with my friends carefree and enjoy my time with Venn without interruptions.

I returned to our bedroom with a clean change of clothes and wet hair. Venn was sitting upright in bed, looking sexy as ever with a bare chest. He had his new phone to his ear. Genevieve had gotten us each one after we returned from the island—in case something went wrong and we had to contact each other.

As soon as I walked in the room, Venn's face fell. He didn't even look at me, as if the news on the other end of the line had pulled him out of reality and placed his mind somewhere else entirely.

The blood drained from my face, and I rushed over to him. "Venn, what's wrong? Your brother?"

Venn didn't say anything as the guy on the other end spoke, though I couldn't hear what he was saying. Slowly,

Venn focused on the world again, and his gaze turned to mine. My heart sank in response to the worried look on his face. The seconds ticked by slowly, each one pounding like a drum in my ears.

"Thank you, Cory," Venn finally said. "Let me know how I can return the favor."

"No problem, man," I heard Cory reply. "What are friends for?"

Venn pulled the phone from his ear and pressed the screen to end the call. He stared down at it for several seconds, his fingers shaking, until he finally lifted his gaze.

"Is your brother okay?" I asked softly as I placed a hand over his.

"I'm not sure," he replied in a shaky tone. "But I know where to find him."

"That's great!" I exclaimed.

"Cory's an old friend from high school," Venn explained, almost like he didn't want to go into the more important details. "We had a bit of a falling out when he got into some bad deals with a group of vampires."

The room went silent for a beat before I spoke. "Did he... did he ever change?"

"Cory?" Venn shook his head. "No. He's a shifter—gorilla, and a big one, too."

I snickered. "A gorilla?"

"Ever seen a gorilla? They're scarier than you think. He worked with some vampires on some gambling deals, nothing like blood slaves or anything. But it still wasn't a good situation. They kept him around for intimidating their debtors. I think it was more than that, too."

Venn's meaning was clear. The vampires never changed Cory because they liked the taste of his blood.

"Anyway," Venn continued, "with his connections to different vampire gangs, I thought he might know something about my brother. He had to put in a few calls for me, but it sounds like he's found him in Detroit."

Venn's expression slowly shifted, like it had taken him this long for it to sink in. He was going to see his brother again. Nothing could replace the feeling of getting to see your sibling after so long, after you'd given up hope of ever seeing them. His lips twitched at the corners and finally spread into a hint of a smile. He looked like he could hardly believe it.

"Venn, I'm so happy for you," I said genuinely. "When do we leave?"

A moment of shock crossed his features. "Rae…"

He didn't have to finish his sentence. I could tell by the look in his eyes what he was about to say.

"You don't want me to come with?" I asked. The hurt was evident in my tone.

"Everyone else needs you here," he said softly.

"No, they don't," I argued. "They can figure out what to do about Matias without me. Besides, I don't want to be separated from you again."

Being imprisoned on Gregor Island and feeling like I'd lost Venn had nearly broken me. I couldn't imagine what I'd do if something happened to him.

Venn reached up to brush dark strands of hair from my face. He blinked back tears as he stared deep into my eyes. "I don't, either, but I think this is something I have to do alone."

A hole tore through my chest. My voice came out small and fragile. "You don't want my help?"

"It's not that," he said, his voice cracking. "I feel like two different people—the guy I was before my parents died and my brother was changed, and the guy I am now, the one I am with you and the rest of our family. I can't explain it, but I feel like I need to find my brother as the guy I used to be—the one I was when we were together."

He took a deep breath and raked his fingers through his hair. "I'm not explaining it well. It has nothing to do with you. Please try to understand that."

I nodded, though it still felt a bit like a rejection. More than that, though, I worried for him. I knew he could handle himself, but I still wanted to be there for him. "Is it dangerous?"

His voice was so quiet I barely heard it. "I don't know."

I chewed the dry skin on my lower lip. I really didn't want him to do this alone. What if his brother was working with a group like Maliya's? The vampires may be cured, but that didn't make groups like that any less dangerous.

"Are you sure you have to do this alone?" I whispered. "You didn't let me go after Jenna alone."

Venn's gaze dropped to mine, and he ran his thumb across my shoulder. "This is different."

"Is it?" I asked. "You don't know what you could be getting yourself into."

Venn closed his eyes and took a breath. "Rae, please. I need to do this alone."

My stomach knotted. I didn't know if he truly meant that, or if he was afraid I couldn't handle myself without my magic —like he was trying to protect me. But I didn't want to fight with him, and I wouldn't be the girl who kept him from his brother.

I took his hands in mine. It hurt to say it, but I wanted him to know I supported him no matter what he decided to do. "Then go. Your brother is more important than anything right now. You need to find him."

God knows I felt the exact same way about my sister. Screw whatever threats we were facing. Family was everything.

Venn wrapped me in a tight hug, and for a moment, I felt that hole in my chest begin to close. Then I thought about being separated from him, and it tore even wider.

"How will you get there?" I asked.

"I've already talked to Richard and Genevieve," he said. "They're going to let me borrow one of their cars. I'll have my phone on me, so you can call whenever you want."

It was probably best if I didn't. I'd talk to him the whole time and slow him down.

"Just promise me you won't get hurt, Venn," I whispered.

He kissed me softly, then drew away to look me in the eyes. "I promise. I love you, Rae. Always and forever."

"Always and forever," I repeated.

I relaxed into his embrace once more as silence settled over the room. I couldn't help but think of what it must've been like for him to lose his brother. It had to be on par with losing Jenna.

"What happened that night?" I found myself asking. "When Tyson was attacked?"

Venn stared up at the ceiling without answering. He shook his head lightly and closed his eyes, like he was trying not to go back there. His heartbreak ricocheted through me. I knew exactly how it felt to revisit old memories. I still hadn't told him all the details of what happened the night my parents died.

"It's okay," I whispered softly. "You don't have to tell me."

"I will," he promised. "Eventually."

9

VENN ~ FOUR YEARS AGO

I remembered it like it was yesterday. I'd spent years of endless nights replaying the events over and over again so that each detail could never escape my memory. I suppose I tortured myself because somewhere deep down inside of me, I had hoped I could go back and change it. But no matter how much I replayed it, nothing would ever change. Each morning I woke, I was still alone. My brother was gone.

Gramps had been drinking that night. I wished I could say there was a reason for it, like he was trying to drink away the memory of Grams, but he'd picked up the whiskey bottle long before Grams died. The fact was, the man was trash, and there was no reason for it.

"Give me the damn remote," he muttered under his breath as he snatched it from Tyson's fingers. He plopped down into his old, tattered recliner and took a swig of whiskey straight from the bottle.

My brother and I exchanged a glance from where we sat beside each other on the couch. You never argued with Gramps, especially when he got in these moods. He'd never hit us or anything, but you sure didn't want to hear the old man yell. The neighbors five doors down could hear it through the walls. I was sure of it.

Gramps clicked the remote, and the TV switched from cartoons to boxing. "Ya damn kids and your stupid cartoons," he grumbled like we couldn't hear him. "I don't know why I waste the cable bill on ya."

Tyson's hands curled into fists as Gramps continued to mumble under his breath about how much of a burden we were. It was like he blamed us for our parents' deaths and that we didn't have anywhere else to go.

Three more years, I told myself. Three more years until I turned eighteen and could legally get out of this hell hole. Tyson and I did our best to stay out of Gramps's way and to clean up after him, but we could never get the smell of vomit out of our mattresses that had been there since we'd moved in, or the mysterious rotting stench that came from the kitchen drain. Our clothes were all hand-me-downs, and Tyson was in serious need of a new pair of shoes. They were ready to fall apart. We had to scour quarters from Gramps's recliner to do laundry, and only managed to find enough to do a load every two or three weeks. Gramps didn't care if his own clothes smelled like garbage and had ketchup stains on every white beater he owned. All he cared about was his boxing.

I placed a gentle hand on Tyson's shoulder, shooting him a glance that begged him to calm down. At thirteen, he was still trying to get the whole anger management thing down. Heck, I was no expert, but at least I knew to keep my cool around Gramps.

Without a word, Tyson stood and crossed in front of Gramps to head to our room.

"Get out the goddamn way!" Gramps yelled.

Tyson all but sprinted down the hall to avoid him. He shut the door quietly, but Gramps heard it.

"Don't you go slamming doors around here, boy!" he shouted.

I heard Tyson groan from the next room and decided to join him. I'd much rather be with him than out here with Gramps.

Slowly, I got to my hands and knees and inched my way across the carpet so I wouldn't interrupt Gramps's programming.

"Where you going?" Gramps demanded.

I stopped dead. "Uh, to my room."

"Microwave me a pizza pocket, will ya, Jason?"

I was used to Gramps calling me my father's name. At this point, I hardly noticed. I made it past the TV and got to my feet. The kitchen was small and cramped. I held my breath as I opened the freezer, hoping we weren't out. I breathed a sigh of relief when I found a single pizza pocket in the door.

"What's taking so long?" Gramps demanded. "It's just a pizza pocket!"

I rushed to grab a plate, then shoved his food in the microwave. Two minutes later, I was back in the living room, handing him his dinner. He took one bite and spit it back out, straightening in his chair.

"Goddamn, that's hot!" Gramps yelled. "You trying to burn my tongue off?"

I stepped away on shaky feet. "N-no."

"Get outta here," he snarled. "And take your goddamn disgusting pizza pocket with you."

Gramps shoved the food into my hand. I was dumbstruck.

I didn't know what else to do, so I just turned away and headed down the hall to my room.

Tyson was curled up beneath his blanket, pretending like he was asleep. I placed a hand on his shoulder and shook him lightly.

He groaned. "Go away."

"Are you hungry?" I asked.

Tyson sniffed the air and sat up at the smell of food.

"You want to split it?" I asked.

"Gramps won't get mad?"

The last time we'd snuck food into our room, he threw a fit for hours—said it would attract mice.

"Doesn't matter," I said. "Are you hungry?"

Tyson gazed down at his hands. "Yeah, I guess so."

I ripped the pizza pocket in half and gave him the bigger chunk. He nibbled on it quietly.

"I'm sick of living here," Tyson said, breaking the silence.

I sank onto my bed across from him. "I know. I am, too. Once I turn eighteen, we can leave. I'll become your guardian or something."

Tyson remained quiet for several moments. "What if... what if we left tonight?"

I just stared at him, unsure if I heard him correctly. "You want to run away?"

He lowered his voice so that even if Gramps was standing outside the door, he wouldn't be able to hear. "This isn't a life, Venn. Mom and Dad wouldn't have wanted this for us."

I frowned. "Mom and Dad are gone. They don't have a say anymore."

"Well, *we* should," he argued. "We should have a say in our own lives."

"It's not that simple," I said.

Believe me, I'd thought about leaving Gramps's place plenty of times, too, but I knew it wasn't realistic. As soon as someone found us, we'd be right back where we started, and Gramps would never forgive us for putting him through that. And if we told the state what a hell hole this was, we could end up somewhere worse.

At least Gramps never laid a hand on us. That was what I kept telling myself. To be honest, it didn't make my life any less miserable.

"The only person who has a say is the state," I pointed out. "If they want us here, we have to stay. It's the law."

Tyson finished off his pizza pocket and crossed his arms. "Not if they don't find us. If you want to stay, fine. But I'm done."

Tyson threw the covers off himself to reveal he was already fully clothed, with his tattered shoes on and everything. He reached beneath his bed to pull out his backpack, which was so full that it got stuck for a second.

"You can't be serious," I hissed.

"Yes, seriously." Tyson stood and swung the strap of his bag over his shoulder.

I caught him by the wrist before he could reach the window. "Where are you going to go? Do you have any idea what kind of monsters roam the streets at this time of night?"

Tyson scoffed and pulled a pocket knife from his jeans. I had no idea where he'd gotten it. Probably traded it with one of his buddies at school. "I'm not afraid of a vampire. I can handle myself. Besides, we've been out at night plenty of times and been fine. It's like the vamps don't even know we're there."

"You *should* be afraid," I snapped. "These aren't the city streets we grew up on, Tyson. Nocton isn't safe at night."

"Well, I can't exactly run away during the day," he shot back, ripping his arm from my grasp. "Are you coming or not?"

"Tyson, you can't go," I said firmly, putting my foot down.

He raised an eyebrow at me. "Watch me."

He flung open the window, but I sprang forward to catch him around the waist. He threw an elbow back and caught me in the corner of the eye. I longed to cry out, but I knew that would only get Gramps's attention. He didn't need to know what was going on in here.

"Let me go," Tyson demanded, squirming out of my grasp.

I clawed out at him, but my vision was still blurry from the blow. I couldn't hang on.

Tyson slipped from my grip and hurried out onto the fire escape. I blinked the world back into focus and rushed behind him, but he was already racing down the rickety metal stairs.

"Tyson!" I hissed, but he kept going. I made a split-second decision. Screw the rules. Screw what Gramps might think. I had to go after my brother.

I crawled out the window and sprinted down the fire escape. Tyson reached the bottom level and jumped onto the pavement below before I'd made it down one story.

"Tyson!" I called again. I tried to stay quiet to avoid attracting any attention. The dark street below us was empty, but there was no telling what kind of monsters lurked in the shadows.

"Come on, Venn!" Tyson spun around, his arms wide out, like he was on the top of the world.

I reached the bottom level of the fire escape, which ended a good ten feet above ground. The ladder that was supposed to descend to let you all the way down was broken off. Gathering my courage, I took the leap.

My ankles ached as they twisted under me, but I caught myself with my hands and hurried back to my feet.

"This is great!" Tyson exclaimed again. "Let's go."

"Tyson, get back—"

I never finished the sentence before a figure leapt out of the shadows. It all happened so fast that I never saw it coming. One second Tyson was standing there with his arms spread proudly, and the next he was on the pavement, writhing beneath a vampire with a newborn bloodlust in his silver eyes.

My blood ran cold, and for a second, I just stood there. Looking back on that night, I always wondered what would've happened if I hadn't frozen up. Would I have reached him in time to keep the vampire venom from entering his veins?

It felt like an eternity had passed, but that eternity had lasted a mere millisecond. When I caught sight of those pearly-white fangs glistening under the light of the street lamp, I sprang into action. No bloodsucking parasite was going to touch my brother!

A primal urge to protect rose up inside of me, and a strong tingle like I'd never felt spread across my skin. The buildings around me seemed to grow taller as I fell onto all fours, but I couldn't make sense of the different proportions around me or the way colors swam differently in my eyes. All I could focus on was my brother and the vampire rolling around the pavement with him, trying to get a shot at his neck.

I didn't realize at the time how strange it was that Tyson was able to fight back, that the vampire didn't just snap his bones under his supernatural strength. I wouldn't realize it until hours later that that was the moment Tyson's shifter genes switched on and he came into his own supernatural strength. I didn't even realize the same thing was happening to me—my first ever shift into a wolf.

Protect. Protect. Protect.

That was all that went through my head as I sprinted forward and slammed into the vampire. He rolled across the pavement, but he sprang to his feet a second later, like he hadn't felt a thing. Blood covered his fangs and dripped down his chin as he curled back his lips to snarl at me like some wild animal.

Anger unlike anything I'd ever felt before swept through me when I realized that the blood dripping down his chin was my brother's. He'd managed to get a bite, and I hadn't even noticed.

"Venn," Tyson's voice called to me through the darkness.

Relief washed over me, but I couldn't take my eyes off the angry vamp facing me, looking as if he was about to attack. A deep growl bubbled up from my throat, and I bared my canines at him.

In the blink of an eye, the vampire lunged, taking me down from all fours and onto my back. I yipped and howled as he squeezed, as if trying to break bone. I kicked my wide wolf paws at him, trying to use my sharp claws to tear at anything I could find.

I swiped at the guy's face, barely able to make out the black fur coating my body. I knew *something* was different, but I didn't have the luxury of questioning it at the moment.

The vampire reeled backward and hissed. It was enough to allow me the upper hand. I pressed my back paws against his chest and kicked outward. The vampire flew through the air and landed with a *thud* beside my brother.

I realized my mistake a moment too late. Tyson was lying on the ground, clutching the bleeding wound on his neck. The vampire took one look between us and decided to go for Tyson—the weakest of the two.

Faster than I could process, the vampire grabbed Tyson and tossed him over his shoulder like a ragdoll.

"Venn!" Tyson cried as sheer terror swept across his features.

I sprinted after them as the vampire disappeared into the dark alley with my brother. I ran as fast as I could, trying to follow the sound of my brother's voice. Even long after the footsteps faded, after my brother's cries were no longer anything more than an echoing in my own mind, and after my legs started to ache and my chest started to burn, I still pressed on.

I must've been wandering the streets of Nocton for hours, but it felt like years. Thick fog had settled over the streets, so much that the street lamps above my head seemed almost invisible. It was like walking through a dream. The streets were so quiet, so lonely. It didn't feel real.

"Tyson!" I tried to call out, but it only came out as a wolf's howl. It was like an ominous chord cutting through the night, signaling death.

He can't be gone, I told myself. *I will find him. I will find him.*

I must've repeated those words to myself a thousand times before they seemed to lose all meaning. My limbs felt so numb that it was as if they'd fallen off my body. I tried to push forward, but eventually, I could no longer move my feet. I curled up at the side of a brick building I didn't recognize and began to weep. I had no idea where I was and no idea how long it'd been. How had I lost him?

"Tyson," I whispered, but again, no words came out. It sounded like a whimper.

That was when I heard a whimper return, one that wasn't

my own. I sprang to my feet immediately and forced myself to follow the sound of the voice. It sounded so familiar. Could it be…?

I turned down an alleyway between two tall buildings. Another whimper came, and I was certain this time that it was real. I rushed forward toward the noise, and a lone figure began to take shape.

A child sat curled up beside a dumpster. His chest rose and fell quickly, and little sounds kept escaping from his lips like he couldn't control the agony inside of him.

My heart turned to water in my chest. As it did, my limbs grew, and I finally stood upright again. The cool night air brushed across every inch of my naked body, but I didn't care. I'd found my brother.

I knelt beside him and placed a gentle hand to his shoulder. "Tyson?"

He started when I touched him, and his gaze darted to mine. Silver momentarily flashed across his irises before they returned to their normal dark brown. He blinked a few times, as if trying to process whether I was truly there or not. The wound on his neck had healed from the vampire's saliva, but his skin had paled, as if he'd lost a lot of blood.

When my brother looked at me—like he was part my brother and part something else entirely—I felt as if my spirit left my body. My limbs moved without my command, and all I could feel was an icy coldness enter my chest. It was like I was watching the scene from up above.

"Venn?" Tyson asked through labored breaths.

"It's me," I whispered. "Are you okay?"

Stupid question. Of course he wasn't okay. He was lying there shivering in the cold after being attacked by a vampire. No one would be okay after that.

Tears rose to Tyson's eyes. "It hurts, Venn. It hurts so bad. Like fire…" He bit down on his lower lip, like the pain was too much to allow him to finish the sentence.

I wrapped him in my arms and pulled him close to me. "We need to get help."

Tyson shook his head. "I'm too far gone, brother."

I knew it was true. I'd heard stories about the transformation before, but I wasn't willing to believe it was something that would ever happen to us.

"No," I protested. "We'll get you to a hospital, get the venom out of you."

Tyson went into a coughing fit, and it felt as if my heart was breaking into a million pieces. I pulled him tighter, like I could wish the venom away with enough love. But even I knew spells didn't work that way.

Finally, Tyson found his voice. He gazed up at me. "I'm sorry. I'm so sorry I dragged you into this."

I shook my head as tears streamed down my cheeks. "It's not your fault."

"You warned me." He sucked in a deep, pained breath as silver flashed across his eyes once more.

My shoulder shook in sobs. "No, Tyson. Stay with me!"

"You have to go, Venn," he cried.

"I'm not leaving you." I buried my face into his shoulder.

"I don't want to hurt you," he insisted in a groggy voice.

"You won't hurt me," I told him.

"You know how new vampires are," he said. "You've heard all about the bloodlust. There will be nothing I can do to stop myself."

"You will." I only said it to try to convince myself. I wasn't ready to lose my brother, the true only family I had left.

Tears streamed down Tyson's face, and he shook his head. "I won't. You have to leave me. Please."

The pleading look in his eyes was almost too much to bear. It was like he was asking me to let him suffer and die alone. I couldn't do that.

"I'm staying right here," I promised.

Tyson's brows knitted together in anger. "I will bite you, Venn. So help me, I will."

This time, I couldn't convince myself otherwise. Tyson was telling the truth. He'd use his new fangs just to get me to leave, to protect me from himself.

Now who's the one protecting who?

In that moment, I'd never hated myself more. I was the big brother. I was supposed to protect him… and I'd failed.

"Venn, I'm a goner," Tyson groaned. "Just let me have one last wish. Go."

I could hardly believe he was asking such a thing from me, but I also knew what would happen if I stayed. I'd be right where he was, vampire venom pumping through my veins, pain unlike anything imaginable—or so I'd heard.

Against my will, I decided to follow my brother's wishes. Slowly, I lowered him back onto the pavement and stepped away.

Of all the details I remembered from that night, the one thing I could never recall was what it felt like in that moment. It should've been the single thing that stuck out above all else, but it didn't. I used to wonder if maybe I was just so numb from everything that had happened that I felt nothing when I let my brother go, but I'd come to realize it was the exact opposite.

All the emotions I'd felt tore through me like a black hole, ripping me apart from the inside. There was so much pain and so much sorrow that my mind had blocked it all out. It was just too much for one man to bear.

I remembered crying. I bawled like the ocean itself was trying to push its way out my eyes. But everything else… everything else was darkness.

"Venn," Tyson whispered before I was out of earshot.

I turned back to him, hopeful that he still wanted me by his side while he made the transformation. "Tyson?"

He sucked in a sharp breath, like the venom was doing something bad to him again. "Don't come after me. I don't want you getting hurt."

I hesitated. "I won't."

"Promise?" he asked.

I didn't know how I could manage to make such a promise. I felt like the worst brother in history, leaving him to suffer alone just because he asked me to. I should've stayed. I should've comforted him when he needed it the most. But instead, I followed his wishes.

"I promise."

I barely remembered the walk home, when I knocked on Gramps's apartment door early in the morning and he answered with a string of curse words, only to find me naked and covered in dirt at his doorstep.

It was the first time Gramps laid a hand on me, after I'd told him what had happened. For whatever reason, I remembered every blow, every shot of pain that radiated across my skin. I drank all that in and seared it into my memory. I supposed that was because I thought I deserved it. When Gramps said it was my fault, I believed him.

10

The morning seemed to darken as we gathered in Genevieve's kitchen for breakfast and Venn said his goodbyes. Like the rest of the house, the kitchen was bathed in dark tones and soft lighting.

Genevieve, Jenna, and Ronark were already seated around the long mahogany table, while Teagan stood behind the island at the stove cooking eggs. Clarita, Amalia, and Richard hadn't made it down for breakfast yet. The rest of us—Sondra, Ryland, Fiona, and me—were all crowded around Venn.

"Don't be gone too long," Fiona said as she hugged Venn.

Venn hiked his backpack up on his shoulder. "I won't."

"Stay safe," Teagan said, as if in warning.

Ryland took Venn's hand and gave him a one-armed hug. "You sure we can't come with you?"

"Guys, I'll be fine," Venn insisted. "You have bigger things to worry about in the meantime."

Sondra wrapped him in a hug. "That doesn't mean we won't be worrying about you. Our intuition is crap these days. If something goes wrong—"

"Nothing is going to go wrong," Venn assured us. "I'm going to find my brother and bring him back. That's it."

"Maybe you should wait until you have more information," I suggested nervously, even though I knew there was nothing I could say to stop him from going.

"It's not like Tyson's location is plastered all over the Internet," Ryland said. "With groups like this—"

He cut off when Venn elbowed him. The meaning was clear. Tyson was hanging out with a dangerous, secretive group of ex-vampires. And Venn was walking straight into their nest. It was all too familiar. If he was anything like me, the more I pushed him to take precautions, the more reckless he'd be.

But I knew Venn wasn't like me, and that was the only thing giving me solace at the moment and keeping me from following after him. He would take precautions. He would think things through. He would take care of himself.

Right?

Venn pulled me close to him. "I'll be fine, Rae. You do your planning against Matias. I'll be back with Tyson before it's all over."

"You better be," I said. "I love you."

"I love you, too."

He gave me a kiss on the lips, then that was it. I watched at the window as he got into Richard's SUV and drove down the street. I didn't look away until he was long gone. Teagan's voice pulled me out of my daze.

"You hungry?" she asked. She stood at the table with a spatula full of scrambled eggs hovering above my plate.

I shook my head but sat anyway. "I'll eat later."

Jenna took my hand under the table and gave it a light squeeze.

"Venn can take care of himself," Sondra said reassuringly, though she didn't sound convinced.

"I know," I replied as I stared down into my full glass of orange juice. I wasn't sure I could stomach it right now. "It's just that he came after me when I went to find Jenna alone. I wanted to help him."

"He'll be back," Genevieve said from the head of the table. "In the meantime, we have work to do."

"What's the plan?" Ronark asked as he dug into his eggs and sausage.

"I know a few locals I'd like to approach to help us," Genevieve said. "There's a man who runs an underground spell shop. He might be willing to supply protection charms and potions."

Oh, God. I hoped she didn't mean Devin, my old boss at Bloodstone. I hadn't heard from him since I quit so I could go after my sister. If I knew him at all, he was already in Chicago cozying up to Matias. Asking for his help wouldn't be my first choice. His spells never were great to begin with.

"What's this guy's name?" I asked, finally taking a sip of orange juice.

"Alexander Morris," Genevieve replied.

Huh. Never heard of him. Wait…

"Alexander, as in Xander?" I asked.

I'd heard of the guy before, but I'd never met him. Devin had talked about him when I worked at Bloodstone. He always complained the guy was his biggest competitor. He even joked about doing some questionable things to him, though he never followed through with any of it. I always got the impression that Devin was a little intimidated by Xander's magic. The guy was at least a mid-witch bordering on a high witch.

"I've tried to reach him, but he hasn't been answering his phone. I want Sondra to visit him today to see if he'll help us." Genevieve handed Sondra a set of car keys.

"You're not going?" I asked, a bit surprised.

She shook her head. "Clarita, Amalia, and I will be going through our inventory today and cataloguing any potions that might be useful to us. Besides, Xander and I haven't exactly gotten along in the past. He likes Sondra."

"I'm coming, too," I said immediately. No way was I sitting around here all day without getting in on some of the action.

"Me too," Fiona chimed in.

"And me," Ryland insisted, puffing up his chest.

Genevieve frowned. "You might scare him off."

"Yeah, he's pretty paranoid," Sondra said. "I think it should just be us three girls. He won't be as intimidated by us."

"But what if—?" Ryland started.

"We can handle ourselves." Sondra shot him a pointed expression.

Ryland gaped at her. "But without your magic…"

"Babe." Teagan placed a gentle hand on his shoulder. "They'll be fine. No one else has magic either, remember?"

"Maybe Tea should come with us, too," Fiona suggested. "She's been fighting vamps for ages without any magic."

Teagan poked at her food. "I'm actually not feeling great today."

"Can I come?" Jenna asked. "I'd really like to get out."

"Sure," Sondra said.

While they spoke, I eyed Teagan curiously. She had been acting weird lately—like she didn't want to fight anymore. Had something happened on Gregor Island that scared her? Something she hadn't told us about?

"You okay, Tea?" I asked.

"Yeah," she assured me. "Just a stomach bug. I'll start on the next pile of books you guys were reading through, see if I can find something."

"Well, girls," Sondra said. "Should we get going?"

Jenna, Fiona, and I got to our feet.

"Hold on." Teagan rose and started for the door. "Before you go, I think you should have some weapons on you. No one has magic anymore, but that doesn't mean they aren't dangerous. Follow me."

The four of us exchanged quick glances as we followed Teagan down the hall and to her guest room. Her room was almost identical to mine, but she had a pile of knives spread out on the bed. There must've been at least two dozen of them, all in different shapes and sizes.

Fiona gasped and reached for the closest one, running her finger along the blade to test how sharp it was. "Where did you get all these? I thought you lost yours."

Teagan smirked, looking proud beside her display. "Genevieve has been very generous after I told her I'd lost the ones she'd given me."

"Wow," Sondra said, like she couldn't believe it. "She really has changed, hasn't she?"

"What did she used to be like?" I asked, reaching for a dagger with a rose-petal design etched into the blade.

"She seems really nice to me." Jenna grabbed a large pocket knife and flipped it open. The blade was at least an inch wide and as long as my hand. She beamed, then closed it and slid it in her pocket.

"Let's just say she wasn't the best mentor to work with," Sondra admitted. "She was very hard on me."

Fiona crinkled her nose. "She wasn't exactly kind when I first met her, either. She wasn't even willing to mentor me because apparently fox shifters are weak. Like that has anything to do with witch magic."

Teagan held up a belt to Fiona, which had multiple sheaths built in for throwing knives. Fiona took it and began securing the belt around her waist.

"Honestly, I think meeting Richard has helped," Teagan said.

"They haven't been together long?" Jenna sounded surprised. "I assumed they'd been together forever."

Sondra shook her head as she secured a sheath onto her hip. "A lot has changed in her life over the past few years. She didn't have Richard or the house until later. It was all around the time I finished mentoring with her a few years ago. Her business took off, and everything just sort of fell into place for her. That was when she loaned me the money to start my own business, but that only hurt our relationship even more."

I slipped the dagger into my boot. "It sounds like she finally figured out magic."

"I think so," Sondra said. "I'm happy for her. I'm glad she changed."

Teagan handed Fiona her leather jacket. "Here. This will hide the knives."

Fiona put it on and grinned. She turned to the mirror above the dresser and spun around to take in her new look. She always looked so sweet in her jeans and flowery tops. Today, her red hair was piled on her head instead of down in waves. In skinny jeans, a deep green tee, and Teagan's leather jacket, she looked totally badass. It was like she'd aged five years in a matter of days.

"Wow," I said, coming to stand beside her. "You look awesome."

She smiled into the mirror nervously. "Do I?"

Teagan patted her on the shoulder and whispered in her ear. "You're a vampire slayer. Embrace it, girl."

Fiona grinned. "Can I still call myself that now that there are no vampires?"

Sondra raised her eyebrows. "You've killed a vampire before, haven't you?"

"Yeah," Fiona admitted. "Tons."

Jenna wrapped an arm around her and looked at Fiona's reflection in the mirror. "Then you're a vampire slayer."

I couldn't take my eyes off the mirror as I looked at our group of five. We were all dressed in dark colors and tight clothing. We kind of looked like a team of assassins. Maybe Xander *would* be intimidated by us.

"Should we go see what kind of trouble we can get ourselves into?" I asked. Excitement sizzled in my bones.

"Hopefully not too much," Teagan said as we all started for the door.

Ryland was already on his way down the hall when he caught sight of Fiona stepping out of the room. He stopped dead in his tracks.

"What?" she feigned.

Ryland looked gobsmacked seeing Fiona dressed in anything but her usual attire. "You look… different."

Fiona crossed her arms. "You mean I look like Teagan?"

"Well, that *is* Teagan's jacket, isn't it?" He eyed it like he wasn't quite sure.

Sondra stepped forward and draped an arm around Fiona's shoulder. "I think she looks great."

"You sure I can't come with? Help protect you?" Ryland begged.

"It's sweet you're worried about your sister," Sondra said, "but I think she can handle herself."

Ryland's jaw tightened. "She's only seventeen."

"And I've been fighting alongside you for years," Fiona shot back. "Why the sudden change of heart?"

Ryland gaped at her. "Because…"

"Because I don't have my shifter strength?" Fiona's irritation grew with each passing second. "I don't need it."

Ryland looked her up and down. He opened his mouth like he was about to protest, but before he could, she sprang on him. Fiona had a knife out of her belt in under a second. She pressed her forearm against Ryland's huge chest and shoved him up against the wall. Her arm came down to stab the knife into the wall just inches from his face before he could even blink.

Ryland's eyes went wide, and he held his hands up in surrender.

"Holy shit, Fiona!" Teagan cried proudly.

Jenna clapped and whooped, while Sondra tried to stifle a laugh. My jaw dropped, and my hand slapped over my mouth.

"You go, girl!" Jenna exclaimed.

Fiona smirked at Ryland. "Tell me again how you don't think I can handle myself."

He stumbled over his words. "I-I guess I was mistaken."

"Damn right you were." Fiona ripped the knife from the wall and turned to us to hide the look of utter disbelief written across her face from Ryland.

I held my hand up and gave her a high-five.

Sondra started down the hall, swaying her hips and snapping her fingers. "And that, cousin, is how a girl gets 'er done."

Jenna, Fiona, and I followed, swaying our hips in the same manner.

Jenna laughed. "You tell him, sister."

Fiona turned toward Ryland, walking backward to keep up

with us. "Love you, brother!" she said as she kissed the ends of her fingers and blew the kiss to him while simultaneously flipping him off.

Teagan elbowed Ryland in the ribs. "Oh, don't look so surprised."

That was all I saw before we turned the corner and headed outside.

Fiona jumped down the front porch stairs and hopped excitedly on the sidewalk. "Wow! That felt good."

"It should," I said. "Your brother's an asshole."

Fiona rolled her eyes. "Only sometimes."

Sondra led us to the garage, where we found a black sedan waiting for us. "I'm proud of you, Fiona, but we're all going to have to tone it down once we get to Xander's. He's not expecting us, so we have to tread carefully."

"What do you mean by that?" I asked as I slid into the passenger seat. Fiona and Jenna took the back.

Sondra started the car. "It means he's a great witch, but it's going to take some convincing to get him to join our side."

Fifteen minutes later, we pulled up to a three-story brick building. It looked old, with shop windows on the lower level and apartments on the upper. I'd only been in this part of town a few times before, but I'd never seen much vampire action around here.

We stepped out of the car. The air was chilly for a summer day, and clouds were rolling in. A few people walked along the street, roaming in and out of shops, but in general it was quiet and felt a bit ominous.

I glanced to the shoe shop on the lower level, but Sondra cocked her head toward the alley.

"This way," she whispered.

The three of us quietly followed behind her. I was acutely aware of the dagger in my boot, prepared to use it if something bad happened. The path between the buildings reminded me of the many alleyways I'd killed vampires in. I half expected one to jump out from behind the dumpster and attack us. But there was nothing except an old newspaper tumbling across the pavement in the wind.

Sondra stopped dead in her tracks and held a hand out to stop us. Warning bells went off in my head, sending my heart thumping. I followed her gaze to see the door we were headed for was cracked open. It creaked as we approached, giving way to a dark descending staircase. Tingles spread across my skin.

"Should my intuition be going haywire right now if I don't have any connection to Synchrony?" I whispered.

"It's not just you," Jenna said, stepping cautiously toward the door.

"Intuition or not, this is a little creepy," Sondra said.

Fiona shrugged. "Eh, we've dealt with worse. Let's check it out."

Sondra opened the heavy metal door wider. When we saw what lay at the bottom, she started sprinting. "Xander!?"

I was right behind her, my heart racing. The door at the bottom of the stairs had been knocked off its hinges. Beyond it, the spell shop had been completely ransacked. Shelves were knocked over, and empty potion vials lay everywhere. Pages had been ripped out of spell books and littered the floor. Most of the merchandise was missing. The fluorescent lights above our heads flickered on and off.

"Xander?" Sondra called again as she climbed over the shelving and tried to avoid the broken glass shattered everywhere.

I could hardly take in the horrifying scene as I followed behind her. Jewelry cases that once held trinkets and charms were completely empty, as were the bookcases along the far wall. The only sign Xander once sold herbs was the bag of sage busted on the floor.

"Who would do this?" Fiona asked breathlessly.

Jenna looked around to take it all in. "You think whoever did this got him?"

Sondra opened her mouth to say something, but a muffled voice cut through the momentary silence.

"Help!"

I immediately raced toward the back room to the sound of the voice.

"Sondra, is that you? Help!"

The back room was just as bad as the main shop. A heavy bookcase had been knocked in front of a closet door, where the voice was coming from.

"Xander!" Fiona called.

"Who is that?" he called back.

I reached for the case and began lifting it. Damn, I was really missing my shifter strength right now. This thing felt like two hundred pounds. Jenna and Fiona rushed over to help.

"I'm here," Sondra said. "You just hold tight. We're going to get you out of there."

We pushed the bookcase upright. Sondra kicked old books aside and yanked open the door. Inside, an old man with white hair shivered in the corner of the dark closet. He put his hand up to shield his eyes from the light. Xander?

He looked so frail—so afraid.

Sondra reached down to help him to his feet. His whole body shook as he took in the destruction of his shop. I grabbed a chair that had been knocked over and set it upright for him. Fiona rushed out of the room and came back a few seconds later with a paper cup full of water.

"Here you go, Mr. Xander," she said as he sank into the chair.

He took it with shaky hands and sipped the water.

"Xander, what happened here?" Sondra asked.

His eyes glossed over, like he couldn't believe what happened. "The Department of Magical Regulation found me."

We each shared a collective gasp.

"But your protection spells," Sondra pointed out. "They should've held, right?"

Xander shook his head regrettably. "I thought so, too. But they broke through it somehow. When the spell broke, it was like a bomb going off. Potion vials shattered, and shelves fell over. I drank a chameleon potion and hid in the closet. Then they came in and took everything. I heard all of it. By the time they left, the door was blocked."

"How long have you been in there?" I asked breathlessly.

Xander raked his fingers through his gray hair. "I don't know. A day, maybe…?"

"What's a chameleon potion?" Jenna asked.

"It basically renders you invisible," Sondra explained. "It's not true invisibility. It's a type of hypnosis spell. If someone looks at you while you're under the influence of it, they'll be compelled to look away. It's like putting a blind spot in someone else's mind. Lasts about twelve hours. What I'm more concerned about is how the DMR broke through your protection spell. It's supposed to keep any threats out of your shop."

Xander shook his head. "I don't know."

"The DMR must be using magic," I said in thought.

"What do you mean?" Fiona asked. "Like Matias is working with them?"

"I don't think so," I said. "Leon Cavanaugh told me the DMR keeps and catalogues all magical artifacts they confiscate. They must have loads of potions and artifacts that they're using to serve their purpose."

Jenna crossed her arms. "Well, that's just sick. Using the magic they despise to fight magic? A little ironic, don't you think?"

I rolled my eyes. "It's like Ryland said. It's the lesser of two evils for them. At least they can control the magic they have their hands on."

Xander seemed to relax now that he'd had a drink of water. He looked up to Sondra. "What are you doing here?"

"We came to ask for your help," she replied. "But we can talk about it later. Let's get you something to eat."

Xander stood to follow Sondra's lead, but he looked a little disoriented, like he was still trying to take it all in. Sondra helped steady him while I stood on his other side and helped him over fallen shelves and to the door.

He finally seemed to steady himself as we ascended the stairs. "Thank you so much for helping me. I didn't know how long I was going to be stuck in that closet."

"I'm glad we came when we did," Sondra said.

Xander stepped into the alleyway and glanced around with squinted eyes, as if the daylight was blinding.

"There's a café two doors down," Sondra said, pointing out of the alleyway. "Is that okay?"

"Yes, of course," Xander replied. "I'll eat anything right now."

We left the alley and entered a small café. The place was quiet, and there was only one other couple there. We claimed a corner booth far away from them so we could talk in private.

Our waitress arrived as soon as we sat, and she handed out menus. She pulled a pad and pen out of her pocket. "Welcome.

I'm Terry, and I'll be your server today. Can I start you folks off with some drinks?"

"Water for me, please," I said. I still wasn't hungry since breakfast.

"You guys can order whatever you want," Sondra offered. "I'll pay."

"Ooh!" Jenna's eyes lit up, and she flipped to the back of the menu. "Do you know how long it's been since I've had a soda? And French fries!"

Fiona glanced up to the waitress. "I'll have a water, too, thanks."

Sondra stuck with water as well, while Jenna ordered soda and Xander ordered coffee. His fingers continued to shake as he tore open the sugar packet and poured it in his cup. No one spoke until the waitress took our food orders and disappeared back into the kitchen.

"What can I help you ladies with?" Xander asked without meeting any of our gazes.

Sondra leaned her elbows on the table from where she sat next to him. "You've heard about Matias Vayne?"

Xander took a sip of coffee. "I've been stuck in a closet for a day. I haven't been living under a rock."

"We plan to go after him," Sondra admitted. "We're looking for witches willing to join us."

Xander set his coffee down. His hand shook as he pressed his fingers to his lips to steady them. I was starting to wonder if his shaking was a normal tick and not due to being locked in a closet for the past twenty-four hours. "I fail to see how I can help, seeing as my magic is useless now."

Sondra frowned. "You know that's not true. You said yourself you used a chameleon potion just yesterday. Your potions and charms still work."

Xander shook his head. "No, no. I'm afraid I can't. The DMR took everything."

"Everything?" I asked breathlessly. There was nothing left in his apartment? Nothing he'd kept secret from his patrons?

Xander shot me a pointed expression. "Yes, everything. I can't help you."

He started to stand, but Sondra's hand shot out to grab his wrist. "Xander, please. We need you."

He hesitated. His gaze traveled around the table, taking in each one of our pleading expressions. We needed all the help we could get.

"Also, you need to eat something," Fiona pointed out.

Xander glanced to the kitchen, then relaxed back into his seat. He took a sip of coffee again, as if it might steady his nerves. "What exactly do you want from me?"

"Whatever assistance you can offer," Sondra said. "I know there's more to your spell shop than you keep out in the open."

Sondra had said Xander was a paranoid man. He must've had protection charms galore in hidden corners of his shop. Which meant whatever the DMR used to break through them was powerful.

"And none of that would be any use to you," he snapped. He crossed his arms over his chest, like he was protecting himself from something.

"We could use information," I added. "You could join us and help us find other people willing to support us."

"No," he answered immediately, sounding bitter about it. "I'm done. My shop is ruined, and my protection spells broken. I'm going into early retirement."

"You don't have to follow us," Fiona said gently. "We're just asking for any potions, charms, or trinkets that could help us face Matias and get our magic back."

Xander gaped at her, then hugged himself even tighter. "I told you. The DMR took everything."

"Do you know of anyone else who might be willing to help?" I asked, feeling hopeless. This guy clearly wasn't willing to get involved in any of this.

"I can't give out names," he insisted. "I won't put any other supernaturals at risk."

"That's not what we're asking." Jenna sounded offended. "No one will be at risk. We'll give them a choice."

Xander's voice became more aggressive. "It would be a breach of my clients' confidentiality!"

Just then, our waitress returned, and the whole table went silent. She placed a burger and fries in front of Jenna and a plate of pancakes in front of Xander. The rest of us hadn't ordered anything.

"You folks enjoy your meal!" Terry said kindly before heading to check on the other patrons across the café.

"Look, Xander," I said as softly as I could. I felt for the guy. I really did. But I also had a feeling he was hiding something. "What happened to you yesterday never should've happened. The DMR is abusing their power now that the magical community is vulnerable. We plan to change that. If we can restore magic, you can set up your protection spells again. All of us will get back a piece of ourselves that we lost when Matias took it. So if you know anything that could help us defeat the guy controlling magic, then please... help us."

My throat began to close up. If the magical community wasn't willing to step up against Matias with us, we would never defeat him. We couldn't do it on our own.

Xander's arms slowly relaxed, and he dropped them to his

side. He shot a quick glance at Sondra, who was gazing at him with a pleading expression.

"You really think you can defeat him?" he asked skeptically.

"Yes," Fiona and Sondra answered in unison. I nodded, while Jenna was barely paying attention as she dug into her burger like she hadn't eaten in two years. Which, to be fair, was pretty close to the truth. She hadn't had a decent meal in that long, at least.

"And what happens when you do?" Xander asked. "Everything goes back to normal?"

"Yes," Sondra said, but her answer rubbed me the wrong way.

I didn't just want things to go back to normal. I wanted them to be better. I wanted things to change. I didn't want to keep hiding who I was, performing magic in secret and always watching my back when I shifted to make sure no one was watching me. I was a witch. I was a raven shifter. I'd embraced that, and it was time the Department of Magical Regulation embraced that, too.

Xander took several bites of his pancakes, then set his fork down. He inhaled a deep breath, like he was thinking hard about it. "All right. I will help you. But you must understand that I'm putting myself at great risk to do so."

Xander began reaching into his pockets. He dropped a handful of all sorts of random objects on the table: hair barrettes, jewelry, coins, even a small pencil eraser. Then he dug into his other pocket to pull out even more. My jaw dropped as I watched the pile grow taller and taller. To the normal eye, it all looked like junk, but I knew better. They were trinkets, the type of protection charm Fiona had found in the book we'd read. They'd suppress another supernatural's powers.

Xander reached up and pulled three different necklace chains over his head, which had been tucked into his shirt. He left one remaining for himself.

"Trinkets," Sondra whispered under her breath. "I thought of those, but they're not very strong."

"Not on their own," Xander agreed. "They won't win you any fights against Matias, but they can give you a bit of an edge."

"That's very generous of you," I said.

"Yes, well, it's all I have," Xander replied.

"It's more than enough," Sondra told him, staring down at the pile in fascination. "There will be enough for each of us to have one."

"Well, go on." He gestured to the pile. "Take them before I change my mind."

"Thank you, Mr. Xander." Fiona reached across the table and began gathering the trinkets into her jacket pockets.

I gathered the few she couldn't fit and put them in my own pockets.

"Just one thing." Xander leaned across the table and pointed a finger toward each of us as he spoke. "If this doesn't work out, I want the trinkets back. Every. Single. One."

I swallowed hard, acutely aware of the trinkets in my pockets. His words echoed in my mind. *If this doesn't work out.*

It had to…

Right?

"I knew trinkets were a good idea," Fiona raved proudly as we pulled into Genevieve's driveaway. A maroon sedan that wasn't there earlier was parked beside our spot.

"Is that another one of Richard's cars?" Fiona asked.

Sondra's eyebrows came together, as if confused. "No, I don't think so. I think I might recognize that car, but—"

Her eyes traveled to the front door, where a pretty blonde stood. She looked vaguely familiar from the back, but I couldn't place her.

"Oh my God!" Sondra exclaimed. She shoved the vehicle into park and cut the engine, then kicked her door open.

I quickly followed behind her. By the time I reached the front door, Genevieve was standing in the open doorway and inviting the girl inside.

"Zoey!" Sondra called, holding her arms out wide like she was going in for a hug.

The blonde turned, and a wide smile spread across her face. "Sondra!"

The girl hurried down the stairs and into Sondra's arms. And I. Stopped. Dead.

Instinct overcame me, and I suddenly had the urge to reach into my boot and stake my dagger through the girl's heart.

The shape of her nose, the Cupid's bow shape of her lips. I'd met Zoey before… except then her skin was paler, and her eyes were silver.

Fiona rushed up to greet Zoey like she was her long-lost sister, but I took a step back, completely dumbfounded.

Jenna stopped next to me. "What's wrong, Rach? You know this girl?"

I swallowed the lump in my throat, then finally found my feet. I grabbed Jenna's wrist and pulled her down the walkway so we couldn't be heard. "I met her in a bar once. She tried to flirt with me."

Jenna shrugged and gazed at Zoey like she wasn't at all a threat. "So? Flirt back."

"Jenna." I swatted her shoulder. "It was a *vampire* bar."

Realization crossed Jenna's face. "She was a vampire?"

I nodded and shot a disgusted look at her. Fiona and Sondra were raving over Zoey like they were best friends. Ew.

"Okay," Jenna said, like it was no big deal. "So she's cured now. Why are you acting like she's still cursed?"

The question hit me like a slap in the face. I didn't have an answer.

"Come on," Jenna said, tugging at my arm. "Let's not be rude."

Jenna walked straight up to Vamp Girl and stuck her hand out. "Hi, I'm Jenna. I'm Rachel's sister. She's the one who killed Valkas and broke your curse."

The blood drained from my face. Jenna grabbed on to my

shoulders and shoved me in front of her, forcing me to take Vamp Girl's outstretched hand. Her fingers were cold—just like a real vampire's.

"Hi, Rachel. I'm Zoey." She tilted her head, as if trying to remember where she'd seen me before. "We've met, haven't we?"

I cleared my throat and lied straight through my teeth. "I'm not sure."

"We have!" she cried. "I remember you. It was at Red Whiskey. We danced together for a few minutes."

I shifted my weight between my feet uncomfortably. I didn't talk to vampires. I slayed them. This whole encounter left me feeling uneasy. And they were just going to let her into Genevieve's house?

"Oh," I said, pretending to remember. "Yeah, I guess so."

"Is it true?" she asked. "That you broke the curse?"

"Yeah," Fiona said, draping a casual arm around my shoulder. "She was totally badass."

Vamp Girl smiled. "Well, thank you."

I gaped at her. I'd gone completely speechless.

"I'm happy to be back," Zoey said, then she turned and followed Genevieve into the house.

I whirled on Fiona and Sondra immediately. "You know Vamp Girl? She's a *vampire*."

The two shared a look I couldn't read.

"Her name is Zoey," Fiona said, "and she *was* a vampire."

"How… how do you know her?" I asked. How had they ended up becoming friends with a vampire? They were supposed to kill them.

"Zoey and I were both students of Genevieve's," Sondra said. "Before she changed."

"Exactly. She changed," I pointed out. "Which means she's dangerous now."

Sondra crossed her arms and frowned at me. "Honestly, Rachel. The way you talk about vampires, you make it sound like they're an entirely different species."

"You of all people should know that," I stated.

"They're cured, though," Fiona argued. "I, for one, am thrilled to have Zoey back."

"But—" I started, but Sondra cut me off.

"Give Zoey a chance, Rae. I think you'll like her." Sondra turned and headed toward the door, and Fiona followed.

I just stood there dumbstruck, trying to take in the new information.

Jenna waited for me. "I'm not too keen on this vampire thing either, but I think Sondra's right. Zoey looks harmless."

I gaped at her. Shouldn't she be siding with me—after what the vampires had done to her?

I forced my feet to move beneath me, and I started up the steps and followed everyone else inside. Voices traveled into the hall from the kitchen. I found everyone gathered around the table, where Clarita and Amalia were exchanging greetings with Zoey. Only Richard, Ronark, Ryland, and Teagan were missing.

I lowered myself into a chair on the other end of the table, keeping a close watch on Zoey. I couldn't help but picture her with elongated canines. Yeah, she looked normal, and her eyes were no longer silver, but I couldn't shake the feeling that she shouldn't be here.

"How'd it go with Xander?" Amalia asked, turning to Fiona.

"Great!" she replied. "He gave us these trinkets to help suppress Matias's abilities."

Fiona dug into her pockets and spread the trinkets out on the table.

Clarita picked up a golden ring with a red stone to examine it. "A good idea. Not the strongest magic by any means, but we can use whatever we can get."

"Rachel," Jenna prodded, gesturing to the trinkets at the other end of the table.

Sighing, I stood and added my trinkets to the pile.

"Oh, wow!" Zoey gasped. "That's a lot. There must be dozens."

Genevieve pursed her lips, like she was thinking hard. "I want everyone to take one and keep it on themselves at all times. If Matias is using the locket to watch us, it should keep his visions fuzzy."

I took the golden ring and slipped it on my finger.

"So, Zoey," I said, trying to force my voice not to waver. "Will you be staying with us?"

Zoey glanced to Genevieve. "No. I heard all the guest rooms are full. I'm just here to help. No point in taking up extra room anyway. I'm only a few minutes away."

I didn't need a reminder of how many vampires roamed these streets... or used to roam them. Damn it. I was really itching to go out on patrol. Those days were over, though.

Sucks to be me.

"What can I help with?" Zoey asked, sounding enthusiastic to be on the team.

"We're still finishing up some cataloguing." Genevieve gestured for them to follow her. "I have a box of potions you brewed while we were working together, but they're unlabeled. I was wondering if you could help identify them."

"Sure thing." Zoey followed behind Genevieve and gave a little hop.

Ugh. She was way too bubbly for her own good.

As soon as the other witches were out of the room, Fiona turned on me. She crossed her arms and furrowed her brow. What the hell? She'd never looked at me like this before.

"What?" I demanded.

"Why were you being so rude to Zoey?" she asked.

"I wasn't!" I insisted.

"You were," Sondra argued.

Okay, maybe I was being a little cold.

Jenna stepped toward the door nervously, like she didn't want to get in the middle of this. "I'm, uh, just going to check on Ronark." She slipped out of the room without so much as another glance my way, leaving me to face Fiona's and Sondra's narrowed gazes.

I let out a huff. "I'm sorry. What do you want me to say?"

"You don't even know Zoey," Sondra said.

"I know she was a vampire," I shot back.

Sondra grabbed my hand. "Let's go talk in private."

I ripped my arm away. "Talk about what? There's nothing to talk about."

Fiona pursed her lips. "Yes, there is."

I gave in and followed the two to their guest room. Theirs was laid out differently than mine, with two twin beds in either corner and a long chest of drawers between them. I fell onto one bed, while they both sat on the other to face me.

"I feel like I'm being interrogated," I grumbled.

"You are," Fiona snapped.

"Jeez. Calm down," I snarled back. "What's your problem?"

"Zoey and I were close for a long time," she said in a harsh tone. "When she changed, it was like losing a sister. You realize vampires are gone, right? Zoey is human again. She's not going to hurt you."

Sondra held her hands up. "Okay, Fiona. You *do* need to calm down. We can have a civil conversation here."

Fiona took a breath but didn't respond.

Sondra turned to me and spoke softly. "Rae, what's going on?"

I sat up straighter in the bed, unsure how to answer that question. "I… I guess when you see someone as a heartless vampire, you can't really unsee it."

"Heartless?" Fiona asked in disbelief. "Did Zoey hurt you?"

"No," I answered immediately. "I just…"

"You just what?" Fiona raised an eyebrow. She was taking this way too personally. Zoey obviously meant a lot to her.

I switched gears. "We don't know how this curse affected people. What if the vampires are still…? I don't know, evil?"

Sondra looked like she was considering my words. She didn't get all defensive like Fiona did. She just sat and listened. "You think the curse could've damaged their souls permanently?"

I hadn't realized that's what I'd been thinking until she put it into words. "Yeah, I guess so. I mean, we don't know for sure, do we? Look at Matias. He's still out to kill anyone who doesn't agree with him. Maybe we should just be cautious."

Sondra shifted on the bed to sit closer to the edge. "I don't think that's the case, Rae. Everything I know about souls says that a soul only leaves a body upon death. Vampires were never truly dead."

"Yeah, but we don't know if this curse was an exception to that rule," I pointed out.

"We've always known the curse affected souls somehow," Sondra said. "It's why witches who changed couldn't use their powers—since witch power is connected to the soul. But I never once believed that vampires had lost their souls completely."

"You can't know that," I pointed out. "It could've damaged them somehow."

"Cool down," Sondra said. "I'm just trying to explain what I believe. I'm not trying to get into a debate."

I shut my mouth and let her talk.

"I've always believed that the vampire curse was powerful enough to overshadow a person's soul. It took their basic instincts and pushed them to the surface, while pushing their humanity down, the empathy and caring that made them human. But I believe they still had a choice in everything they did."

"Which makes them bad," I pointed out. "If vampires were willing to kill people or enslave them, doesn't that make them bad? If they *chose* that, rather than having it forced upon them through a curse?"

"Not all vampires did those things," Sondra responded. "They didn't all join up with the blood slave trade. Some of them never even tasted human blood outside a blood bank. Occasionally, the good would come out."

"I *never* saw that," I told her.

"How hard were you looking?" Sondra spoke softly, like the question wasn't a slap to the face.

"If you truly believe that, then why did you kill them?" I asked.

"We killed the ones who deserved it," Fiona replied, calmly this time.

What if they all deserved it?

"And what happened to them?" I challenged. "The ones you killed?"

"Their souls would've been released from their bodies, and

they would reincarnate," Sondra said. "We know their souls were there all along now. Their souls have been restored. Otherwise, Matias wouldn't be able to perform magic."

"So he just gets a free pass?" I asked. "Once he dies, he'll be reincarnated to start his work all over again?"

Sondra shook her head. "We don't know that. With cases like Valkas and Matias, where the person is truly evil, we believe that Synchrony will destroy their souls to keep the balance. But that's not for us to judge."

"Then who *does* judge?" I asked.

"*Synchrony*," Sondra emphasized.

"Who's to say Synchrony isn't asking for our help?" I said.

Fiona shot to her feet, like she couldn't take it anymore. "This is ridiculous, Rae. You're just scared to admit that the vampires ever kept a trace of their humanity, because that would mean you've actually killed somebody!"

Fiona stomped out of the room, leaving me staring at her with my mouth agape. My blood boiled.

I glanced to Sondra. "She stands up to her brother once, and suddenly she's grown a pair of balls?"

Sondra stood, though far less dramatically than Fiona had. "Zoey was our friend. You of all people should know what it's like to get back someone you thought you lost."

With that, she strolled out of the room after Fiona, leaving me to consider her words.

Three days passed, and I spent most of it holed up in my room with piles of books I'd dragged out of Genevieve's spell room. Fiona and I hadn't talked, and I'd only spoken to Venn once. He'd made it to Detroit, but it turned out his brother was no longer with the group of vamps he started with. He was still trying to track him down. Jenna and Ronark were getting into more and more arguments, and I had to step in a few times to calm them down. The only thing that seemed to calm Jenna's nerves was an Aspirin and a tall glass of water. The withdrawals were getting worse with each passing day. I kept telling her things would get better, but I didn't know for sure. I just had to hope that was the case.

"This is kind of cool," Jenna said on the fourth night since Venn had left.

I was lying on my stomach on my bed and thumbing through a book on psychic energies. The words on the pages were beginning to blur together. I slammed the book shut and rolled over on the bed, staring up at the ceiling. The mattress shifted under Jenna's weight as she sat up and pulled the book she was reading closer to her.

"Anything useful?" I asked.

She shrugged. "Probably not. This one is all about incantations to control the weather. I just thought it sounded neat."

"Eh." I groaned from where I lay. "Maybe we should take a break."

"Should we get something to eat?" Jenna suggested. "Honestly, I could use another Aspirin."

I wasn't very hungry. I hadn't had much of an appetite these last few days, but my limbs felt a little shaky, and my throat was scratchy. "Yeah. I should probably get something in my stomach."

Jenna and I set our books aside and headed to the kitchen. The house was quiet, but when I entered the room, I found Sondra sitting at the table with a blank sketch pad in front of her. She looked deep in concentration with her pencil to the paper, but she didn't make a stroke. She heard our footsteps approaching and looked up.

"Hey," I said lightly as I headed to the fridge to grab a yogurt, then helped myself to a spoon from the drawer. "I thought everyone had gone to bed."

"Fiona's snoring, and I needed a quiet place to think," Sondra said.

Dishes clinked as Jenna reached into the cupboard for a bowl, then into the next cupboard for a box of cereal.

I took the seat beside Sondra. "How's it been going? Rounding people up, I mean. Teagan said yesterday didn't go too well."

Sondra frowned. "No, it didn't. I went to visit some friends about an hour away, but they refused to help us. They were afraid just associating with me would get the DMR's attention. They basically burned any evidence that they ever practiced magic in the first place."

I frowned. "We need more people, more weapons."

Sondra sighed. "I know. They at least gave me the names of some of their friends who might be able to help—but I think it was just to get me to leave. I've been trying to get ahold of them, but everyone's on high alert these days, especially anyone involved in magic."

Jenna caught my eye. She cocked her head toward the door to let me know she was headed back to her room to eat, then left me and Sondra alone in the dimly-lit kitchen.

The silence left me a little uncomfortable. I took a scoop of yogurt, then turned to Sondra's sketch pad. "What are you drawing?"

She shook her head and set her pencil down. "Nothing."

"Nothing?" I asked in shock.

Sondra dropped her head. "I haven't drawn anything since we've been here."

"But you always have your sketchbook with you. What about the other night around the fire?"

Sondra started fiddling with her pencil. "I was just pretending to draw. I couldn't manage it."

I couldn't wrap my head around it. "But that's your thing."

"It was," she said regrettably.

Her chestnut brown hair fell in front of her face, shielding it from my view. It was like she was trying to hide her pain from me. She sniffled, then pushed her hair back to look at me. When she did, she looked totally fine.

"The truth is, I don't know who I am without magic," she admitted. "I used to draw to make sense of the magic, to remember things from my past lives and sort through all the incantations in my brain, but now… it's like drawing has no purpose."

"Don't say that," I insisted. "You're more than just your magic, Sondra. You haven't even had magic all your life. Who were you before?"

She shrugged, and her lips turned down at the corners. "That's the problem. I don't know. I found myself through magic. It was like a compass guiding me to where I needed to go. Now… I don't know which direction I'm supposed to walk."

"Draw me," I suggested before I realized I'd even come up with the idea.

She furrowed her brow. "What?"

"You said you don't feel like your drawing has purpose. Well, give it purpose. Use me as your inspiration."

"I don't know, Rae." Sondra looked down at her sheet of paper, as if already mapping out the lines of my face on her sketch pad.

"How's this?" I asked, striking a pose with a faraway look.

Sondra looked like she was holding back a smile.

"This?" I threw my head back and bit the tip of my finger, giving her a *come-hither* look.

Sondra chuckled. "Okay, I'll try. Just relax. No sexy poses."

I sat up straight and got comfortable. Sondra shifted in her seat and bit the end of her pencil, studying me.

"You have really good bone structure," she said.

I smiled but held my pose. "Thanks."

"Your eyes are pretty, too."

I fluttered my lashes at her. "You think so?"

She laughed and took my chin to guide my face back where she wanted it. "Sit still."

Silence settled over the kitchen. The only things I heard

were the sounds of my own breathing and the scratch of Sondra's pencil moving across the page. I glanced to her every now and then, and she looked deep in thought, like she was lost in another world while she was drawing.

At least an hour passed. Occasionally, she'd sigh, like she wasn't pleased how it was turning out. She held the pad up so I couldn't see the drawing.

Eventually, I broke the silence. "How's it going?"

Sondra chewed her lower lip. "It's getting there. I think maybe we should take a break. I can finish this up later."

"Can I see it?" I asked.

Sondra pulled the sketch pad protectively to her chest. "It's, uh, not done. I'll show you later, once I fix all the shadows and stuff."

"Okay," I said slowly, eyeing her. Sondra wasn't usually so protective of her art. I was starting to worry, but I didn't want to push her, either. I stood. "Goodnight."

"Night."

The bed was cold when I returned to my room, as if reminding me of the days that Venn hadn't been there with me. I thought he'd be back by now. The fact that he wasn't sent a chill through my body.

After changing into pajamas, I curled under the thick comforter and pulled out my phone. I found Venn's number in my contacts and held my breath as the other line rang.

"Hello?"

My breath came out in a puff of relief. I couldn't read Venn's tone, but I was happy to hear his voice.

"Hey, it's me," I said quietly so I didn't bother anyone in adjoining rooms. "Did I wake you?"

"Rae," Venn sighed, like he was relieved as well. "No, you didn't wake me. I couldn't sleep anyway."

"So… how's it going?" I didn't know what else to say. I just wanted to hear his voice and make sure he was all right. "Will you be home soon?"

"I don't know," he admitted sheepishly. "It's taking longer than I thought."

"Do you think Tyson's okay?"

Venn paused for a moment. "I don't know right now. I'm trying to get a private investigator to help, but the process is slow. It might be a few more days before we find anything."

"Maybe you should come home," I suggested. "Let the detective do his job."

Venn sighed. "I can't, Rae. Not until I know for sure."

I wasn't sure what he meant, but I didn't like the way he said that.

"Venn, are you sure you're okay alone?" I asked. My heart ached for him.

"I'm fine," he insisted, but he didn't sound fine. He sounded scared, agitated, and lonely all at once, though I knew he'd never admit it.

"I'm here for you," I told him honestly. "Don't be afraid to ask for help if you need it."

"I know," Venn whispered, like he couldn't find his voice.

After a beat of silence, he perked up. "How has the studying been going? Find anything useful?"

"Some," I admitted. I sat up and pulled one of the books off the nightstand. I opened it to one of the pages I'd book-marked. "Most of it requires new magic, though. The good news is I've been reading so much that I'm starting to memo-rize some of these incantations, not that it's much help to us now."

Venn chucked. He knew all too well how much I sucked at remembering spells. I was glad to lighten the mood.

"I know," I said. "Can you believe it?"

"Of course." Venn sounded like he was smiling. "You're amazing."

My heart lifted in my chest. "You, too."

Venn sighed. "I miss you."

"I miss you, too," I whispered back.

Silence settled as I listened to the sound of his breathing.

"It's getting late," he said. "You should get to bed."

"What about you?" I teased. "It's later where you're at."

"I'll try," he told me, but it didn't sound hopeful.

My gut sank. "Are you sure you're okay? You don't sound well."

"I'm just stressed," he admitted, but something told me it was more than that.

I didn't press, but I couldn't help but feel like he was hiding something from me.

14

The next morning, I went upstairs to Genevieve's library. I hadn't been in there since the night I'd come to Genevieve for the dagger. The room was all polished dark wood and endless bookcases along the walls. We'd pretty much exhausted all the spell books downstairs, and I wanted to see if she had anything else we could use. My eyes passed by each spine, reading the titles, but none of them hinted at magic. They were all encyclopedias, textbooks, or books on finance.

"Rae?"

I turned to the door to see Fiona standing there. She held a few loose sheets of paper in her hands.

She took a step into the room. "Is it cool if we talk?"

I sighed. "Sure."

Fiona sat in one of the chairs in front of the fireplace. I took the other one.

"First of all, I wanted to say I'm sorry," she said. "I didn't mean what I said about you. I was just upset how you took meeting Zoey, but I get now where you're coming from."

I relaxed. "I'm sorry, too. I know Zoey is your friend."

I still felt uneasy about her, but I shouldn't have said those things in front of Fiona.

She gave a timid smile. "Thank you. I just don't want to keep fighting. We have bigger problems. If we're going to fight Matias, we need to work together."

It took setting all my pride aside to agree with her, but I knew she was right.

"Friends?" Fiona asked.

"Friends," I agreed. I glanced down to the papers in her hands. "What's that?"

"Research." She handed me the top sheet. "I went online to broaden our search, and I found a list of known artifacts. I don't think we have time to search for any of them, but—"

"Oh my God!" I stopped dead in my tracks when my eyes landed on a sketch of cufflinks in the shape of a lion's head. "I know these artifacts!"

"You do?" Fiona straightened in her seat.

"My old boss from Bloodstone, Devin, wore ones just like these all the time. I always thought it was weird because he wasn't exactly a classy guy. He always wore these dirty button-down shirts. I thought the cufflinks were sentimental or something. But what if they were *magic*?"

Fiona's eyes lit up. "Do you think he'd sell them to us?"

"For the right price? Absolutely. Devin's all about the cash." I looked back down at the printed web page. "What exactly do these cufflinks do?"

"They enhance your strength," Fiona answered.

"So we could actually stand up to any shifters Matias is recruiting," I said thoughtfully. "Now Devin's stupid can-crushing trick he always did makes sense. I always suspected he might have some shifter blood in him or something."

"Can-crushing trick?" Fiona asked.

"It was this stupid thing. The guy drank soda like it was candy. Whenever he'd finish a can, he'd crush it against his forehead and toss it out. Some stupid thing about asserting his dominance."

Fiona chuckled. "He sounds like a prick."

"A total prick," I agreed.

The room went silent for a few moments before Fiona changed the subject. "There's another reason I wanted to talk to you. I'm worried about Venn."

"Me too," I admitted. "I wish he would've let someone go with him."

"Have you talked to him lately?"

I nodded. "Last night. He still hasn't tracked Tyson down. He says he's doing fine, but I'm not sure I believe him."

"Maybe he's just—"

My phone began to buzz in my pocket. I shot out of my chair so fast that I nearly knocked it over. The name on the screen sent a shot of adrenaline coursing through my veins.

"Venn?" I asked desperately when I answered.

"Rae." Venn sounded relieved, but there was also a heavy sadness in his tone.

"Venn, what's wrong?"

"I just… wanted to hear your voice." His tone was low, so broken. I'd never heard him sound so down before.

"I'm here. What's going on?" The phone shook in my hands as a worry beyond anything I'd ever felt for him tore through me.

"I'll tell you when I get back."

"Tell me what? Venn!"

"I just wanted you to know I'll be home tonight," he said.

"Did you find Tyson?" My whole body was shaking now. Somehow, I already knew the answer.

"I have to go. I love you."

"I love you, too." Tears rose to my eyes.

The line went dead.

Fiona rose so slowly from her chair that I didn't hear her approach. "What happened? Is everything okay?"

I shook my head. "I don't think so."

My mind raced through all the possible scenarios Venn could've gone through the past few days. I couldn't read or talk about artifacts. I couldn't even eat. I sat at the kitchen window for hours, staring out over the front lawn even though I knew Venn wouldn't be back yet. People passed through the kitchen every now and then, but if they said anything, I didn't hear them. Jenna sat beside me the whole time, but she didn't talk. She just stayed for emotional support.

It felt like I'd been sitting there for days. The sun had fallen low in the sky when a pair of headlights finally pulled into the driveway.

I shot out of my chair and raced out the front door. Fiona was passing through the hall just then, and she quickly followed behind me. I heard Jenna's footsteps as well.

"Venn!" I cried as he stepped out of the vehicle.

Venn looked like hell. There were bruises across his face, and the skin on his lip was broken open, as if he'd been in a fist fight. His eyes looked hollow, like he hadn't slept in days. He looked at me, but it felt as if he was looking *through* me.

"Venn!" I threw my arms around him and stood on my toes to kiss him.

He kissed me back, but the kiss was cold, unfeeling.

I drew away from him, my eyebrows knitted. It was at that moment that I realized my worst-case scenario was real. Tyson wasn't with him.

"Your brother...?" I whispered. My eyes darted between his, trying to find the emotion. But it wasn't there. Venn was just... numb. It was like he'd totally given up.

"He's dead," he whispered so softly that I barely heard him. But the words were like a knife through my gut. I didn't even know Tyson, and I felt for him. It was only a fraction of what Venn must've been feeling, but it was enough to make it feel as if a hole had opened up in my chest. Venn had lost him... for good.

I wanted to help him, to heal him of the pain I knew he was feeling, but I knew nothing could fix this. I drew him into a tight hug, because that was all I could do in the heart-breaking moment. I couldn't bring his brother back, but I could at least show him I was here for him.

I was vaguely aware of several other arms wrapping around us. They weren't just Fiona's and Jenna's, either. Sondra, Teagan, and Ryland had followed us out of the house, and I hadn't even noticed. They all joined in on the hug, cocooning Venn in a safe embrace.

It was then that the tears began to fall from his cheeks. He curled into me, his face pressed into my shoulder. All the emotions he'd held back came out all at once like a broken floodgate. His shoulders shook, and sobs echoed in my ears, but it was like I was seeing the whole thing in slow motion—like the scene was playing far away.

"We're here for you, Venn," I whispered.

"Always," Sondra assured him.

Venn's breath shook against my neck. "I love you all."

"We love you, too," Fiona said.

"With all our hearts," Teagan added.

Ryland looked on the verge of tears. I'd never seen him like that before, but it was clear he cared for Venn's well-being. "Whatever you need, man. We've got your back."

Venn didn't want to talk about what happened to him in Detroit. Fiona had asked him what happened to his face—where the bruises had come from—but he just went silent, like he hadn't heard her. I was dying to know as well, but the more I pushed it, the more he would pull away. I knew it because I'd been in similar places, too.

It was painful not to ask him what was wrong. I wanted to help. But I decided to let him come to me at his own pace. I helped him into a warm bath and gave him a healing potion. Hours later, we were snuggled up in bed together, but he still wasn't talking. It hurt a little that he didn't want to confide in me.

At his own pace, I kept telling myself.

All I could do right now was hold on to Venn. He curled up on the bed with his knees to his chest, while I wrapped an arm around him from behind. At some point, I must've drifted off, because I woke up a few hours later to find the bed beside me empty and cold.

I shot upright and glanced around the room, my heart racing. Where was Venn?

I kicked the covers off myself and raced out into the hallway. My pounding heart began to slow as I heard the sound of his voice coming from the room beside ours.

"You should've seen the vamp," he was saying. "Twice the size of Ryland, and Teagan took him out with one strike."

The door was open a crack, so I pushed it wider. Ronark and Jenna were sitting on the bed laughing at Venn's story, and Venn was sitting in a chair in the corner, looking relaxed. I hadn't seen any of them look this chill since we left the island, not even the night we went star-tipping. What was going on?

The floor creaked under my weight, and three sets of eyes darted toward me. I swung the door open wider and stepped inside.

"What's going on?" I asked.

Their laughter died the second I stepped into the room. Ronark shifted on the bed, looking guilty about something.

"Nothing," Jenna said, though she shot a glance I couldn't read in Venn's direction. "Venn's just telling stories."

I sat beside her on the bed, feeling a little hurt that he was willing to talk to them and not to me. "Mind if I join you? I don't think I've heard this one yet."

Venn dropped his gaze. "It's a long story. And it's really late. I was going to head back soon anyway."

"Oh, okay," I said flatly.

Suddenly, I was twelve years old again, trying to hang out with my sister and her friends at their sleepovers, only to be told I was "too young." Except this time, it was worse, because it was my boyfriend pushing me away.

"Am I missing something?" My cheeks heated as I glanced between each of them. They all stared back blankly, like they were trying to hide their true feelings.

"No," Ronark said. "Nothing at all."

Ronark sounded genuine, but he was a hard guy to read.

You're just being paranoid, I told myself. If something was actually going on, Venn and Jenna would let me in on it.

"Well, we should probably get back to bed, then," I said.

Venn stood and shot Jenna and Ronark a frown. "Rae's right. I'll see you guys later."

Back in our room, I asked, "What was all that about?"

Venn shrugged as he crawled into bed beside me. He kept his back to me so I couldn't see his face. "I couldn't sleep, and I heard them up. They helped me relax."

"Did you tell them about Detroit?"

"No," he replied honestly, but something still didn't sit right with me.

"I don't like being lied to, Venn."

"I'm not lying," he insisted. "I'm not ready to talk about it yet."

"Okay. I just wanted to make sure we're clear on that."

Venn rolled over to look me in the eyes. "There are things you don't know, Rae, but it's not because I don't want you to know them. I'll tell you when I'm ready."

He took my hand and kissed it. It was all he was going to give me, and it wouldn't be fair of me to ask for more.

"Okay," I said. "I'll be ready whenever you are."

Except, I didn't know if he'd ever be ready.

15

VENN ~ FIVE DAYS AGO

Four years had passed since the night I lost my brother. Four years since I promised him I wouldn't go after him. And I was finally saying screw it to that promise.

The vampire curse was broken. My brother was human again. Whatever promise I'd made that night was under the assumption that he'd remain a vampire forever. Now, everything had changed.

I'd been thinking about it since the night the curse was broken, but I hadn't planned to mention it to Rae until we'd had a chance to rest. She'd just killed the most powerful vampire in the world. She deserved a moment to breathe before I told her I was running off on my own.

I knew she'd fight to go with me, but I couldn't let her. I had no idea how dangerous it might be, and I didn't want to put her in more danger than she already was.

But more than that, I had to make amends with my brother. Alone.

The fact was, I was still ashamed. I still blamed myself. The closer I got to my brother, the more questions she would ask.

And eventually, I would break. I would tell her how I walked away from him that night, how terrible of a person I was. She wouldn't want to be with me anymore, not once she knew that I could walk away from someone I loved so easily. But if I fixed this with my brother, if I did it on my own without her help, maybe she'd see that I had changed—that I could love just as hard as if I had stayed.

Truth be told, I didn't know where to start. I'd spent years in the vampire crowd. After Tyson had changed, I ran away—for good, just like he wanted. Scared and with nowhere to go, I had no choice but to follow the vampire who had found me scouring dumpsters for scraps of food. Maliya had promised me a warm bed and fresh meals, as long as I pledged myself to her. Years, and never a single mention of a Tyson Michaels.

So I turned to the one guy I could, someone who knew more about the vampire community than I ever did. Cory Reid, a gorilla shifter I knew from high school. He fell into the vampire crowd long before Tyson ever changed. He was the only guy I thought might know how to find him—the only one who would help me, anyway.

It took a while to track Cory down, considering we hadn't spoken in years.

"Venn?" he'd asked in surprise when I'd finally got ahold of him. "Venn Michaels? It's been forever. How are you, man?"

"Not great," I admitted. "You remember my brother, Tyson?"

"Your sidekick? Sure I do. How is he?"

"That's what I'm calling you about," I admitted. "I need to find him."

"Oh." Cory's voice flattened. "He changed, didn't he?"

I didn't like that word. *Changed.*

"Yeah," I said, my throat going dry. It wasn't from the withdrawals, either, but damn it, that was getting to me, too.

I'd been fed on while on Gregor Island, which sent all the cravings rushing back. I'd spent the last two years, all my time with Sondra, trying to get over that. I didn't want to have to go through it again… so I'd ignore it as long as I could.

I didn't know how he did it or who he had to talk to, but Cory managed to track Tyson down to Detroit.

The drive was brutal. Eight hours alone in the car. It gave me way too much time to think. What would it be like to see his face again? Would he be happy to see me?

A horrifying thought kept pushing its way in. Or would he hate me for breaking my promise?

I won't know until I get there, I kept telling myself.

I got more than I bargained for when I arrived. Cory warned me to be careful, that the group my brother had fallen into was ruthless. It sounded a lot like Maliya's nest.

I decided to scope the place out, see what I was up against. The address Cory gave me led me to an old warehouse. I parked the car several blocks away.

Night had fallen, and I slipped through the shadows and tiptoed to a back door I hadn't seen anyone use. Inside, I navigated endless hallways, following the sound of voices until I came to a huge room with a tall ceiling. It was practically the size of a football field, with endless rows of shelving.

"What is this?" a male voice snarled.

I peeked around a dark aisle to see a group of a dozen men in an adjoining room. They were gathered around a small table beneath a dim light. Tyson was nowhere in sight.

The guy in charge threw a bag of white powder to the guy across the table from him. "I asked for a *strong* batch of chrysanthemum, not this weak ass shit."

The blood drained from my face. Chrysanthemum? It wasn't just a beautiful flower. It was a slang term for a type of drug made with magic. Everyone who knew anything about magic knew that all the magical drugs were named after flowers. Cory hadn't told me my brother was involved in a magical drug cartel. My pulse quickened. This was definitely dangerous.

"The price of this stuff has gone up tenfold in the last week," the boss snarled. "Supply is down, and demand is higher than ever. But we need the best if we want to charge these kinds of prices. Tell your sorry excuse for a witch that we won't accept such a disgusting insult."

"Yes, Maverick, sir," the man replied in a shaky tone.

"Don't come back without the quality we expect," Maverick spat. "You don't get another shot at this, kid. Don't screw it up."

The guy huffed and left the room. I sank back into the shadows, only to back into something solid. My heart pounding, I turned and looked up to what I'd run into. A pair of blue eyes stared back at me from several inches above my head. Thick biceps twice the size of mine crossed over the man's chest.

I had only a split second to make a decision. It momentarily crossed my mind that without my shifter magic, I stood no chance against this guy. Before I knew it, my feet were moving under me, and I was making a run for it.

"Hey!" he barked. His footsteps echoed through the warehouse behind me.

Suddenly, a dozen voices were screaming and shouting as I raced toward the nearest door. I was almost there—

Arms tangled around my legs as I went crashing to the ground. I rolled over and caught a glimpse of the guy's face a split second before I slammed my foot into his nose. Blood spurted everywhere, but it only made him smirk.

"Big mistake," he said in a deep voice.

His fist connected with my face, and everything went dark.

I didn't know how much time had passed. All I knew was that my head hurt like hell when I came to. A dark room came into focus, and I noticed three figures standing in front of me, though I couldn't make out their faces past the blinding light shining in my face.

I tried to lift my hand to shade my eyes, but I couldn't move them. They'd been tied behind my back. My throat burned with more thirst than ever. Had these guys still been cursed, I might've begged for a hit.

I hated myself just for considering it.

The guy in the middle stepped forward until he was beneath the light. *Maverick.*

"Well, well, well, what do we have here?" He clicked his tongue and narrowed his eyes. "Do I know you?"

"No," I answered quickly, but I wasn't sure that was the right answer.

"He looks a little like Michaels," one if his cronies pointed out.

"Michaels?" Maverick spat. "You better start making sense, Cal."

"The little vampire shifter you recruited a few years ago," Cal clarified.

Every muscle in my body tensed. Tyson!

"Remember the coyote Remy used to pick fights with just

to watch him squirm?" Cal glanced to the big dude who'd knocked me out—Remy, I assumed. Remy and Cal both chuckled, but they stopped dead when Maverick turned to glare at him.

"We don't talk of traitors around here!" Maverick snapped. "That kid left us for Diego's gang across town. Took our trade secrets with him, too. If I ever see that son of a bitch again, so help me I will slit his throat myself."

I tried not to let my surprise show. I came all this way, and Tyson wasn't even here? If he had truly betrayed them, they'd kill me just for being associated with him.

"Don't ever bring up that traitor's ass again," Maverick snarled, glaring between the two of his cronies.

"Look," I said, forcing my voice to stay calm. I was anything but calm. My strength was near non-existent, so there was no way I was getting myself out of these ropes without talking my way out.

"I don't know any Michaels," I lied. "I got your name from a friend. I'm here to buy some flowers."

Maverick turned back to me with a smirk. "Is that so? We don't tend to do business with people who *sneak* around our warehouse."

"Could be one of Diego's spies," Cal suggested.

Maverick's face lit up, like he approved of the suggestion.

"What should we do with him?" Remy asked, cracking his knuckles. "Send Diego a message?"

"No, I'm not Diego's," I said quickly. "I've never even heard of him. Honestly. I'm from out of town. I just need something to get me by while I'm here."

"Maybe we should—" Cal started, but Maverick cut him off.

"We don't want to be turning away good business, boys."

Maverick leaned so close to me that I could feel his breath on my face. "Who sent you?"

I hesitated. I could give them Cory's name, but I didn't want to get him into trouble with these guys. The only other name I could think of was a guy Cory had mentioned he worked with. I jumped on it.

"Brent from Chicago," I lied.

Maverick relaxed, then scoffed. "Brent from Chicago. I should've known. Show us the money, kid."

"In my wallet." I lifted my hip the best I could and nodded toward my back pocket. I'd visited the bank before I left Nocton and pulled most everything out of my account for this. I was grateful I'd left some of it in the car. These guys wouldn't hesitate to clean house; then I'd be left without anything to get back home on.

Remy snatched my wallet out of my pocket and flipped it open. He pulled the bills out and tossed the wallet back to me without digging through the rest of it. The wallet bounced off my stomach and landed several feet away on the concrete floor. Remy handed Maverick a wad of cash. Maverick flipped through it with a satisfied smirk on his face. There was at least a few hundred dollars there.

"Let him go, Remy," Maverick ordered.

Remy drew a blade from his hip and cut the rope restraining me. I quickly grabbed my wallet, then followed behind Maverick as he cocked his head toward the door.

"What exactly is it you're looking for, kid?" Maverick asked as we started down a dark hallway.

I said the first thing that came to mind. "Magnolia."

"A great choice," Maverick said. "One of my favorites. Have a seat."

Maverick gestured to an open doorway leading to the

room I'd seen him in before, though we came in on the other side. I took a seat at the end of the table. My hands shook as I waited, but I forced them to remain steady. All I had to do was get out of here with my limbs intact.

Maverick sat across from me. Remy and Cal stood behind my chair with their arms folded in front of themselves, like they were standing guard.

"Tell you what, kid." Maverick laid my money out on the table, then leaned back in his chair. "What you've got right here will buy you an eight ball of magnolia."

"That's it?" I balked before I could stop myself. In Nocton, that amount of cash would buy at least three times that.

Maverick shrugged. "Prices have gone up. You're not going to find a better deal in these parts. Are you going to take it or leave it?"

I heard the threatening sound of Remy's knuckles cracking. I didn't want the drugs, but I knew that if I didn't accept their offer, I'd be walking out of here with nothing in my pockets. At least if I took it, I could resell it and get my money back.

"I'll take it," I said, wanting nothing more than to get out of there.

Maverick smirked and pulled a small baggie filled with a light pink powder out of his jacket pocket. He set it on the table between us, then scooped up my cash. "It's been a pleasure doing business with you."

I grabbed the bag of magnolia and started for the door. Remy and Cal followed behind to escort me out.

"Oh," Maverick said before we got far. "And tell that son of a bitch Brent he knows the drill. He better not screw up next time."

A shiver ran down my spine. I hadn't meant to get anyone else in trouble. "Yes, sir."

I increased my pace as soon as I left the building. The door clanged shut behind me. I kept throwing quick glances over my shoulder to make sure I wasn't being followed. These weren't the kind of guys I wanted to mess with. I reached into my pocket and clung tightly to my keys, just in case some bastard jumped out of the shadows.

I breathed a sigh of relief when I made it back to the car in one piece. I quickly climbed inside and hightailed it out of there as fast as I could. Every muscle in my body tightened and remained on high alert.

"Stupid, stupid!" I screamed to the silence, slamming my hand against the steering wheel. How could Tyson have been so stupid to join up in a drug cartel? And how could I have gone in there so unprepared, with no weapon or anything?

On second thought, a weapon would've only made things worse. They would've found it and never bought my story.

All that mattered was that I was out of there. I had a general idea of where Tyson was, and I was one step closer to finding him.

***

It took one call to Cory, and I already had the details of where to find Diego and his men.

"Bro, I'm sorry," Cory had said. "You gonna bust up Diego's on your own, too?"

"That's the plan," I told him. All I needed was to get a glimpse of Tyson. Once I knew for sure he was there, I'd find a way to get him out.

"Man, you're crazy," Cory had said.

I approached a two-story home the next day. It wasn't much smaller than ours back in Nocton—the one that burnt down. I knocked on the door.

Silence.

I glanced up and down the street. It was quiet… and a little eerie. I already had a bad feeling about this. The door popped open a crack.

"Yeah?" A guy at least ten years older than me peeked out through the door.

I hesitated a moment. He had an angry look in his eyes that made me want to run. But I stood my ground.

"What the hell do you want?" he snapped.

"I need a fix," I lied. "Just one. I'll pay whatever you want."

His lips tightened. "Who gave you this address?"

I huffed, playing my part. "I dunno, man. He never said his name."

I tried to peek past him and into the house, but he took up the whole doorway. *Come on, Tyson. Hear my voice.*

"You ain't gettin' anything without a name," he growled.

"Okay," I caved, quickly modifying my story in my head. "Truth is, I don't remember. It was Ty… Ty-something. He didn't give me the address. I followed him."

The guy scoffed. "Ain't no one by that name here. Get lost."

"Wait!" A hand shot out to grab the door before the guy could swing it all the way shut. The door swung open to reveal another man in a tattered white shirt and scruffy beard. "You talking about Tyson?"

Hope surged in my chest. He recognized his name!

I played it cool and shrugged. "Could be. Don't know for sure. Bring him out here and I'll let you know."

"You kind of look like him," he said thoughtfully. "You some sort of relation?"

I hesitated.

The man swung the screen door open so hard that it nearly slammed into my face. I jumped backward, but his hands were already on me, fisting into my shirt. He shoved me up against the porch's support pillar. His rotten breath rushed across the side of my face.

"I asked you a question," he spat.

I shoved him off of me and ducked beneath his arm. "Get off me!"

"Diego!" one of the men called.

Diego kept a firm hold on my shirt as I tried to struggle out of his reach. My foot slipped on the top step, and we went tumbling down to the sidewalk together. He landed on top of me, then drew his fist back and slammed into the side of my face. At least six people had flooded out of the house to watch. Their cheers filled the otherwise quiet street.

"What the fuck, man?" I screamed. I shoved him off of me, but I didn't punch him like I wanted to, not if it meant they'd hurt Tyson because of me.

He stumbled back, then ran for me again when I righted myself. His fist clipped my jaw.

I held my hands up. "Whoa—"

He took another swing at me, but I dodged around it. His fists tangled in my shirt again. I ducked and slipped out of my shirt. He looked at me with fury in his eyes.

"No one comes 'round here like this!" he screamed. "You hear me? You're looking for Tyson? That asshole sold us bad secrets! You want to find him? Join him in hell."

He lunged at me again, and this time, I fought back. My fists slammed into his gut, but it couldn't have felt any worse than the gaping hole opening up in mine. Tyson wasn't here.

Good God, brother. What had you done?

The men on the porch quickly came to the aid of their friend. Suddenly, fists were flying at me from all angles. I aimed my foot at one of the men, and he went stumbling backward, then I swung my elbow out to connect with another guy's nose.

But there were too many of them. Their hands were all over me, dragging me to the ground until I couldn't stay upright anymore. Their feet slammed into my ribs, my legs, my face—anything they could reach. Pain radiated all across my muscles. I tried to block their blows, but they just kept coming.

Get to your feet! A voice sounded through my head. I tried to do as the voice said, but each time, I was just knocked down again.

Get up! You're going to die!

That sent a wave of determination through me. I brought my knees to my chest, then kicked them outward. They connected with one guy's abdomen. At the same time, I caught one of the feet aimed at my head, then twisted. The guy stumbled sideways into his friend beside him.

It was just enough to give me an opening. I scrambled to my feet and took off running as fast as I could. Hands reached out to grab me again, but they couldn't hold on.

I raced across the street and jumped into my vehicle, quickly locking the door behind me. The first guy slammed his body against my door, going wild like a rabid dog. I hastily started the car, my heart racing, then shifted into drive and shot out into the street. Two of the men had raced in front of my vehicle, like they could slow it down, but they jumped out of the way when they saw I wasn't screwing around and would run their asses over if I had to.

My heart finally slowed when I returned to my hotel

room. I called Rae that night because I missed the sound of her voice. She sounded worried, and I just couldn't bring myself to tell her what had happened. She'd demand I leave, and I couldn't do that until I knew for sure where Tyson was.

I met with a private detective the following day, seeing as I'd run into a dead end. It was going to cost a fortune, but I'd do anything to find my brother. I didn't care about the cost.

After giving the detective everything I could possibly think of, he assured me there was nothing more I could do and suggested I go back to my hotel and get some rest.

That day stretched for an eternity and into the night as I waited to hear back from the detective. The next day, the eternity continued. It felt like the waiting would never end, like I might never know where to find him—like he'd be lost forever.

I tried to drink away my worries that night, but if anything, it made it worse. Time seemed to slow to a crawl, stretching out that eternity even more. It didn't help quench the aching thirst in my throat, either.

Rae called me that night. The sound of her voice was the one ray of sunshine in an otherwise dark set of days.

The next day, the call finally came.

"Did you find him?" I asked the detective hopefully.

"I'd like you to come in," he said.

I didn't know if that was a good or bad sign. I decided to take it as neutral to keep my hopes up. But the second I walked into his office, all hope had vanished. I could see the sorrow and regret in his eyes.

"Please, Mr. Michaels," Detective Olson said, gesturing to the seat beside his desk. "Take a seat."

"It's not good, is it?" I asked, already feeling it in my bones.

Detective Olson sat and shook his head. "I'm afraid not. Your brother… he's dead."

I didn't hear much after that over the ringing in my ears. If I weren't already sitting, I would've surely collapsed.

"When a vampire dies, almost all evidence is wiped away, including DNA evidence," he said. "Most vampire deaths are identified through the IDs left in their clothing, but your brother never applied for one. What I did find…"

Detective Olson turned his computer screen toward me. He hesitated with his finger over the keyboard. "Are you prepared to see what I'm about to show you?"

"Yes," I lied.

My hands shook in my lap as the video began to play. A surveillance video overlooked an alleyway. Tyson's terrified face came into view as he retreated into the narrow space, looking on high alert. He didn't look a day older than the last time I'd seen him. Five men pursued him, looking like they were speaking to him. I recognized the build of the man in the middle.

It was Diego and his men—the ones who'd tried to beat me to death.

"Is that him?" the detective asked.

I couldn't take my eyes off his face. I felt magnetized to the screen. I ran my finger across his moving figure, like I might be able to touch him through time and space.

"Yes," I said, my voice cracking. "That's my brother, Tyson."

Diego raised his arm, aiming a gun straight at Tyson's head. All it took was a blast of light, and my brother was reduced to nothing but a pile of ash.

Detective Olson sighed, then turned the screen back toward himself.

I blinked back the tears, and my hands formed into tight

fists. My gut twisted, and I thought I might hurl. I shot to my feet and started for the door.

"Mr. Michaels." Detective Olson stopped me.

I paused with my hand on the doorknob.

"We can get the men who did this," he said.

I hesitated a moment. Hell, yeah, I was going to get these men—but not in the way Detective Olson was talking.

I shook my head. "I didn't come here for revenge. I came for my brother."

And he's gone.

The words echoed in my mind on the way to the car. Once in the driver's seat, I finally let my frustrations out. I slammed my hands against the steering wheel and let out a rage-filled scream. My anger melted into heavy sobs. I couldn't believe he was gone. I didn't *want* to believe it.

I'd never be proud of what I did next.

I waited outside of Diego's house, watching. I called Rae while I waited, because I thought the sound of her voice might help right my unsteady world. But then I saw Diego coming out of his house, and I knew I was going to pursue him. I told her I had to go, and I followed him on foot. I wore my hood up to conceal my features and keep my skin dry from the misting rain.

Diego came to a large park and glanced around before ducking into a thick patch of trees. I figured he was working a drug deal—and he wasn't going to finish it if I had anything to say about it. I quickened my pace and entered the trees behind him.

"You're late—" he started, but he cut off when he saw it was me.

"You murdered my brother, you son of a bitch!" I growled.

I was on him in under a second. He fought back, but I

barely felt the pain. I was so pumped up on adrenaline that I felt ten times stronger than normal. Diego managed to get hold of me and shoved me hard into a tree. The back of my head cracked against the trunk. It only fueled me more.

He drew a gun and pointed it at me, but I lunged for him. The gun fell from his grasp as we tumbled to the ground. Over and over, my fist pummeled his face, until he was so swollen and bloody that he was hardly recognizable. I grabbed his gun from the ground and stood, pointing it at him.

He held his hands up in surrender. "Don't shoot! I'll give you anything you want."

You can't give me Tyson.

I could've done it. I was so enraged that I had it in me. But as my finger curled around the trigger, it really hit me. Even if I did this, it wouldn't bring Tyson back. Nothing could.

A moment of hesitation was all it took for me to know that this wasn't who I was. This wasn't what Tyson would've wanted.

I dropped the gun to my side, and Diego breathed a sigh of relief. "Consider yourself spared," I snarled. "But know this. The next person you piss off won't be as merciful as I am. Your days are numbered, Diego. Have fun watching your back."

I left the trees fuming, but I was glad I hadn't gone through with it. I tossed the gun in the bushes. I couldn't stand to hold on to it.

My hands shook when I returned to the vehicle. I leaned my head against the steering wheel and let the tears flow until they could flow no more. When I finally lifted my head, it was pounding, and there was a large hole widening in my stomach. It felt like I was falling apart, and I didn't know how to hold myself together right now—not without Tyson.

I reached into my pocket to pull out my key, but my hand found the little plastic bag of magnolia. I pulled it out and examined the pink powder. The thirst in my throat never seemed worse than in that moment.

A thought took root, and once it did, I couldn't get it out of my mind.

Maybe this will help me forget.

I already knew how stupid it was, how much I'd regret it later, but I also knew how much everything hurt—and how magnolia would help numb that pain.

Even if it were only temporary.

16

"Fiona found something," I told Genevieve over breakfast the day after Venn returned. "I think Devin has it."

She cocked an eyebrow at me. "Devin, as in the guy who runs Bloodstone?"

I didn't miss the look of disgust on her face. "Yeah, I know. That place is a shithole, but Fiona found an artifact I think he has, and it might help us."

Fiona already had the stack of papers in her lap. She reached across the table to hand the paper to Genevieve. Genevieve glanced over all the images on the page.

"I recognize the cufflinks," I said. "The website says the owner can increase his strength tenfold just by possessing one of them. We can buy them off him."

Genevieve pressed her lips together. "That sounds useful. Take whoever you want with you. Give Devin whatever price he asks for them."

I gaped at her. "You want me to arrange my own party?"

Genevieve shrugged. "Why not? You're the one who knows him. I guarantee he'll not be interested in doing business with me. He always saw me as a competitor. Was very bitter about it, too."

"If he doesn't like you, is he going to trust your money?" I asked.

She shrugged. "He doesn't have to know it's mine. I'll send you with the cash."

I nearly choked. Genevieve's house was nice, and she and Richard had a lot of cars, but it wasn't like she was living in a castle. If she had the kind of cash lying around that I knew Devin would ask for this sort of thing, she was living well below her means.

"Okay. I want Sondra…" She was always my first pick.

I was about to say Venn, but he still looked a little out of it, and I needed my team at the top of their game. Devin was the kind of guy who would release a poisonous airborne potion if he felt threatened.

"Fiona…" I decided next, because she was eyeing me eagerly, and also because she was the one who'd found out about the cufflinks in the first place.

I glanced around the table, looking for more eager eyes, but Jenna and Ronark were both staring down at their food. Ryland and Teagan shared that look again, the one I was still struggling to read. What was going on with them lately?

"What about you, Tea?" I asked. "Ready to get back out there?"

She froze. "Oh, uh, I—"

"I'll go," Clarita offered.

Amalia looked relieved beside her, like she was glad she didn't have to volunteer.

"Do you know Devin?" I asked Amalia.

She bit her lower lip. "A little. He was my mentor for a few months when he lived in Chicago. A useless mentor, honestly. He doesn't know half as much as he claims."

I knew exactly what she meant. Devin was an idiot.

"Well, it looks like I have my team. Should we get going?"

Fiona stood and bounced on her toes, looking eager. She already had Teagan's knives strapped to her waist. She caught me eyeing them. "Teagan's been teaching me. I've been practicing."

"Good," I said as I stood. "Let's hope we don't need them."

I wrapped my arm around Venn and kissed him on the back of the head. "I love you, babe."

He rubbed my hand. "Love you, too. Stay safe."

"I will," I promised.

Bloodstone was hidden in the back of a bakery. When we pulled up outside, it was like stepping back in time to my old life. I hated working here, but it'd paid my rent.

"That's weird," I said, eyeing the front window. The lights were off, and the sign on the door read *Closed*. "Devin was never late for work. It was the one good thing about him."

"Maybe he shut down with the DMR investigations?" Fiona suggested from beside me in the back seat

I shook my head. "He'd still keep the bakery running, even if he got rid of all his magic in the back."

"Unless he was caught," Sondra said thoughtfully.

"There's only one way to find out." Clarita opened the passenger-side door and climbed out of the car. The rest of us followed.

I cupped my hands around my face and peered into the dark shopfront. The case beneath the counter that held donuts and bread was empty. I could see part of the kitchen from this view, but I spotted no movement.

I pushed away from the window. "This is just too weird. It isn't like Devin. He likes money too much to just shut everything down."

"What are you suggesting?" Clarita asked.

"I'm suggesting we investigate," I replied. "Follow me."

I started around the side of the building toward the small parking lot. It was squeezed between the bakery and a coffee shop next door and fit only eight cars.

"Breaking and entering?" Fiona hissed.

"It's not breaking and entering if you have a key," I said with a smirk.

Devin always left a spare beneath a pile of landscaping rocks near the side door in case he ever got locked out. I'd told him it was a good way to lose the key, but when he challenged me to find a better place for it, I couldn't.

I glanced around the street, like I might see Devin's little red sports car, but I didn't know why I bothered. He always parked it around the block to save the other parking spaces for patrons.

I found the key where I expected and unlocked the door. The hall was dark and looked ominous. I held a finger to my lips to signal everyone to be quiet. I tiptoed inside, remaining on high alert the whole time. The hall smelled mostly like a mixture of herbs, but there was also the slight hint of decay in the air. Was Devin dealing with another mouse infestation? I'd told him last time that if he didn't deal with that quick, the inspector was going to shut him down and both the bakery *and* Bloodstone would be out of business.

"Devin?" I called down the hall.

No answer.

"Devin, it's Rachel. You around?"

I was met with only silence.

I reached the door to Bloodstone. It wasn't anything fancy, just a backroom where we kept crystals, herbs, charms, and other magical objects. Devin had torn down the wall between two rooms so that Bloodstone was almost as big as the front of the bakery and looked like a shop of its own.

The door was left open a crack. All I could see was a sliver of red carpet and the dark black display cases along one wall. My hands shook as I reached for the door and pushed it open.

I leapt backward in horror at what I saw. My hand slapped over my mouth to keep from spewing my breakfast all over the floor. Three equally horrified gasps came from behind me.

Devin's body lay sprawled across the floor in a pool of his own blood. A hole larger than my fist went straight through his chest and to the carpet below, as if something had burned through it. His eyes were clouded over and stared lifelessly toward the ceiling. His round face was so pale that he barely looked like himself, but there was no denying his signature buzzed hair, thin beard, and slight pot-belly.

"What happened here?" Fiona asked breathlessly.

I finally found my feet and took a step into the room, being careful to avoid getting too close. I shook my head. "I have no idea. Devin worked with some shady people, but he was smart enough to never piss them off."

Clarita knelt close to the body to inspect the wound.

"Are you thinking what I'm thinking?" Sondra asked her.

Clarita didn't take her eyes off Devin's chest. "If you're thinking this was done with magic, then yes."

Fiona furrowed her brow. "There's no way he's been here long, so this couldn't be just any magic. An artifact, maybe?"

Sondra pressed her lips together. "It would have to be a very powerful one."

I looked around the room. Everything was in its proper place. Even the cash register at the counter hadn't been disturbed.

"What do you think they wanted from him?" I asked.

Fiona walked around the room, inspecting it for clues. "You knew him. Maybe someone had a grudge against him."

I shook my head. "I don't think so. He was an asshole, but not enough to get him killed. The only thing I can think of is they wanted something from him, something magical. But in that case, why not take the rest of this—the potions and everything?"

I thought back through the days of running inventory and tried to think back to the most powerful thing he sold. Devin never did sell anything you couldn't find in any other underground shop. Mostly herbs, spells, and charms. They were harmless on their own.

I stared down at the body, and my eyes caught something on his wrist. *The cufflinks*.

I knelt beside Clarita, who was still looking him over for clues. "Look. He still has the cufflinks. If someone killed him for an artifact, why didn't they take these?"

"Maybe they didn't know they had power," Sondra theorized.

"Or *maybe* it was for revenge," Fiona said again.

I reached out for the cufflinks, but Clarita grabbed my wrist.

"We don't want to tamper with anything," she warned. "We don't have magic. We won't be able to cover it up."

"This is what we came here for," I reminded her. "Who's going to notice them missing?"

Sondra looked conflicted, then finally dropped her shoulders. "Rae's right. We're preparing for a war. We don't have the luxury of leaving here without our arms full. We'll take whatever we can get."

"Fair enough," Clarita said. "But we have to be careful."

"There are plastic bags behind the counter." I pointed. "Fit whatever you can in them."

Clarita was careful not to touch anything but the plastic bags. She turned the first one inside-out and used it as a sort of glove to gather potion vials so she wouldn't leave any fingerprints behind. Sondra and Fiona followed her lead.

"Make sure to get those clear potions in the corner," I told them. "They're healing potions. And those yellow ones? They enhance the senses. We might want some of those."

I pulled the cufflinks off Devin's wrists, but as I drew away, my hand brushed by something cold. The phone in his pocket shifted and fell out another inch.

An idea suddenly hit me, and I was too curious not to investigate. I didn't care if I got my fingerprints all over everything. I had to know what happened here.

I pulled Devin's phone from his pocket. The screen came on when I touched it, but the battery was only at seven percent. It prompted me to enter a PIN. I held my breath and tried the one I'd seen Devin enter a thousand times before —5262.

To my relief, the screen unlocked. Devin was so predictable.

It opened up to the camera right away. I was about to go to the home screen and check his messages when a circle in the corner caught my eye, where the phone showed the last picture taken. It was blurry, like it'd been taken in motion.

I clicked on it, and a video started playing.

"Thank you for the offer, but I'm going to have to decline," Devin's voice came through the speaker. The screen went dark, like Devin had been hiding the phone while he recorded.

Clarita gasped from behind me. "What are you doing?"

She rushed over to me, but I hit pause and pulled the phone away from her.

"I think this might give us a clue to what happened," I said.

"I said not to touch anything," she hissed.

I shrugged. "Too late. Do you want to know what happened, or not?"

Clarita couldn't hide her curiosity.

"I want to know," Fiona said, coming up behind me.

I looked up at Sondra. "And you?"

"Yeah," she admitted. "I do."

The three gathered around me, and I hit play on the screen again. Another voice came over the speaker, lower than Devin's and slightly familiar.

"You owe me, Devin," the man snarled.

My heart started to pound violently in my chest. That couldn't be who I thought it was, could it?

"We settled that debt a long time ago," Devin shot back. "Look, I have a teenage daughter. I can't leave her now."

"Does she have magic?" the other man asked coolly.

Devin hesitated. "She… Lana's practicing."

"Then bring her."

My face paled. I didn't look up to see how the others reacted, but they must've been thinking the same thing I was.

Matias Vayne.

"No," Devin objected. "I won't get her involved in this."

"She's been involved since the day I gave you that loan," Matias growled back at him.

It was clear as day. It was definitely Matias. What was he doing in Nocton, trying to recruit Devin of all people? Was he that desperate for allies?

"I paid you back!" Devin shouted. "I don't owe you anything."

"Then come because you want to," Matias pressed. "You never could resist a good magic trick. Come join the greatest one of all."

"I told you," Devin said. "My daughter… she's still in school, and—"

Matias's tone turned hostile. "If you don't join me, you will die. Only the best can survive in the new world I'm creating."

A moment passed, then Devin said, "I guess you're just going to have to kill me, then."

Matias chuckled. "With pleasure."

A loud blast sounded through the speaker, then came the *thud* of a falling body. My hand shot over my mouth, and my whole body trembled.

I thought the recording would end there, but it didn't. Matias's voice continued. "It's a real shame. I do hate wasting good magical blood."

The sound of heavy boots followed, then the creaking of hinges as the door swung behind him, then… silence. Nothing but silence.

After several long seconds, I lifted my head and glanced between the three other women with wide eyes.

"Matias," Sondra whispered, like she didn't quite believe it yet.

I was so shocked I could hardly speak. "I-I can't believe he didn't go with him. I would've thought Devin… I forgot about Lana."

Fiona's voice wavered. "Matias isn't screwing around. If people don't take his side, he'll kill them."

Clarita looked deep in thought, but she snapped out of it a moment later and got to her feet. "Let's get out of here."

"Are we just going to leave him?" I asked.

"We don't want anyone to know we've been here," Clarita said. "Let's hope whoever finds him thinks Matias robbed him."

"What about security tapes?" Fiona asked.

"He doesn't use them," I assured her. "He doesn't want that kind of record of the type of business he runs."

Clarita started pulling more items off the shelves. "Rae, wipe your prints off the phone, then come help us fill these bags."

"I'll bring the car around," Sondra said quickly.

I was still trying to wrap my head around it. I knew Matias was bad, but this? It was clear Matias was worse than I initially thought. And it was going to take a hell of a lot more manpower than we had to defeat him.

17

The sound of screams met us when we pulled into Genevieve's driveway. I shot a quick glance at Fiona, who wore the same shocked expression as I did. I kicked my door open before Sondra had shifted into park, then grabbed the dagger out of my boot and raced up the front steps.

"You're being an asshole!" Jenna shouted.

I ran through the kitchen and toward the sound of voices in the living room, where the TV was playing loudly. Three pairs of footsteps followed behind me.

"And you're being a *bitch!*" Ronark snarled back.

"You're both acting like little bitches," Venn snapped. He grabbed for the remote in Ronark's hand, but Ronark pulled back so they were both fighting to take it from the other. Their expressions were hostile, like they'd burst into a shifter fight at any moment of they could.

Ryland shoved himself between them, trying to wrestle the remote out of their hands. "You jackasses are going to hurt each other."

Teagan brought her knees to her chest and screamed, "Everyone just shut up!"

Nobody did. They all just kept shouting obscenities at one another.

"What the hell is going on?" I demanded.

No one even looked my way, as if I weren't there.

"You dirt bag," Venn growled at Ronark. I'd never seen such an angry expression on his face.

"Douche!" Ronark snapped back.

Venn let go of the remote with one hand to slug Ronark in the shoulder. Ronark's eyes blazed with fury, and he yanked back as hard as he could. He wrenched the remote out of Venn's and Ryland's hands and reeled backward onto the couch. The remote went flying out of his grip. He landed on top of Teagan, and his elbow slammed into her cheek.

Teagan screamed. Immediate rage burned in her features. She drew her arm back and punched Ronark in the side of the head. "Dick!"

She went to punch him again, but Ryland got there first. His hands fisted in Ronark's shirt, and he dragged him to his feet. "You're going to pay for that, asshole."

Ronark flinched as Ryland drew his arm back, but Jenna leapt forward. She let out a high-pitched battle cry and jumped on Ryland's arm, practically wrapping her whole body around him.

"Leave him alone!" she screamed.

I was about to jump in and call a stop to this madness, but I suddenly didn't know whose side to take. One second Jenna was cursing at Ronark, and the next she was defending him. All this over the remote? This was so not normal.

Venn tried to peel Jenna off Ryland, all while her legs flailed and she screamed.

"Guys! Guys!" Fiona tried to get their attention, but it was to no avail.

Sondra pushed past us and grabbed Venn and Ryland by the ears.

Venn whirled around and slapped her hand away. "Get off me!"

I returned the knife to my boot, then rushed across the room and scooped up the remote. I hit the power button, and the TV went silent. Everyone froze. All eyes turned to me.

"What. Is. Wrong. With. You?" I demanded.

Ryland looked to Venn, who looked to Ronark, who looked to Jenna.

Teagan was the one who answered. "They're all being a bunch of pricks."

"Yeah, I got that," I snapped. "The question is why."

"Ronark wants to watch the report on the DMR crackdowns, and Jenna wants to watch the ones on Matias," Teagan answered.

"The reports on Matias are more useful to us," Jenna insisted.

"That's not a reason to turn on each other," I said. "For God's sake, you're acting like children. You're supposed to be on the same team."

I looked to each of them to see a guilty expression fall across their faces. My eyes settled on Venn. His eyebrows were tightly knitted together, and his jaw was tightly clenched. He held my gaze for several seconds before huffing and storming out of the room.

What the hell? Venn had never looked at me like that before.

Anger bubbled up inside of me. "Grow up. All of you. Then come help us unload the car. We have shit to talk about."

We unloaded our bags at the dining room table. Genevieve looked completely shocked. "He sold you *all* of this?"

"Not exactly," I said.

Her eyes brightened. "He agreed to help?"

I bit my lower lip. "Uh, no."

Genevieve looked suspicious. "What happened?"

"When we got there…" Sondra took a deep breath and dove into the story of what happened at Bloodstone.

Everyone around the table went speechless. We were all here except Venn, Ronark, and Jenna. Those three were all still salty about what happened earlier—whatever that was—and had gone to hide away in their rooms. I wanted to talk to Venn, but I couldn't get the look he'd given me out of my head. Something told me he wasn't interested in my company right now. Besides, I had plenty of other things to worry about.

Okay, maybe *I* was salty about earlier. Might as well admit it.

"Do you want help cataloging these?" I asked Genevieve after our story finished and people started to disperse.

"That'd be very helpful," she said. "You're familiar with all this?"

"Most of it," I replied. "I worked there long enough. Most of it's labeled, but I can help you determine the potency of the potions and things like that."

Genevieve glanced into one of the bags. "Healing potions?"

"Yes," I said. "They're not nearly as potent as the one you gave Sondra, but they're better than an Aspirin."

"Perfect," she responded. "Fiona, do you mind taking these upstairs with the others?"

"Not at all." Fiona took the bag and left the room.

By now, Genevieve and I were alone in the kitchen. She sat across from me and started going through the bags. "Ooh, a sensory enhancement potion. I definitely want this one."

"I also got these." I took the cufflinks from my pocket and set them on the table between us. "I was thinking Ryland should take one since he's already so strong. It'll give him a bigger boost. And the other one could maybe go to Fiona, since she's—"

"Weak?" Genevieve cocked an eyebrow at me.

"I was going to say fragile." That sounded just as bad. "All I mean is that I care about her. I don't want her getting hurt thinking she can take on someone bigger than herself."

"She's stronger than you think, Rae. She's been doing this a long time."

"I know, but..." I trailed off.

"But what?" Genevieve prodded.

I paused. I shifted in my chair and picked at my nails. "I guess you're right. I underestimate her. I've been known to be a bad judge of character from time to time."

I immediately thought of Zoey.

"That's something you can work on," Genevieve pointed out as she dug through the bags and set things upright on the table.

I gave her a slight smile. "People are wrong about you."

Genevieve chuckled. "Is that so?"

I joined her in organizing the items in front of us. "Everyone makes you out to be scary. I don't think you're scary."

"Darling, you don't know a thing about me." She sounded amused.

"I know you're helping us," I said. "I know you're a very

powerful witch. Would someone with a heart as black as they say be capable of what you are?"

She scoffed. "A black heart? Is that what they say about me?"

"No," I replied quickly. "No one's actually ever said that."

Wow. I was totally sticking my foot in my mouth. That was meant to be a compliment.

Genevieve smiled. "I know what people think of me, and they have every reason to think those things. I have a very dark past, Rae. It's only been recently that I've been trying to turn that around."

"Trying?" I couldn't help but fixate on the word.

She started on a new bag, ignoring my eyes on her. "It could take a lifetime or more to make up for what I've done."

I hesitated. I wanted to know what she meant, but I didn't know if I could ask.

"Do you want to know the truth, Rachel?" She could totally sense my curiosity.

"If you're willing to share," I said.

"You're sure? It could very well ruin your perception of me," she warned.

My mouth went dry. How could I resist this information? "I'm sure."

Genevieve leaned toward me and folded her arms across the table. "I lie. I cheat. I steal. Worst of all, I kill."

My body froze, and a chill ran down my spine. My voice shook when I spoke. "We've all done those things, haven't we?"

She shook her head. "I'm not talking about little white lies and petty theft. I'm not talking about killing vampires. I'm talking about human beings. No mercy."

Genevieve was starting to scare me, but a part of me still trusted her.

"I'm sure they deserved it," I said in a shaky tone.

"Did they?" she asked curiously. "I think they did, but who am I to judge?"

"What… what did they do to you?" I asked.

Genevieve got a blank, distant look on her face, as if she was traveling back to a painful past. "Horrible, horrible things. It started with my father, and then my husband."

"Richard?" I asked, unsure what she meant.

"No, not Richard," she said. "My first husband. When magic returned, I turned to dark magic as a means to escape. I tortured people to get to the men who hurt me, Rachel. Innocent people."

I swallowed hard as bile rose to my throat. I wasn't sure I wanted to hear the rest, but she continued anyway.

"I made my father watch as I tortured his new wife and children," she said, dropping her gaze. "I burned him alive in his own house. And my ex-husband… well, he suffered a far more painful death. He went mad before his body finally gave out."

I shuddered at the thought.

Genevieve shook her head, like she was trying to push aside the memories. "I started mentoring others shortly afterward. I was hard on my mentees. Sometimes I'm shocked they learned anything from me at all."

"Why are you telling me all this?"

"Because it's not a secret, Rachel—not among those who know me, anyway. Part of healing involves admitting what happened, asking for forgiveness, and moving on instead of hiding from it."

Her words hung in the air for several moments.

"How did you change?" I finally asked, cutting through the silence.

"Mostly magic," she answered simply.

"Is there, like, a spell for it?"

"No. Not even magic can change a person who doesn't want to change. Not permanently, anyway. I stopped trying to *force* my magic and started *trusting* my magic. Suddenly, magic became easier, and I knew it was working."

"Magic isn't that easy," I argued. That's why I preferred killing. Killing was easier.

"Magic is one of the easiest things in the world," Genevieve replied. "Attuning yourself to it, on the other hand, is one of the hardest things to do."

"Isn't that the same thing?"

Genevieve didn't get a chance to respond as the sound of footsteps entered the kitchen.

"Venn!" I shot to my feet eagerly.

He wore a dark hoodie with the hood pulled up over his head. His gaze fixed on the ground, and he continued through the kitchen like he didn't hear me. He headed to the refrigerator, pulled out a bottled water, and chugged the whole thing.

"Venn?" I stepped toward him cautiously.

He wiped water from his lips and looked to me with tight eyebrows.

"Do you want to talk?" I asked softly.

"No," he replied in a clipped tone that stung more than it should've.

"I just want to help," I told him. "I know things are hard right now. You don't have to tell me everything, but at least—"

"I said I didn't need your help," he snapped. It was so unlike him.

I reached out for him. "Venn, I understand—"

"You don't understand shit!" he roared, swatting my hand away.

I stepped backward as tears rose to my eyes. Why was he shutting me out?

"Then help me understand," I insisted.

"You barely understand magic," he snarled. "How can you understand this?"

My stomach turned hollow as Venn whirled around and stomped out of the room.

18

I shot a desperate look at Genevieve, like she might be able to explain Venn's erratic behavior. She looked just as shocked as I felt. A split second passed before I rushed out of the room after him.

"Venn!" I called. "Wait."

The door to our guest room slammed behind him. When I tried to open it, the door handle wouldn't twist. What the hell? He'd locked me out!?

"Venn, please," I said through the door. "Let me in."

He didn't respond. Anger swept through me. I got that he was upset, but he didn't have to make it personal.

"Venn!" I screamed.

The door beside me swung open. Jenna stepped out with her hair a mess, looking like she'd just woken from a nap. "What's going on out here?"

"Venn's shutting me out," I told her.

Her expression became more alert. She shifted into big sister mode and pushed me out of the way to bang on the door. "Venn Michaels, you open this door right now, or so help me I will break it down!"

"Jenna, that's not necessary," I said.

She turned to me with a stern expression on her face. "Nobody hurts my Rugrat."

"Thanks, but—"

"Venn!" She pounded on the door again.

"Go away!" he called back.

"You can't shut her out forever!" Jenna snapped.

"Go. Away!" he repeated.

"Venn, please," I begged. "I love you, but this is starting to get out of hand. If I did something wrong, please tell me so I can fix it."

"I told you," he shouted through the door. "You don't understand."

I just about snapped. What made him think I didn't understand trauma? Had he not listened to any of the stories I'd told him?

"Seriously? Seriously!" I yelled at him. "You think I don't know what it's like to lose someone I love?"

"No!" Venn shouted. "You don't. You found your sister. I lost my brother!"

All the blood drained from my face. My knees shook as I absorbed the weight of what he'd just said.

Jenna turned to me. "Rach, he didn't mean it."

I barely heard her. "Venn... Venn resents me?"

"No," she assured me, but I didn't believe it. "He's just going through a lot."

"Then why would he say that?" I snapped. "People don't say things like that unless they mean it."

I turned back to the door and softened my tone. "Venn."

He didn't answer.

"This is hurting our connection," I said. "Remember what

you told me on the island? Being soulmates isn't easy. We're not perfect. We just have a strong connection. The connection dies if we don't nurture it."

I was paraphrasing.

Still, he said nothing.

I gave a light knock at the door again, but I was met with nothing but silence. Worry and anger knotted together in my gut, twisting everything around until I thought I might puke.

"Venn!" I shouted. "Jenna wasn't kidding about breaking this door down."

I thought I heard motion behind the door, but I couldn't be sure. I reached for the handle and shook it, but it was still locked. I was ready to knock this door down myself. With all my strength, I kicked at the door, and it gave way.

When I saw Venn, it was like the world was at a standstill yet shifting from side to side all at the same time. I couldn't move or breathe. I only stared.

Venn froze in place as he brought the back of his hand to his nose, where he was about to inhale a pink powder.

The world seemed to move again. Anger flooded through me. So much anger. I didn't even know what to do with myself in that moment. It felt like I was watching myself outside my body as I marched across the room and slapped his hand away from his face. The pink powder rained down to the floor.

"Drugs!?" I exploded. "You're doing *drugs*!"

Venn shot to his feet. His face came only inches from mine. "I told you that you wouldn't understand!"

I threw my hands up. "Congratulations. You were right. I don't understand how you can be doing drugs and didn't even tell me about it. Do I even know you at all? How long has this been going on?"

"Rachel," Jenna tugged at my arm, but my feet remained firmly planted in place.

"I knew you were hiding something from me," I accused, shoving my finger into his chest. "I knew it!"

"Rachel, calm down," Jenna begged. "It's not as bad as you think."

I turned on her. "This shit is dangerous, Jenna!"

"Stop it, Rachel," Jenna said. "Venn's right. You don't get it. You don't know what the withdrawal is like."

I drew in a sharp breath. "*You*! You've been doing this, too? That night you were all *just hanging out*, you were—"

"Yeah," Jenna admitted with gritted teeth. "So what? It helps us deal with it."

"This is not how you deal with it!" I screamed. "It's just one more thing to get addicted to."

"You don't know what it's like to be addicted to a vampire's bite," Jenna argued. "This isn't half as bad as that."

"It's still clearly a problem," I growled back. "You've all been so irritable lately. This is going to ruin relationships. Is that what you want?"

"That's not what—" Venn started, but I cut him off.

"Is. That. What. You. Want?" I repeated.

"Rachel, stop it!" Jenna yelled.

"No, Jenna," I shot back. "Ever since we got off that island, you've changed. What happened to the girl who was all about making the best out of a bad situation?"

"I *am*!" she shouted. "I'm dealing with it. Just because it's not in the way you think I should be doesn't mean I'm not doing something about it. It's going to take time."

I pressed my fingers to my temples. "I can't believe we're seriously having this conversation. I know what it's like to hit rock bottom, but I was *never* stupid enough to turn to drugs to deal with it."

"Really?" Venn asked. "So we're stupid now?"

"No, I just—"

"You just what?" Venn growled. "You just want to control everything. You want life to be a perfect place where you can slay your vampires and save the day and everyone bows down at your feet at the end of it. Is that it?"

"This is what I'm talking about!" I yelled. "This isn't you, Venn!"

"Well, it sure as hell isn't the drugs talking," he snapped.

I was so angry I wanted to stab something. Couldn't he see how reckless this was? How dangerous it could be for him?

"Forget it." I whirled around and stormed out of the room. I didn't know where I was going, but I had to get out of there before I hurt somebody.

Venn's voice followed me down the hall. "So that's it? You're done nurturing that connection?"

"No. That one's on you."

My legs carried me outside to the back yard, where I found Teagan and Fiona flinging knives at a target set up beside the long fence. Sondra and Ryland sat at the firepit close by, though there was no fire in it. They were snacking on potato chips. It was already past lunch. I hadn't eaten, but my stomach twisted just thinking about food.

I stomped over to Teagan and Fiona, fuming. "I need a knife."

Teagan raised her eyebrows. "Who won the fight?"

"You heard that?"

"Not really," Fiona admitted. "Enough to know you and Venn are fighting. Not enough to hear what you said."

Teagan handed me a knife. Before she could demonstrate how to use it, I hurled it at the target. It bounced off and landed in the grass.

"Another," I demanded, and Teagan handed the whole pile over to me.

I vented, accenting each word when the knives left my fingers. "Venn thinks it's *cool* to start doing *drugs* and to share with my *sister* and hide it from *me*. How stupid can he be? Doesn't he know how that shit messes with his body?"

I ran out of knives, and not a single one stuck.

Fiona's eyes widened, and her hand shot over her mouth. "Venn's been doing drugs? How long?"

"I don't know," I said. "Since he came back from Detroit, I guess. Maybe even since we got off the island."

Teagan froze and blinked a few times, like she was trying to absorb it. "I knew he'd been acting strange, but I thought it was from losing his brother."

"Look, I get trying to deal with the pain, but why didn't he come to me?" My anger began to melt into pain. The three of us started toward the target to retrieve the knives. "I know he's been going through withdrawals, too. I can tell by the way he's been acting. But I don't get it. I was fed on more while we were on Gregor Island, and I feel fine now."

"But Venn had been fed on for years," Fiona pointed out. "If a vampire bit him on the island, all of that would come rushing back. He'd have to go through the whole recovery process over again."

"The whole thing?"

"It wouldn't be as bad as last time," Teagan said, "but it'd be worse than what you've experienced."

We all just stood there in silence for several moments, like we were waiting for someone else to say something. Fiona's eyes were beginning to brim with tears.

"Come on," I said.

We returned to our spot in front of the target, and I started throwing the knives again. The first one stuck in the target, and I felt a small surge of victory.

I sighed. "I'm just conflicted. I think he's right that I don't know what he's going through, but he's not even giving me a chance. We're supposed to be a team, and I don't think we can do that when he's hiding things from me."

I bit my lower lip. "The truth is, I'm worried about him."

"I think we need to get you out of here," Sondra suggested. I hadn't even realized she'd come up behind me, or that she'd been listening. "You and Venn both need to cool down, then you can talk once you're both in a better mindset. How does that sound?"

"It sounds great," I said honestly. "But Venn…"

"We'll talk to him," Teagan offered.

"Yeah," Fiona agreed. "You don't have to worry."

"What are we going to do?" I asked Sondra.

"I'm still unable to get ahold of those friends of a friend I was telling you about. I'm starting to worry. I'd like to visit them in person. Are you up for a drive?" Sondra asked.

If this was anything like our last two visits, there was no way I was missing out. I had to burn off some of my energy if I was going to face Venn with a clear head.

"Absolutely."

19

The car ride was under an hour, but it seemed longer. Teagan insisted Ryland come along because she knew he'd only make things worse if he spoke to Venn about the drugs. Ryland agreed because he was *sick of missing out on all the fun*.

"And here I thought you were just scared," I teased.

"Hey," he joked back. "You want a rematch on that arm wrestle?"

"No thanks."

Ryland would crush me.

Genevieve also came along. We thought she'd be able to help us convince these people to join us.

It was late afternoon when we exited the highway. We drove another twenty minutes past endless farm fields. I was starting to think we might be lost, but then Genevieve pulled off the road and down a long country driveway. We stopped at a large house nestled in a small cluster of trees. It was large and looked only a few years old. It had multiple peaks made of different colored bricks and a large porch on the front. It looked like it belonged in some sort of architecture magazine.

"You're sure this is it?" Ryland asked.

"This is the only address listed for Carla and Adrien Bell," Sondra said. "So it better be right."

The air was unusually cool for the end of summer when we stepped out of the car. It was quiet, too, like the family had abandoned the property. I glanced around for signs of a vehicle, but I didn't see any, though that didn't mean no one was around. There was a two-car garage attached to the house.

Sondra knocked on the door.

"Maybe they're not home," I suggested while we waited.

"Or maybe they're just being cautious," Sondra replied.

I glanced to Ryland. Yeah, he'd definitely send off alarm bells. He was kind of scary.

Sondra knocked again. I continued to scan the property. As my eyes roamed over the porch we were standing on, I noticed movement in the nearest window. As soon as I spotted it, the curtains returned to their proper place, as if nothing had been there at all.

"They're home," I whispered lowly.

Sondra frowned, then raised her voice. "Carla and Adrien? We're sorry to drop in like this. I'm friends with Jordan Chase. She gave me your names. I've been trying to get ahold of you for a few days. When I didn't hear back, I wanted to check to make sure you were okay."

The front door opened a crack. A man in his forties peeked out at us. He was dressed casually and had a sort of *dad* vibe going on. The screen door remained closed between us, like it would protect him if we were unfriendly.

"You're Sondra?" he asked.

"Yes," she said kindly. "These are my friends, Genevieve, Rae, and Ryland."

"Adrien." A woman's voice came from behind the door. "Let them in. We need them."

Adrien hesitated, then opened the screen door.

The woman came into view. She looked Adrien's age, with dark blonde hair and a friendly smile. "Any friend of Jordan's is a friend of ours. Please, come in."

We stepped into the house, and the woman extended her hand out to each of us. "I'm Carla, and this is my husband, Adrien."

Greetings traveled around the entryway as we introduced ourselves, then Carla gestured for us to sit in the living room. Their house was filled with warm tones and family pictures, making me feel right at home. Sondra, Genevieve, and I took the couch. Ryland crossed his arms beside us like he was standing guard. Carla and Adrien both took a seat across from us in individual chairs.

"You'll have to forgive us for not getting back to you," Carla said.

"I understand," Sondra said. "None of us can be too careful with the way things are right now. Jordan didn't tell me you had children."

Adrien's face went white, but he quickly recovered when he glanced to where Sondra was looking. A family picture hung above their mantle. In it, Adrien and Carla sat in a pile of autumn leaves with a son and daughter who looked around the ages of five and seven.

Carla folded her hands over her knees. "Yes. Jordan said you might be contacting us, but with the kids, we were just afraid it'd be too much."

"We're glad to see your family is okay," I said. "Sondra was really worried."

"We should've called back," Carla admitted. "Things have just been really stressful around here lately."

I shifted uncomfortably on the couch. The way she said it made me uneasy.

An immediate look of concern crossed Genevieve's face. "Is your family in trouble?"

The couple exchanged a glance.

Adrien leaned forward to rest his elbows on his knees. He glanced down to his hands, like telling the story was difficult. "About a week ago, the Department of Magical Regulation came to our house with a search warrant."

I gasped. "Did they find anything?"

Carla shook her head. "No, thank heavens. But you can understand our caution."

"Of course," Sondra replied. "But you do… practice magic, don't you? Jordan said you did."

Adrien looked to his wife with concern, but he turned back to us with a sigh. "Yes, we do, but we don't profit off any of it. It's more of a hobby. We meet with a group of local witches about once a week, and we use our magic to bring fortune to our lives and others', but that's it. We're not actually sure how the DMR found out about us."

"We think maybe one of our group members exchanged our names for a reduced sentence," Carla theorized. "We haven't heard from most of them since everything changed, so it's impossible to know who."

"Jordan wouldn't," Sondra said with certainty.

"No, of course not," Adrien said. "We trust Jordan with our lives. In fact, she was the one who suggested we get rid of all our evidence before the DMR arrived. She basically saved us."

"The investigation is still ongoing, though," Carla told us. "Look, the reason we're telling you this is because Jordan said you might have an offer for us. She said you could help."

Genevieve sat up straighter. "We actually need *your* help. As Matias has been building an army, we've been building our own. We have over a dozen groups in the local area who have either donated potions or magical objects to help us or who have agreed to help us go up against Matias."

"You intend to get your magic back from him?" Adrien asked with raised eyebrows, like it was impossible.

"Precisely," Genevieve said confidently.

Carla narrowed her eyes, looking skeptical. "How exactly are you going to do that?"

Genevieve held her head up high. "Through any means necessary."

"Yes, but *how*?" Adrien pressed.

"I'm working out those details," Genevieve said confidently.

Carla sighed. "Look, we'd really like to help you, but this sounds dangerous. With the kids... we just can't commit to something like this."

Carla shot Adrien a glance, and he nodded back.

"However, we have something that might be of use to you." Carla stood and unclasped the bracelet on her wrist. "This is the only thing we kept since the DMR crack-downs."

She held it out toward us. Since I was closest, I took it and examined the bracelet. It wasn't anything spectacular, just a silver chain with fake diamonds embedded along it.

"Adrien is a therapist who works with victims of domestic violence," Carla explained. "We were working on designing artifacts that would protect women in these situations. This was our prototype. If the wearer is in danger, it will send a strong blast of air back at their command. It disorients their attacker to help them escape a dangerous situation."

"Are you sure you want to give this to us?" I asked.

Adrien nodded. "If you can defeat Matias and we get our magic back, we'll be able to make hundreds more artifacts just like this one."

"That's very generous of you," Sondra said. "Thank you."

"No," Carla replied. "Thank *you*. What you're doing is very—"

Carla cut off when the sound of tires came from outside. More than one set, too.

Adrien rushed to his feet and raced toward the window. Ryland was at his side in less than a second, and they both peered out past the curtain.

Adrien swore under his breath. "It's the DMR! What are they—?"

"Everybody down!" Ryland shouted.

Before I knew what was happening, Ryland flung himself away from the window. He spread his arms wide and knocked the three of us on the couch to the floor. My head narrowly missed being smashed against the corner of the coffee table. Carla immediately dropped to the floor and covered her head.

A second later, the sound of shattering glass filled the room. Something hard bounced across the floor. Then came a sharp hiss. The room began to fill with visible gas.

"Everybody run!" Adrien shouted.

Carla's face went stark white. "Adrien, the kids!"

Ryland dragged Carla to her feet. "Where are they!?"

I shot to my feet as fast as I could and raced after them down the hall. Gas was starting to fill the house. I could hardly breathe. Carla raced into the kids' room, and Ryland followed close behind. I paused outside the door to make sure the other three were behind us. Sondra and Genevieve stumbled down the hall, covering their faces.

"Adrien!?" I cried. "Where's Adrien?"

He rounded the corner and pushed past the other two to get to the kids. Ryland burst out of the room carrying both of the children. They were each wrapped in a blanket.

Carla grabbed clothes out of the basket near the door and shoved them at the children. "Cover your mouths! Don't breathe it in."

Both children had a look of terror fixed to their faces. The boy had frozen up, while the girl was crying and reaching out for her father.

Adrien leapt into father mode and took his daughter from Ryland's arms, cradling her. "This way!" he shouted.

Just as we all took off down the hall again, the front door burst open. My heart leapt into my throat. I stole a glance toward it as I rounded the corner into the kitchen. All I caught was the sight of men in gas masks and holding guns flooding into the house.

"Everyone on the ground!" one of the soldiers shouted, but we were already moving far back into the house.

My eyes burned, and my lungs felt like they were on fire. Adrien threw open the door to the garage and ushered his wife and Ryland through. I was next, but I paused when I looked behind me to see that Genevieve had stopped to catch her breath beside the kitchen island.

Sondra backtracked to take her hand. "We have to go!"

Genevieve took another deep breath, but she looked a little disoriented. I ran back to her and looped her arm over my shoulder. Whatever gas they'd fired into the house was seriously messing with Genevieve's respiratory system, because she was hacking up a lung.

"Genevieve," I said sternly, "there's no time—"

"ON THE GROUND!" a harsh voice sounded behind us.

Genevieve, Sondra, and I all froze up at once.

"Go," I mouthed to Adrien, who the soldiers couldn't see from the doorway.

Adrien's eyes went wide, but one look at his daughter, and he knew what he had to do. He turned and swung the door shut behind himself.

"I said on the ground!" the soldier demanded.

I twisted my head to see at least a dozen guns pointed in our direction. My heart slammed against my rib cage. I'd never had to go up against guns before.

"This residence is hereby found in violation of DMR regulation three," one of the men said.

"Please," Sondra said as she held her hands up in surrender. "We don't even live here. We're just visiting—"

"Arrest them," another deep voice commanded.

As three men with guns stepped toward us, instinct kicked in. Suddenly, I was back on the streets, surrounded by a group of vampires who'd like nothing more than to suck me dry. No way in hell was I going down without a fight.

Anger and fear rose within me. I could feel the strong emotions sweeping across my body like the tingle I used to get from shifting into raven form. My whole body felt like it was alive with fire, as if for just one moment, my magic had returned. I didn't know exactly what was happening. All I knew was that I had to run.

Arrest this, you asshole!

Boom!

Everything happened so fast. One moment, I could feel the magic from the bracelet tangling with my emotions and offering to save me. The next, the air in front of me exploded, blasting back all the soldiers. Fire shot out of one of their guns, and the deafening sound filled the kitchen.

A split-second passed in which I had to process everything that had just happened. It all sank in in a flash.

"Let's go!" I took Genevieve's arm and dragged her behind me.

She stumbled, like she couldn't quite find her footing. It felt like she was fighting me, but we were in too much of a hurry. I didn't slow.

Sondra, Genevieve, and I ran through the door to the garage to find a minivan waiting there for us.

"Get in!" Ryland shouted from the open side door. He gestured frantically for us.

We stumbled inside and fell across each other in the second row of seats.

"Go!" Ryland yelled to Adrien in the driver's seat. The children sat in the back, huddled up against their mother.

"Everyone hold on," Adrien warned.

He clicked a button above his head, and the door to the garage slowly opened. I didn't even catch a glimpse outside before the door to the house burst open and a soldier in the doorway was pointing a gun at the window.

"Drive!" Ryland shouted.

Adrien didn't wait for the garage door. He slammed his foot against the gas, and we went flying backward. The minivan tore through the door, and Adrien wrenched on the wheel. Six big DMR vans were parked in the driveway, and another line of soldiers were pointing their guns at us.

He shoved the shifter into drive, but hesitated a moment.

"Go!" Carla snapped.

The car jerked as Adrien floored the pedal and swerved

around the soldiers. I ducked my head as bullets rained down on us from the back. The children sobbed.

Suddenly, three different vans were following behind us. Adrien shot a glance in the rear-view mirror.

"Faster!" Carla demanded of him. "They must have evidence against us. Otherwise, they wouldn't be here. They aren't going to give us a fair trial. This is our only chance!"

Adrien turned the wheel once again, and the van jolted as we sped over the side of the driveaway and into the field behind their house.

"Let's see how well they keep up with this," Adrien challenged.

I tried to sit up, but we were bouncing around so much that it was hard to stay upright. Beside me, Genevieve was starting to wheeze. I was concerned she might've been allergic to the gas, but when I looked over to her, I saw she was clutching her stomach.

"Oh my God!" I cried.

I didn't see the blood staining her dark dress right away, but then I noticed the liquid seeping around the wound.

"Genevieve's been shot!" I yelled.

I threw my shirt up over my head so that I was only in my bra. I balled it up and shoved it against her abdomen.

Sondra immediately jumped to Genevieve's aid as well.

"It's going to be okay," she said while she tried to get Genevieve in a comfortable position against the seat. She sounded calm, but she had worry written all over her face.

Tears streaked Genevieve's cheeks, and she stared up at the ceiling, like she couldn't quite focus on our faces.

"I'm sorry, Genevieve," I said desperately. "I shouldn't have used the artifact."

"No," she said between labored breaths. "You had to. The DMR would prosecute you, and—"

She gasped in pain as we went over another large bump.

"Stay with us!" Ryland reached over Sondra to help keep Genevieve's head up.

Genevieve groaned.

"No. No!" I screamed. "Genevieve!"

Genevieve kept one hand pressed firmly to her abdomen and lifted the other to take mine. She squeezed it tightly. She looked straight into my eyes and said, "Don't let the DMR get you. You *have* to defeat Matias."

My throat closed up, like invisible hands were trying to choke me. "Don't talk like that."

"You're going to make it," Sondra assured her. "We have those healing potions back home."

Genevieve shook her head and blinked tears away. The strong, determined expression she usually wore had melted away. She looked so frail. My chest felt heavy as I watched her. It felt as if a cinderblock were sitting on it.

"I'm sorry for everything I did," Genevieve whispered to Sondra. "I'm ready for a new start."

"No!" Sondra sobbed. "We need you!"

Genevieve didn't seem to hear her. She turned to me and never took her eyes off mine. She reached into the folds of her dress and placed her phone in my hand. "The passcode is 7427. Matias is coming. Make sure you're ready for him."

Another breath passed through her lungs, then she went still. Her hand went limp in mine, and her eyes glossed over. My stomach had never felt so heavy as I wrapped my arms around Genevieve's lifeless body. It all happened so fast. I could hardly process it.

Genevieve was dead.

20

Hours must've passed, but it felt like seconds just as equally as it felt like days. I couldn't process the time. All I knew was that it had gotten dark out and I hadn't slept yet.

We'd lost the DMR, thank God. I didn't think I could handle those bastards after what happened today. I vaguely remembered Sondra calling Fiona and explaining what had happened.

"You need to pack everything up and get out of there as fast as you can," Sondra instructed. "The DMR has Genevieve's license plate. They could be on their way now."

"Where are we going to go?" I'd heard Fiona ask. "The lake house?"

"No," Sondra said. "The house is in her name. The DMR might suspect that."

"What's going on?" Teagan yelled in the background. "Is Ryland okay?"

"Yes," Fiona said. "Just give me a second."

"Put Sondra on speaker," Teagan barked.

"I'll call Zoey," Sondra said. "In the meantime, get everyone to help you pack the cars. We need all the potions, trinkets, everything. I'll keep you updated. Can you put Richard on the phone?"

I basically didn't process anything after that. All I could do was relive the moment over and over again in my mind. I tried to shut it out—to stop feeling anything at all—but I couldn't. The feel of Genevieve's hand in mine, the look in her eyes as her soul left her body… it would all be seared in my memory forever.

An emptiness akin to the days following my parents' murder tore through me. I'd seen too much death in my lifetime. Now that I'd seen it again, it brought everything else back. It was like a black hole of death had opened up in the pit of my stomach and was trying to swallow me whole.

At some point, we arrived at Zoey' house in Nocton. It was a small one-story ranch-style house with an attached one-car garage. I barely saw the neighborhood as Ryland wrapped me in his arms and guided me to the front door.

I sat with a blanket around my shoulders in the living room, staring at the carpet but not really seeing anything. I wore Ryland's shirt he offered me and still held Genevieve's bloody phone in my trembling hands.

My hands. I tried to pretend those didn't exist, either. Because if I admitted they did, if I felt their existence in any way, I'd have to acknowledge the blood dried onto them.

I didn't really know what was going on other than Richard was dealing with the police and coroner—making up some elaborate lie that would keep the rest of us out of it, I was sure. Carla and Adrien had taken their family to a hotel, but I didn't know what their plans were after that. Would they help us fight Matias? Would they go on the run from the DMR?

I didn't know. Honestly, it didn't seem to matter right now.

"Rae." Zoey stepped into the room with a pile of clothes in her hands.

She gently set the bundle beside me on the couch. I shied away from her, turning to Ryland, who still had his arm around me. It was totally platonic and didn't really help, but I appreciated it nonetheless. Ryland always put up a tough guy front, but I knew he actually cared.

"I brought you a towel and a change of clothes for when you're ready to clean up," Zoey said.

"I'm good," I declined, but it was clearly the biggest lie I'd ever told. Genevieve had just died in my arms. I wasn't going to be *good* for a long time.

"Maybe you should clean up," Ryland encouraged. "Everyone else will be here soon."

I sighed. He was right. Nobody else had to witness the blood on my hands. It would just be cruel to shove the aftermath in their faces.

I looked up to Zoey. "Thank you."

I took the pile of clothes in my hands and stood on shaky feet. The blanket around my shoulders fell away, and cool air rushed across my skin. A chill ran down my spine.

"It's okay," Zoey assured me. "You'll all be safe here. You don't have to worry."

I shot a nod her way, but I couldn't find my tongue to speak. I *never* stopped worrying.

I carried myself to the bathroom and shut the door behind myself. I set the clothes and towel on the counter, along with Genevieve's phone beside mine. I slipped Ryland's massive t-shirt over my head, then stripped down the rest of the way and climbed in the shower.

Warm water rushed over me, but I sank down to the bottom of the tub and curled my knees to my chest. Genevieve's blood dripped off my body and swirled down the drain. I couldn't bear to look at it, so I didn't. I closed my eyes and forced myself to breathe, but it was like I kept forgetting how.

I didn't know how long I sat there, but I finally gave up on trying to breathe when the water started to get cold. I rose to my feet and scrubbed off with the shampoo and soap I found on the lip of the tub.

When I stepped out of the shower, I heard Jenna's voice from the living room, though I couldn't make out what she was saying. Some of the weight in my stomach seemed to ease. I dried off and dressed quickly, shoved Genevieve's phone in my pocket, and then hurried out into the living room.

Teagan sat on the couch next to Ryland, and Fiona sat on her other side. Jenna and Ronark stood and both fidgeted, like they couldn't sit at a time like this. Venn paced around the room, listening to Ryland's long-winded explanation of what had happened. Zoey stood watch next to the small dining room. I didn't know where everyone else was.

Venn's eyes immediately connected with mine. He rushed forward and scooped me up in his arms. I buried my face in his shoulder, as if our fight from earlier had never happened. He set my feet back on the ground and took my face in his hands. A split second later, his lips were on mine. I melted into him.

He drew away to look me in the eyes. "I was so worried after I heard..."

"I'm fine." It was mostly true. I hadn't been hurt. I just felt... sick.

Venn pulled me to his chest again. "I'm sorry about earlier."

Ugh. I didn't even want to think about that.

"Yeah, yeah, lover boy." Jenna shoved Venn out of the way and threw her arms around my neck. "You're officially no longer allowed out of my sight."

"Stop, Jenna," I said. "I'm fine. Genevieve…"

I choked on her name.

"I miss her already, too," Fiona said softly. She stood and came to my other side to offer a hug of her own.

I nodded and wiped at my eyes. If I spoke, I knew I'd start crying again.

"Why don't I show you where you'll be sleeping?" Zoey offered.

I lifted my head and nodded.

Zoey led us to the basement. It was wide open and completely finished. A couch and fifty-inch TV with endless gaming consoles sat against one wall, while a large computer desk took up another corner. In the middle of it all was a pool table. There were two other doors, one that I could see led to a bathroom and the other I assumed was a storage room.

Zoey walked over to the couch, which was piled with stacks of pillows and blankets. "I'm sorry I don't have extra beds, but there should be enough blankets for everyone."

Teagan stepped forward and took a dark navy blanket off the top. "This is more than we could ask for. Thank you for letting us stay."

"We're in this together, aren't we?" Zoey asked. "You guys take your time. We can unload everything in the morning. Feel free to raid the kitchen if you get hungry."

The thought of food made me want to hurl.

Zoey went back upstairs, and the basement fell silent. I liked the silence… but I couldn't stand it at the same time.

I took a blanket and pillow off the top of the pile. I spoke just to break the silence. "What took you guys so long to get here?"

"Ugh, don't ask," Fiona said as she grabbed her own pile of bedding. "Jenna, Ronark, and Venn were out, and we had a helluva time getting ahold of them. Basically Amalia, Clarita, and I had to load everything up ourselves."

That weight in my stomach returned. I avoided anyone else's gaze as I started to make up my sleeping spot near the computer desk. Venn was setting his up beside me.

"Where were you guys?" I prodded, though worst-case scenarios were already racing through my head. I felt betrayed.

"We were just out," Jenna said with a shrug. "It's not a big deal."

"If it's not a big deal, then you can tell me," I snapped.

"Chill, Rae," Ronark said. "It's not what you think."

I turned toward all of them, my face flaming. "How can I even trust you three after you *lied* to me?"

All three started talking at once.

"Stop it, you guys," I growled. "I don't want to hear it."

Venn reached for my arms to help calm me, but all it did was piss me off. I swatted him away and shot to my feet. He stared up at me with sad eyes before standing beside me.

"All we did was go get a cup of coffee," he assured me.

I tilted my head at him. "Is that code?"

"No! You're overreacting," he insisted.

"I'm not!" I cried. "You're acting like it's not a big deal, but it is, Venn. We aren't supposed to keep things from each other!" I lowered my voice and grumbled. "You should probably sleep on the other side of the room tonight."

"Everybody timeout!" Teagan threw herself between us. "Can't we talk this out without tearing each other's faces off?"

I crossed my arms and stared at Jenna, Ronark, and Venn.

"It's not a big deal," Jenna insisted.

"It is!" I shouted. "Because we're family, and we care about each other. We can help you."

"No, you can't," Ronark shot back. "There's nothing that can fix this but time."

"Then stop doing drugs!" I screamed.

Jenna's eyebrows knitted together, and her lips tensed. She looked about ready to slap me, but there were too many people between us. Venn's hands clenched into fists, and Ronark looked like he was about to explode.

Ryland shook his head, like he still couldn't believe it. "Venn, you said you'd never…"

Teagan pressed her fingers to her eyes. When she lifted her head, she was fuming, nostrils flared and everything. "Are we seriously going to go through this again?"

"Again!?" I exploded as pieces began to fall into place. "That's how you got over the addiction last time, isn't it?"

Venn gaped at me, like he didn't know what to say. What a jackass.

"Tell me the truth!" I demanded.

Venn raked his fingers through his hair, looking more distressed than I'd ever seen him.

I sucked in a sharp breath. "It *is* true. Why didn't you ever tell me?"

"Because it wasn't important," he insisted. "It's not who I am anymore."

"Clearly, it is!" I shot back. "Because you're doing the exact same thing."

"Well, it worked last time, didn't it?" he snapped.

Oh, hell no. Was he seriously trying to justify this? It was dangerous! I wasn't going to let him do this to himself.

"And what if it doesn't work this time?" I challenged. "We've already lost Genevieve. We don't need to lose you, too!"

The room went dead silent as everyone absorbed my words. Slowly, Venn's shoulders fell, and he took a step forward. His tone softened as he looked me in the eyes. "I never meant to keep anything from you, Rae. I just wanted to get through this on my own. I didn't want to burden you."

Was he serious right now?

"I don't believe you," I stated. "I think you're just trying to salvage your story."

Venn tried to take my hand in his, but I pulled away. "Rae, I mean it when I say that I love you with every fiber of my being. Some things are just too difficult to face—too hard to talk about. That has nothing to do with you. I told you there were things you didn't know, and I wanted to open up. But I just... I didn't mean to hurt you. I never want to hurt you, so from here on out, I'll tell you everything."

A warm, soft feeling settled in my gut. I knew he was telling the truth, but it was difficult to accept. He'd acted like he didn't trust me.

"I'm sorry," Venn whispered. "If this ruins your trust in me, I understand. But you should know that I'd give up anything to be with you."

I sniffled as I took in his words, but I didn't know how to respond. I was still mad, and I wanted to yell at him, but I also wanted to kiss him and tell him everything was forgiven. I didn't want to keep dragging this out. I just wanted to make up already.

"I'll prove it," Venn said, mistaking my silence. He reached into his back pocket and pulled out a small baggie with pink powder inside. "I'm giving it up. Now."

"Venn!" Jenna protested.

"Seriously, dude?" Ronark sounded horrified.

Venn whirled around and stomped past both of them.

I quickly followed. "What are you doing?"

He stopped in the bathroom beside the toilet. "I'm getting rid of it. It's hurt you, and I can't have that. I'd rather suffer through the thirst for a thousand years than lose you."

Venn looked to Jenna and Ronark in the doorway behind me. "I suggest you two do the same."

Venn threw his baggie into the toilet and flushed. Ronark let out a small whimper, like he couldn't bear to see it go. Jenna threw her hand over her mouth.

The moment the drugs were gone, Venn breathed a sigh of relief. It was as if they'd been weighing him down.

It seemed as though a minute of silence passed as I processed what has just happened. Venn had been right. I could never comprehend the full weight of what he'd been going through. But I knew one thing. Venn had just made a huge sacrifice for me.

I stepped forward and wrapped my arms around his neck. His body was warm and comforting. He pulled me closer to him and buried his nose in my hair. It felt like coming home after a very long time away.

"I love you, Venn," I whispered.

Tears rolled down his face and into my hair. "I love you, too. I'm sorry. I'm so sorry—"

His words cut off as I pressed my lips to his. For the first time all night, I felt like I could breathe again.

When Venn and I finally parted, I turned to Jenna. She looked on the verge of tears as she stepped forward into the small bathroom. She looked at me a moment, then threw herself forward and pulled me into a hug.

"I'm sorry, too, Rugrat," she said. "I made rationalizations I shouldn't have. I shouldn't have hidden it from you. I just thought…"

"You thought what?" I asked.

She shook her head and wiped her eyes. "Nothing. I don't want to hurt you, either, so I'm getting rid of my portion, too. I'll find a different way to get through this."

She reached in her pocket and tossed her baggie into the toilet, then turned to Ronark with expectation in her eyes.

He hesitated in the doorway, then sighed. "Believe me, I want to find another way through this, too, but…"

"We can do it, Eli," Jenna said, holding her hand out to him.

"You know I hate it when you call me that," he grumbled.

She took his hand and pulled him inside the room. It was started to get far too cramped in here, and everyone else was still watching from the doorway.

"You survived eight years on that island," Jenna pointed out. "That's a helluva lot worse than what we're facing now. It's going to be hard, but we're going to make it through."

Ronark took his baggie out of his pocket and stared down at it. "I was just hoping it would be easy…"

"This isn't an easy button, Ronark," Venn said softly. "It's a pause button. Sooner or later, you still have to walk through the fire. I know."

Jenna's hand closed around Ronark's. "We'll walk through that fire together. And get this over with as soon as we can."

Ronark took a deep breath. "Okay. Together."

Jenna and Venn spoke at the same time. "Together."

Ronark tossed his baggie into the toilet, and Jenna flushed it. She smiled as the drugs disappeared.

I took her hand. "See? I told you you were strong."

She took a deep breath. "We'll see."

"Guys!" a terrified voice came from the top of the steps. It sounded like Amalia.

"We're all down here!" Ryland called up to her.

She pounded down the steps until she was standing at the bottom where we could all see her. "It's Matias again. Something's happened."

21

We all raced upstairs and gathered in the living room, where Sondra, Clarita, and Zoey sat.

"What's going on?" I asked breathlessly. My heart pounded in preparation for whatever bad news they were about to say.

Sondra's hands shook. "Matias has attacked the DMR branch in Chicago."

The TV played footage of the destruction. The entire building had been leveled to the ground, and buildings all around it were in shambles. It looked as if a tornado had gone through the area. The images were dark, with nothing but nearby city lights to illuminate the scene. The TV anchor spoke, but I could barely process what she said as the images flashed across the screen.

"How do they know it's him?" Jenna asked. The color had drained from her face.

Clarita pursed her lips. "Keep watching."

"*At this time, fifty-seven are confirmed dead, and another twenty-four have been severely injured,*" the anchor said.

The TV flashed to a cell phone video from earlier in the

night. The five-story Department of Magical Regulation building was still standing, but high-speed winds whipped through the parking lot. The camera panned to a group of three dozen men in suits looking confidently up at the building.

Matias stood at the front of the group and looked directly into the camera. "The Department of Magical Regulation has overstepped their power, and they shall pay for it. The magical community will not stand this persecution."

Matias waved his hand like a signal to his followers. Magic of all colors swirled out of people's hands, while others looked to the skies to control the clouds. The magic wound together and swirled around the building, increasing speed until the colors blurred into streaks.

At Matias's command, the magic exploded outward in a flash of white light. The camera whipped backward, and the feed cut out.

I gaped at the TV. This was straight-up terrorism. How could Matias still think he was in the right?

"What the hell?" Teagan exploded.

"I can't believe he's killing people like this!" Fiona said at the same time.

Ryland scoffed. "I can."

"Yeah, okay," Fiona said. "I don't agree with what the DMR is doing, but those people in that building are just doing their jobs. It's the *system* that's the problem. Those people were innocent."

So was Devin.

"This is what Matias does," I growled. "He's determined to build this new world and will kill anyone who gets in his way."

"This is getting out of hand," Venn said. "We can't wait any longer. We have to end this now."

"What are our options?" Jenna asked.

"Genevieve was in contact with Matias," Clarita said. "She was trying to lure him here, to bring the fight to home field and try to get him away from the majority of his army."

"Without her..." Zoey hesitated. "Without her, we're doomed."

"No," I stated sternly. "I don't believe that."

"Then what do we do?" Fiona asked. "Take the fight to him?"

"That's too risky," Sondra said. "His army is bigger than we can take on."

"What if we partner up with the DMR?" Teagan suggested. "By now they have to take this threat seriously. Maybe they'll actually consider our offer."

"We can try again..." Sondra said, but she sounded skeptical.

Amalia stepped forward. "I'll be honest. I don't think *any* of us are in the right mindset to make a decision right now. Why don't we all get some rest and we'll reconvene after Genevieve's memorial in the morning?"

"We're having a memorial?" I asked.

"Just something for us," Amalia said. "In the back yard."

"We don't have time for this," Ryland said. "We have to fight—"

"Nothing is going to happen overnight," Amalia argued. "Besides, if we're going to fight, we need to be at the top of our game."

Sondra stood. "Amalia's right. Let's take the night to each give it some thought and we'll figure out what to do in the morning. It's been a long day."

Everyone agreed, and the group dispersed.

Downstairs, Venn and I lay next to one another on the floor. I snuggled tightly under my blanket and faced him. His face was only inches from mine as we talked in low whispers.

"Venn, is this mission hopeless?" I asked.

He thought about it for a moment, then shook his head. "No. I don't think so."

"Maybe this whole thing was a bad idea," I said, though I wasn't sure I truly believed that. "Going after Matias, I mean. The DMR will take care of him, right?"

Venn frowned. "His men just leveled a DMR branch."

"Yeah, but the DMR has a whole freaking SWAT team behind them," I pointed out.

Venn shrugged. "What's that against magic? If they can't stop him, we need to be ready."

"How are we going to do that without Genevieve?" I asked desperately. "She was orchestrating this whole thing."

Venn brushed his fingers across the side of my face. I realized I was on the verge of tears as her face flashed through my memory.

"Can we talk about something else?" I suggested.

"Yeah, of course," Venn said. "I think I'm ready to tell you about what happened in Detroit."

I sat and listened as he whispered lowly so only I could hear. He spared no detail. The thought of what he'd been through sent my stomach into knots, and for the first time, I was starting to understand why he'd turned to drugs.

I reached out and wiped the tears from his cheeks. "Tell me something happy."

Venn laced his fingers through mine. "Do you want to hear about my brother?"

His eyes brightened, like he was already thinking back to happy memories.

I nodded. "Yeah. I would."

Venn and I stayed up talking for hours. Eventually, my eyelids became heavy, long after everyone else had fallen asleep. Venn couldn't keep his eyes open any longer.

"Thank you," I whispered.

"For what?" he asked.

"Making me feel better. Tyson sounds great. I wish I would've met him."

"You would've liked him," he said.

"I think so. We should probably get to sleep."

Venn leaned over and kissed my nose. "Goodnight, Rae."

"Goodnight."

Venn closed his eyes and was out in an instant. I had to use the bathroom so badly that I crawled out from beneath my secure blanket cocoon and tiptoed across the room.

It was only when I was in the privacy of the bathroom that I realized I still had Genevieve's phone in my pocket. I pulled it out and cleaned it off, the whole time contemplating why she'd given it to me. There must be something important in it.

I sat on the toilet lid and turned on the screen. I closed my eyes, trying to remember the passcode she had given me. Five... seven... were there two sevens? No, it was two fours, definitely two fours. I entered 5474 into the screen. It buzzed once and prompted me to try again. What was the number again?

"Matias is coming. Make sure you're ready for him," she'd said to me.

Why couldn't I remember what she'd said right before that?

7454?

7427!

The code suddenly clicked, and I entered it in. The screen unlocked.

I just stared down at it for at least a minute until the screen timed out and shut off again. Where did I even start?

I opened the screen again and started with Genevieve's call history. She'd made a lot of calls in the last few weeks. A few were names I recognized, like Zoey and Clarita, but others I didn't know. It all had to be part of our plan to round people up. Should I call these people?

The thought sent a wave of nerves through me, so I closed the phone app and opened the messenger app. My heart stalled in my chest.

At the top of the screen was a conversation with Matias's name on it. With my heart pounding, I opened the conversation. The most recent message was from Matias and read, *"Okay. Let's meet. When and where?"*

I quickly scrolled up to read through the whole conversation. Each text message came days apart, like Matias couldn't be bothered by Genevieve.

> G: It's Genevieve. I want to meet.
> M: Genevieve who?
> G: Genevieve Morgan. You've heard of me.
> M: Of course.
> G: Can we meet?
> M: Meet?
> G: I'm considering joining you.
> M: Come to Chicago. We'll talk it over.
> G: I unfortunately have business in Nocton. Can you meet me here?
> M: I don't make house calls.

G: Do you want me on your side or not?
M: Okay. Let's meet. When and where?

With each text message, my fingers trembled more and more. Was Genevieve trying to double cross us? Or was she doing this to lure Matias away from Chicago? I didn't know. It was hard to tell the tone of the text messages.

She was on our side, I told myself. Deep down inside, I knew it. If Genevieve truly wanted to join him, she wouldn't have ever helped us. Besides, Clarita had said this was part of her plan.

And Genevieve had placed it right in my hands.

2 2

———

I didn't know what to do. I shivered the entire night, contemplating it all. Genevieve had left the choice up to me. Did I bring Matias here right now? Or did I wait until we had more people on our side?

You can't waste any more time, I told myself. *We have to do this now—with whatever we have.*

Before I could make a formal decision, I drifted off to sleep.

I woke the next morning to an empty basement, all except for Venn, who was sitting up against the wall watching me sleep. I rubbed my eyes and sat up beside him.

"Where is everyone?" I asked in a groggy voice.

"They're about to start the memorial," he said.

I was instantly awake. "The memorial. We can't miss it!"

I took Venn's hand and shot to my feet. The house was quiet as we hurried up the stairs. French doors led out of the dining room and to a patio in the fenced-in back yard. It was dark and dreary outside, like it was about to rain.

I slowed as we approached the doors. Sondra and Clarita

stood inside, looking out over the lawn. I could see everyone else outside sitting in folding chairs with their backs to us. They whispered amongst themselves, but I couldn't hear what they said.

"Rae. Venn," Sondra said. "We've been waiting for you. Are you ready?"

I started to nod, but I found myself taking a step backward. Images of my parents' funeral flashed through my mind. It was a day like this one—dark, dreary, and cold. My mom's friend, Kathy, had planned the whole thing. I'd told her I didn't want to say anything because I was afraid I'd cry the whole time, but I didn't. Not one tear.

In the months that followed, my sorrow turned into anger. I went from grieving my parents' death to obsessing over my sister's return. When that hit a dead end, all that was left was a burning desire for revenge. Now that seemed futile.

I didn't want revenge for Genevieve's death. I just wanted my chance to grieve.

"You don't have to do this, Rae," Venn said.

I took a deep breath. "No, I want to. Genevieve deserves this."

We stepped outside and took a seat in the back row. I kept my head down to avoid everyone else's sad gazes. Richard took a cue from Clarita and stood to say a few words. He had a hard time finding his voice.

"Thank you all for being here," he said, choking up as he spoke. "Genevieve would've wanted you all here like this. The other night, she rolled over to me and said, 'You know what, Richard? I'm glad this happened.' I asked her what she meant, and she told me, 'I'm glad we lost our magic. It brought me closer to so many people. I got to tell them I was sorry. Whatever happens when we face Matias, at least there's that.' I didn't know what she meant at the time, but I get it now. Genevieve was ready to lay down her life for the rest of you, because through you, she finally found peace."

Dry sobs bubbled up in my chest. Once they started, I couldn't shut them off. Venn noticed and wrapped me in a hug, but that only made me shake harder. The image of her blood all over my hands entered my mind again. As soon as I saw that, I saw everything. Genevieve's lifeless stare turned into my parents' eyes. I was standing in their bedroom again the night the Soulless attacked, staring down at their bodies. Blood soaked my nightgown at my knees from where I'd sunk down into the pool of blood, too shocked to stay on my feet— too shocked to speak or move.

I pushed away from Venn and raced toward the back door into the house. His footsteps were close behind me. I buried my face in my hands and sank onto the couch in the living room.

Venn wrapped me in his arms and kissed the top of my head. "It's okay. You can cry."

I didn't want to cry. It made me feel weak. The Ravenite never cried.

But I didn't want to be the Ravenite right now. I just wanted to be Rachel Collins. I wanted to mourn the loss of my parents and my friend. Was that too much to ask?

Soft footsteps padded across the carpet, but I didn't look up to see who they belonged to. I already knew by the cadence that it was my sister.

"I've got this," Jenna said softly to Venn.

"I'm not leaving her," Venn replied in an equal tone.

"I'd like to speak to her privately," Jenna whispered.

He hesitated, then turned to me. "Is that okay, Rae?"

I nodded without looking up.

Venn headed back to the yard while Jenna took his spot on the couch. I leaned into her and sobbed.

"I miss them all so much," I cried.

She rubbed my back. "I know, Rachel. I miss them, too."

"Mom, Dad, Genevieve… none of them deserved this."

"Rach, did you ever talk to Mom and Dad after they died?" Jenna asked gently.

"What do you mean?" I sniffled. Was she suggesting some sort of séance or something?

"Did you ever just talk to them… like pretend they were there and they could hear you?"

"Jenna, that's ridiculous."

"Is it?"

I drew away to look her in the eye. She shot me a pointed stare.

"No. I never talked to them," I admitted.

Jenna rose from the couch. "Give me a minute."

She stuck her head out the door and gestured to Zoey, who rose from the last row and came to talk to her. They whispered a few things back and forth I didn't hear, then Zoey placed something small and metallic into Jenna's hand.

"What's going on?" I asked when she returned.

She grabbed my hand. "Come on. I need to show you something."

I pulled against Jenna as she dragged me toward the front door. "Where are we going?"

"You'll see," she pressed.

"We're in the middle of a memorial service!" I hissed.

"You need help," she insisted. "I think you really need this right now."

Jenna led me outside and to Zoey's car in the driveaway.

The keys jingled in her hand as she opened the driver-side door.

"Jenna, we can't," I objected. "I have something important I have to—"

"Whatever it is, it can wait," she said, cutting me off. "Come on."

Jenna was already in the driver's seat and had started the engine.

I sighed and slid into the passenger seat.

"Close your eyes," she instructed.

I placed my hands over my eyes. "This better be good."

"Jenna, where are we going?" I asked in a rather irritated tone. "Can I open my eyes yet?"

I'd had them closed for half an hour already.

Jenna helped me out of the car. She held my arm and guided me across what felt like a soft lawn. "Not yet. Keep walking."

"I'm going to trip over something," I argued.

"You are not. We're almost there."

Jenna came to a halt, and I stopped beside her. She grabbed my shoulders and turned me to my left.

"Okay," she said. "You can open your eyes now."

My stomach bottomed out when I saw where she'd brought me. A long stretch of grass spanned in front of us, dotted with evenly-spaced headstones. Just feet in front of me were two matching marble headstones with my parents' names engraved on them. Dean and Marissa Collins.

My legs became numb as the weight of where I was

slammed into me like a ton of bricks. I fell to my knees, shaking. I hadn't been here since the funeral.

I forced my gaze away from my parents' death dates and up to Jenna. My voice cracked when I spoke. "How did you know where to find them? You weren't at the funeral."

"I looked into it when we got back from the island," she said softly.

"Why would you bring me here?"

She knelt beside me. "Because I think you need to talk to them."

I closed my eyes and turned my head away. "This is cruel, Jenna."

She reached for my hand, and I let her take it. "I'm not trying to hurt you, Rachel. Please understand that. Can you just try… for me?"

A silent beat passed before I whispered, "I'd do anything for you, Jenna."

She squeezed my hand. "Tell them how you feel."

My throat closed up as I turned back to my parents' graves. "I… I miss them."

"Don't tell me," Jenna said. "Tell *them*."

Tears began to well in my eyes. I squeezed them tightly shut, until my eyes could no longer take the weight of the tears. Without a single sound, they began to trail down my face. I opened my mouth to speak, but my breath wavered.

"Take your time," Jenna encouraged.

"Mom. Dad." I dashed the tears away. "I miss you."

I expected Jenna to say something, for her voice to cut through the momentary silence, but she didn't. It was all up to me now.

"I miss the sound of your voices. You sang so pretty, Mom.

And Dad… you always knew what to say. When you weren't there, I didn't have anyone to tell me what to do anymore. I felt lost. All I wanted was those Thursday game nights back. I wanted to bake cookies with you again and help you on that old car I always told you was a lost cause. I wanted Mom to hug me again and tell me to eat my vegetables or whatever. I regretted not watching that cheesy horror film with you guys the Friday before it happened and not going to that Home and Garden Show Mom asked me to come to with her that past spring. I wished I would've made you breakfast in bed more often and told you just how great of parents you were. You guys did everything for Jenna and me, and I absolutely know with every fiber of my being that you loved us. I loved you, too. It's just that sometimes… sometimes I'm not sure you knew it. And I wish you did."

Sobs broke out in my chest, and my head was starting to hurt.

Jenna placed her arm around my shoulder and whispered, "They knew, Rugrat. They knew."

Memories of that night pushed their way into my mind again. This time, I didn't shut them out. This time, I relived every moment until I curled into a ball at my parents' graves and wept until I could weep no more.

It was the summer after my Sophomore year of high school, just days after the school year had ended. I was looking forward to our mini vacation that weekend. Mom and Dad were planning a surprise stay at a waterpark resort for Jenna, to celebrate her graduation. I'd been dreaming about it when the sounds of screams jolted me from my sleep. I'd completely frozen up as my body trembled in fear. I sat straight upright in bed and pulled the blanket close to my chest, as if it could save me from the monsters like it did when I was a kid.

Heavy footsteps pounded up the stairs. I glanced around franti-

cally for a place to hide. Under the bed wasn't an option, since it was too low to the ground to fit under. I raced over to my closet.

"No, she's mine," a deep voice said from my sister's room beside mine.

"Rugrat!" Jenna shrieked. "Run!"

My heart leapt into my throat, and my whole body quaked. A warm tingle rushed down my spine, and the room seemed to grow around me as my pajamas fell to the ground. It was the first time I'd ever shifted. Instinct I couldn't understand at the time kicked in. I flapped my wings and landed atop my bookcase. I crouched low in the darkness, hiding in the small space between the top shelf and the ceiling.

My door burst open, sending my heart pounding a million miles per hour. I held my breath and watched as a huge silhouette stormed into the room. He grabbed for my sheets on the bed but only found them empty. The man growled and flipped my mattress, then angrily stomped over to my closet. He yanked on the sliding door so hard that it came off its track.

"There's no one here!" he barked to the other men.

"Look harder," the other snapped back. "Search everywhere!"

The man in my room stepped into the dim moonlight coming from my window. It was only then that I noticed his pale features and silver eyes. Sharp, threatening fangs protruded from his mouth. I could even see a deep scar above his right eyebrow, which was weird, considering vampires had incredible healing abilities. Someone must've done some serious damage for that scar to stick around.

I crouched down even lower, trying to flatten myself against the shelf as his angry eyes scanned the room. I feared he'd seen me when his eyes flickered upward. My tiny raven heart hammered as he reached up toward me. In the light of the moon, I caught sight of the Soulless mark on his wrist.

He let out a primal scream and knocked all the books off the shelf below me, then stormed out of the room.

"Forget it, Silas," a voice said outside my doorway. "We have the girl. Let's go."

"Let me go, you son of a—" Jenna's words fell dead, as if someone was covering her mouth. It was in that moment that I realized I'd made a terrible mistake. I shouldn't have hidden. I should've fought.

I swooped down from my perch atop the bookcase and flapped my wings as hard as I could. I nearly rammed into the wall across from my room, but I corrected my flight on instinct. The men's footsteps had already faded down the hall and were at the front door. I flew down the stairs and toward the front door, but it had already closed behind them. I quickly shifted back into human form and wrenched the door open as fast as I could. I raced outside in nothing but my birthday suit, only to find a large windowless van already pulling away down the street. My stomach bottomed out.

My sister was gone.

I could hardly process any of it as I turned back inside, my limbs shaking. I was in so much shock that I barely noticed the broken glass everywhere. I didn't know how long I stood there, trying to understand what had just happened. It was like I wasn't even in my own body anymore, like I was watching it all from above and just going through the motions. It struck me to call the police, but my throat was so tight that I didn't think I could speak.

Mom had left a pile of clean clothes in a basket on the couch. When I saw it, a little voice in the back of my head told me to put something on. It was the easy thing to do right now. I grabbed one of Mom's nightgowns and slipped it over my head.

I didn't want to go to my parents' room. I didn't want to see the damage. But I had to check on them—just in case.

My legs carried me down the hall, but it was as if my mind was elsewhere, like it was stuck the moment before I'd heard the screams.

None of this felt real. It was like I was living my worst nightmare. But the nightmare only got worse.

In my parents' room, the moonlight illuminated their bodies. They were both slumped on the floor next to the bed. Blood pooled out from their bodies, mixing together between them. It was like a scene straight from a horror movie, where the blood was slashed all over the walls, on their clothes, the bed... everything.

I suddenly couldn't feel anything at all. My vision clouded over as I sank to my knees in their blood. Long wounds were slashed across their necks, as if the vampires had ripped their throats out with their teeth.

I was still shaking in a pool of their blood when the police arrived. I didn't know who had called them, but I assumed it was a neighbor who'd heard the screams. I vaguely remembered answering some questions and being told "everything would be all right."

All I could remember thinking was, You're wrong. Nothing will be okay every again.

Jenna held me while I cried at the foot of my parents' graves. I didn't know how long we sat there, but it must've been at least an hour of silence. With each passing breath, it felt like I was removing that ton of bricks weighing me down one at a time. When my tears finally dried, it felt like a huge weight had been lifted off my chest. I raised my head and wiped at my face. Jenna's eyes were red like mine, though she hadn't made a sound. I didn't realize until now that she'd been crying.

"Thank you, Jenna," I whispered.

"Do you feel better?" she asked.

I didn't feel like I should. Visiting my parents' graves should've left a hole inside of me the size of a bowling ball. That's why I had avoided coming here for so long. But instead, it was as if that hole had been stitched up.

I nodded honestly. "Yeah. I think I've held those feelings in too long."

"Me too, Rach."

I pulled Jenna into a hug. "I'm glad you brought me here."

"Should we get back?" she suggested.

"Yeah—" I started, but I cut off when I suddenly remembered something. "Oh my God, Jenna! I didn't get a chance to tell anyone this morning."

I reached into my pocket and pulled out Genevieve's phone. The battery was on the verge of dying, but it had just enough juice left that I could show Jenna the text messages. Her jaw dropped when she saw them.

"Genevieve said we had to defeat him," I told her. "We should respond, shouldn't we?"

She looked speechless but said, "Yes, of course we should, but maybe we should consult everyone else first. We don't want to rush anything."

"Right," I agreed. "But I don't think we can wait any longer."

I stood and took a deep breath, feeling more confident than I had in weeks. "Jenna, I think it's time."

23

When we returned to Zoey's house, we called everyone together in the basement to discuss our options.

"I know what we have to do," I announced. "Genevieve planned to lure Matias here. In her last breath, she handed me this and said, '*Matias is coming. Make sure you're ready for him.*' Sondra, can Matias use the locket to see that Genevieve's dead?"

She thought about it for a moment. "I don't think so. If he was watching her, his visions would go blank. He could guess she's dead, but he'd more likely assume she hadn't made a decision yet."

I held up the phone for everyone to see. "Good. We've been given the option to choose when and where this fight will take place. So, what will it be?"

"We're as ready as we'll ever be," Sondra said. "I say we do this as soon as possible."

"Agreed," Ryland said.

"Somewhere out of the way," Clarita added. "We don't want any casualties."

"Right," Fiona said. "But it also can't be somewhere that will raise his suspicions. Matias is smart enough to know if we're conning him."

"Let's put ourselves in Genevieve's shoes," I suggested. "If she were really going to enter into this deal, where would she meet him?"

"Her house?" Teagan theorized.

"No." Richard stepped forward. His eyebrows were tightly knitted together, like he was deep in thought. "Genevieve never met new clients at the house—only those she trusted."

"Matias wasn't a client, though," Zoey pointed out.

"No, but she would've taken the same steps to protect herself," Richard said.

"What about Bryant Park?" Fiona suggested. "It's just outside of town and almost no one ever goes there. Some of us can hide in the trees."

"Is that going to arouse suspicion, though?" I questioned.

"Not if we frame it right," Richard said in thought.

"I think it's a good idea," Amalia chimed in. "Fewer people will get hurt."

"When do we want to do this?" I asked.

Venn spoke up for the first time. "Tonight."

Nods of agreement traveled around the room.

"The sooner, the better," Fiona agreed. "It's time to get this over with."

I took a deep breath and opened Genevieve's phone to the text messages. "Okay. Here goes nothing."

Tonight. Bryant Park. I'll need space for my audition.

My fingers trembled as I hit *send*.

I held my breath. Moments later, the phone chimed.

I'll be there.

I stared down at the phone in disbelief. All eyes turned to me eagerly. "We're going to need more guns."

"It looks like everyone gets one healing potion," Fiona said as we organized the potions, trinkets, and artifacts we had gathered.

Sondra was upstairs, getting in touch with everyone Genevieve had convinced to help us. The rest of us were sitting on the ground in the basement, trying to divvy up the magic so everyone stood a fighting chance.

"I want Ryland to have one of these," I said, handing him one of the cufflinks.

"This is supposed to make me stronger?" he asked, eyeing it.

"Yes," I said. "I figure making you stronger will give us more of an edge over some of Matias's men."

"We don't know how many men he'll bring with him," Venn pointed out.

"I couldn't exactly tell him to come alone," I said. "It would've been super suspicious."

"If they outnumber us, then they'll go after our weakest members first," Venn said.

"Venn's right." Ryland stretched his hand across the pile of stuff in front of us and dropped the cufflink into Fiona's hand. "I think you should have one."

She scrunched up her nose at him. "Are you calling me the weakest member?"

"I'm saying I want to protect you," Ryland stated firmly. "You can fight bad guys. I know you can. We just need to level the playing field a little."

He turned to me. "Rae, you should take the other one."

"What about Teagan?" I asked.

Teagan's face paled. "Oh, I might—"

"Sensory enhancement!" Jenna exclaimed. "I call one of these potions."

My stomach sank. It was the same thing Genevieve had said when she'd seen those potions. I felt awful. I still hadn't had a chance to give a proper goodbye to her.

"Chill," Amalia said. "There's enough for most of us to get one."

"Hey, have you guys seen these?" Clarita held up vials of glowing blue liquid. "These ones are nifty. They give you a range of superhuman powers. The effects are totally random, but I once saw a guy turn invisible from one of these."

Ronark drew a sharp breath and shouted, "Dibs!"

I stood.

Venn reached out for my hand to stop me. "Where are you going?"

"I just need a moment alone," I told him in a low voice.

He dropped my hand, but he looked worried. "Okay. Let me know if you need anything."

"I will," I promised. I left him with a kiss, then climbed the stairs and headed out the back door. My stomach rumbled since I hadn't eaten all day, but I didn't know how much I could stomach right now anyway.

The sky was dark even though it was only mid-afternoon, and it was sprinkling out, but the rain was so light that it only felt like mist. I didn't care as I took a seat in the front row of fold-up chairs that were still sitting out on the lawn. It felt appropriate.

This seemed as good of place as any to talk to Genevieve. I pictured her standing in front of me as a spirit—caught somewhere between life and reincarnation. I didn't have all the details on how the afterlife worked, but I had a feeling she was still around, watching over us.

"Genevieve," I whispered into the damp air.

A light breeze passed through the yard.

"I didn't know you that well, but I know you were a good person. Even after the stuff you told me about your ex-husband and your father, it doesn't change what I think of you. I don't judge you for any of that, even though I know you think that makes you a bad person. All I know is that you've helped me time and time again. I don't think you would've done that if you didn't have a good heart. You changed, Genevieve, and I hope you knew just how good you were before you left. I hope you forgave yourself, because the rest of us have."

I closed my eyes and took a deep breath. The cool mist on my face felt like fingers caressing my skin, as if Genevieve were here telling me she was listening.

"We're going to miss you, but we're going to make you proud," I told her.

Silence settled over the lawn. In this dark, dank weather, it would usually send a shiver down my spine, but now it felt peaceful.

I sat there for several minutes, inhaling deep breaths through my nose and exhaling them through my mouth. I dedicated my thoughts to Genevieve, thinking of all the encounters we'd had—like when she led us to the caves to find The Wise Owl and healed us after we faced Matias there. Or when she let us stay in her lake house, then gave me the dagger that would kill Valkas. People often questioned her motives, but she had been our friend all along. She'd said it was for selfish reasons, but I didn't believe that. I think she truly wanted to help us.

The sound of creaking hinges sounded like a gunshot to my ears. I jumped to my feet and whirled to the side, where a door to the wooden fence surrounding the yard was slowly swinging open. The fence was so high that I couldn't see over it. A dark silhouette stepped through the fog and into the yard. As he came forward, I saw he was wearing a business suit and carrying a briefcase. It was so surreal, like some sort of dream. This guy *definitely* didn't belong here.

"Who the hell are—?" I stopped in my tracks when he took another step forward and I could finally make out his features.

"Leon Cavanaugh?" I balked.

Cavanaugh cleared his throat. "I don't have much time, Rachel. I'm here to make a deal. Would you like to hear it?"

"Why would I want to make a deal with you?" I spat. "You wouldn't take the one we offered."

"Because I'm prepared to offer you something better," he asserted, offering me a chilling smile. "What will it be... Ravenite?"

My blood ran cold. How did he know?

I wasn't registered as a shifter. No one but my friends knew I was the Ravenite. Unless one of those creeps on Gregor Island knew and spilled the beans...

"I don't know what you're talking about," I lied.

Cavanaugh gestured for me to follow him. "Let's not make a scene. I know exactly who you are, Rachel Collins. And I can help you."

"Help me with what?" I demanded.

Cavanaugh turned and started for the fence door again. He

slipped around it where no one would see him if they glanced out the back window.

I couldn't resist my curiosity. I joined him at the door, but I didn't step through it. I let it hang open, where I could slam it in his face if I needed to.

Zoey lived on a corner lot, so this edge of the fence faced the street, as did the front of her house. There was a shiny black sedan parked next to the curb. It was easy to guess who it belonged to.

"How did you find me?" I demanded. Seeing as Cavanaugh was here, I was just waiting for the DMR to break down our door.

"I've been keeping a close eye on you and your friends," he admitted.

My entire body tensed, and I spoke in disgust. "Did you *follow* us to the Bells' house?"

Is that why the DMR had attacked us when we met with Carla and Adrien?

"Are you admitting to being on the premises?" he challenged.

"No," I said quickly.

"The situation at the Bells' house had nothing to do with you." He waved his hand like it meant nothing.

My blood started to boil, and my hands clenched into fists. Genevieve had died! One of his men had killed her. How could he just wave it off?

He started speaking like we were in a business meeting. "I looked into your files after you visited my office, Rachel."

He set his briefcase in the damp grass and opened it, then pulled out a thick yellow envelope. "The more I looked into you, the more I suspected something was missing from your file. I did some digging, some cross-referencing, and I found these."

My heart hammered as I reached into the envelope and pulled out large photographs. They seemed to come from various security cameras. All of them were in black and white, and each of them showed me fighting some asshole vampire. They never showed my face, but it was clear by the hair and height that it was me.

"This doesn't prove anything," I said, shoving the envelope back into his hands. "That's not me."

"We'll see what a jury has to say about that," Cavanagh challenged. "According to my files, the Ravenite is guilty of at least eighty-seven murders that we know of, along with multiple breaking and entering charges and one account of grand larceny."

My eyebrows shot up. Eighty-seven? Wow. I didn't know my count was *that* high. Then again, the grand larceny charge was definitely not me, so I was guessing they'd attributed a few unsolved crimes to my name.

I shrugged. "I don't know who did those things, but they weren't me. Besides, they were all vampires, weren't they?"

"Doesn't matter," he said. "In the eye of the law, they're still human. That defense won't work now that vampires have proven their humanity was inside them all along."

Cavanagh flipped through his papers. "Let's forget about the Ravenite for a second and focus on these other charges. I have your friend Sondra Thompson on at least three murder charges and illegal operation of a magical establishment. Fiona Thompson... no murders that I know of, but definitely illegal shifting. Ryland Thompson, multiple accounts of illegal magic use, and I'm sure a few murders I can get a jury to convict him of. Teagan Perry, accessory to magical misuse. Venn Michaels—"

"Okay!" I shouted. I quickly lowered my tone and threw a quick glance at the house. "What's this deal you want?"

Cavanaugh looked pleased. "The Department of Magical Regulation has attempted to go after Matias Vayne, but each attempt has been unsuccessful—"

"Why haven't we heard about any of this on the news?" I asked before he could finish.

He frowned. "We want people to feel they're safe, Miss Collins."

Which meant they'd been desperately trying to cover up their failures.

"I know you intend to go after him," Cavanaugh said. "Perhaps you will have more luck than we have had."

"What does any of this have to do with that file in your hands?" I snapped.

"I want the Artifact," he stated in a clipped tone.

"So that the Department can control magic?" I asked in disbelief. The thought made me sick. "You're going to use magic to stop magic. Sounds a little ironic, doesn't it?"

And predictable. I knew the asshole wouldn't be able to resist the temptation. He was almost as bad as Matias—stealing people's free will to get the world he wanted.

"I admit, it goes against everything I believe in," Cavanaugh said, "but I do think this is what needs to be done."

"You want me to bring it to you instead of destroying it," I stated. It wasn't a question.

Cavanaugh nodded and waved the file at me. "You retrieve the Owl and give it to me, and I can make all of this go away."

I narrowed my eyes at him. It *was* an attractive offer. He

had enough evidence against me and my family to put us away for a long time.

"How can I trust you?" I asked. "What's keeping someone else from digging up the same information and putting us on trial?"

Cavanaugh pulled a sheet of paper from the file and handed it to me. "This is the contract you would sign with the Department of Magical Regulation. In exchange for the Owl, we would agree to grant you and your friends full immunity in your previous crimes *and* allow you to keep access to your magic."

"So that you can just ding us when we use it?" I snarled.

"No," Cavanaugh said. "If you read through the contract, you will see that you'll be free to use your magic, barring any harm to others."

I hesitated. "And if I don't hand over the Owl?"

"Then this information goes to the courts," Cavanaugh threatened. "You only have one choice in this matter, Miss Collins. Give us the Owl, or you and your friends will spend the rest of your lives in prison. I'll give you a few days to think it over."

Cavanagh left me with the contract in my hands as he turned back to his vehicle. Before he slipped inside, he turned back to me. "Oh, and Miss Collins? You tell anyone of this deal, and the offer's off the table."

I knew instantly what he was getting at. He couldn't have anyone persuading me not to hand the Owl over. With all the research he'd done, he knew I was his best shot at getting his hands on the Artifact. He also knew my family was my weak spot.

And he knew I was actually considering the deal.

24

Cavanaugh left me standing in the lawn, feeling completely torn. How could I pass up this deal if it meant protecting my family? But at the same time, how could I accept if it meant stealing magic from innocent supernaturals?

"Rae?" The sound of Venn's voice came from the back door. "You out here?"

I quickly folded the paper in my hands, shoved it into my back pocket, and hurried toward the door. "I'm here. Just needed a moment to myself."

Venn stood in the doorway looking at me. "I just wanted to check on you."

"I'm fine," I lied. My knees shook as I entered the house. I wanted to immediately tell him—tell anyone—about Cavanaugh's visit, but I knew I couldn't. I still hadn't made up my mind about it, and I knew the second I told anyone, the deal was over.

We started toward the basement, but my mind was racing. There was so much to deal with right now—losing Genevieve, facing my parents' graves, the contract with Cavanaugh… All I really wanted to do was forget about it all for a moment, to find just one ray of sunlight on this dark and dreary day. Jenna had been a huge help earlier, but not in the way I needed right now. I needed to know that once this was all over, everything would be okay. *We* would be okay.

Before I realized what I was doing, I pulled Venn down the hall. I pinned him against the wall and kissed him with everything I had in me. The weight in my abdomen melted away, and my shoulders relaxed. Warmth rushed in to replace all the cold in my bones.

I drew away from him, beaming. God, that kiss was everything. It might be the one thing that would keep me holding on tonight.

Venn smiled, looking pleased. "What's this about?"

I shrugged. The truth was, I didn't know where this came from. I was conflicted about everything right now. I just wanted to be with Venn one last time before we faced Matias.

I wrapped my arms around him and rested my head on his chest. "I just need to be with you right now."

He hugged me tightly and kissed the top of my head. "I'm here. Whatever you need."

I glanced both ways down the hall, then took his hand and dragged him into the privacy of the bathroom.

"In here?" he hissed.

He could take me anywhere he wanted and I wouldn't care.

"Where else are we going to get a little privacy?" I asked.

Venn quickly agreed by pulling his shirt up over his head.

I couldn't believe this was happening again. We'd been through so much these past few days. But I needed Venn right now as much as he needed me. I could see it in his eyes.

We wasted no time. Venn and I were on each other in seconds, our hands roaming over each other's backsides. He grabbed my ass, where I'd tucked the contract into my pocket.

Worry hit me, and I jumped back. He couldn't know I had that on me.

He shot me a confused expression, but then I stripped my pants off, and he relaxed. I tossed my shoes and jeans aside, then lifted my shirt up over my head. I stood in nothing but my bra and panties.

I helped Venn strip down to nothing, then he helped me. Our bodies pressed together as we kissed each other over and over again.

I drew away to catch my breath, then stole a quick glance in the mirror. Before, the sight of my own naked body used to disgust me. I wasn't skinny enough. I wasn't tall enough. My hair was too dark and my skin too pale. But now that I was standing next to Venn, it was like looking at a different girl. She was beautiful, and he was… there were no words.

He caught me staring at him in the mirror. "You like this view?"

"Yeah," I admitted breathlessly. My gaze flickered down our bodies, and I realized I *really* liked this view. Maybe the bathroom wasn't such a bad idea after all.

"Protection?" I asked him.

"Already on it." He smiled as he pulled a condom from his jeans on the floor. "Figured it'd come in handy eventually."

After he put the condom on, Venn guided my shoulders so I was facing the mirror. He pressed himself up against me from behind. I gasped at the feel of his warm body on my back.

"Is this okay?" he asked.

I couldn't take my eyes off us in the mirror. "Absolutely."

I bent over the counter, and Venn pressed into me. He held on to my hips, and I moaned as I watched him move against me. At the sound, Venn reached between my legs from the front and began massaging me. I moaned again. It felt so good that I couldn't help but close my eyes and simply bask in the glory of his hands on me. My breasts pressed against the cold countertop, which I liked even more. Everything felt more sensitive.

Venn rubbed harder, faster, until I couldn't take it any longer and grabbed the hand resting on my left hip. I brought it to my mouth and bit down on his hand to keep from making any noises. Venn increased his speed, until we both finished in a glorious display of mental fireworks.

We both went weak in the knees and fell the ground. The plush rug in front of the sink was warm against my back.

I struggled to catch my breath. "Venn… That was amazing."

He looked to me from where he lay beside me. "You're telling me?"

I chuckled. "I'm glad we're not fighting anymore."

Venn kissed me lightly. "Me too. I'm sorry about all that."

I reached up a finger and placed it to his lips. "Shh… It's over. We're good. Just… let me help you from now on."

He nodded. "I will."

A knock sounded at the door, and we both jumped.

"Occupied!" I called out quickly.

"Hey, Rae. It's Teagan," she called through the door. "Let me know when you're done in there. I need to talk to you."

Venn and I quickly got to our feet. I started cleaning up while he pulled on his pants.

"I'll be right out!" I called.

"That goes for you, too, Venn," Teagan said.

My face went white, and I started laughing hard under my breath. Did she know what we were up to in here?

"Shh…" Venn chuckled, but he didn't seem to care.

I dressed quickly, then smoothed my hair down. When we stepped out of the bathroom, we heard voices in the kitchen. Ryland and Teagan sat at the table, waiting for us. Everyone else was still downstairs.

"What's up?" I asked innocently.

Teagan knotted her hands together and looked to Ryland. "We… we have something we have to tell you two."

My stomach sank as Ryland gestured to a dining room chair. This didn't sound good. I took a seat next to Venn, who looked as clueless as I felt. I grabbed Venn's hand beneath the table, and he squeezed it tightly.

"First off, I want to start by apologizing," Ryland said.

"Apologizing?" I furrowed my brow at him. "For what?"

"I haven't been very welcoming to you," he admitted.

"Don't say that…" I started, but it was kind of true.

Ryland held up a hand. "Let me finish. I never should've blamed you for what happened in your past lives. You had no control over that. Things have been hard on all of us lately. I'm sorry I made it harder for you."

A hint of a smile touched my lips. "Thank you, Ryland. Apology accepted."

I thought for a moment that was it, but I could tell by their faces that they wanted to tell us something else.

"What is it?" Venn asked, sounding worried.

Teagan gazed down at her hands. "We wanted you to know that I won't be able to come with you."

I gaped at her. "But you're our best fighter."

"I know," she said in a small voice.

I'd had my suspicions for a while, but I never knew how to

bring it up. Now seemed like an appropriate time. "Did something happen on Gregor Island?"

Ryland and Teagan shared that look again.

Teagan shook her head. "No, it happened before. There was a reason I didn't go with you into the woods that night on the island, either—why Ryland and I went to the boathouse instead."

"Were you hurt?" I asked. "When they took you?"

She didn't look hurt, but something had definitely changed.

"No," Teagan said. "The exact opposite. I'm pregnant."

My jaw dropped, and Venn went speechless beside me. It took me a moment to process what she'd said, then I leapt to my feet and rounded the table.

I pulled her into a hug. "Oh my God!"

Venn finally found his voice and said, "Congratulations!"

He stood and gave Ryland one of those one-arm hugs guys shared. Ryland beamed, and Teagan hugged me back tightly.

"Thanks," Ryland said. "Now you get why Tea hasn't been able to help you. We just want the baby to stay safe."

"Why didn't you tell us?" I asked as I drew away from her.

Teagan smiled wide. "We were waiting, but we can't keep it in any longer."

"I hope we're not the first people you told," Venn said.

"No," Ryland assured me. "We just told Sondra and Fiona this morning, but we wanted to tell everyone individually rather than in a big group."

"It feels easier that way," Teagan said.

"Well, we're really happy for you," I told them.

Teagan ran a hand across her belly. "Thank you. We're just ready for all this to be over."

Venn chuckled. "Believe me, we all are."

"So, names?" I asked excitedly.

"We haven't decided yet," Teagan said. "We probably won't until we know whether it's a boy or a girl."

"How long do you have to wait?" I asked.

"Just a few more weeks." Teagan looked own at her belly. I hadn't noticed before, but now that I was looking for it, I saw she had a small bump.

"Anyway," she said. "You should probably head back downstairs. We have a lot more preparations to do before tonight, and we still have more people to tell."

When Ryland and Teagan told us about their baby, it felt like maybe things would turn out okay.

We only had a few more hours until we found out.

25

Venn stood at my side in the trees as I fiddled with Carla's bracelet. We'd arrived at Bryant Park over an hour ago, just before dusk, and there was still no sign of Matias.

"Do you think he figured out this is an ambush?" I whispered.

Venn placed his index finger to his lips to quiet me. I distinctly heard the brush of fabric as his arm moved. My senses were on high alert after the potion I drank. I could easily see through the darkness and feel the heaviness in the air, indicting further rain. I was also armed with one of Devin's cufflinks, a healing potion, a few weapons, and my trinket—a golden ring we'd gotten from Xander. I'd also drank one of those potions Clarita had said made one guy invisible, but I had yet to discover what superpower I'd drawn.

I heard the flapping of his suit coat in the wind before I saw him. Matias came down from the skies like an angel of death, levitating himself above the ground. He landed so softly in the grass that I didn't hear it. He straightened a lock of hair, then glanced around. Even without the silver eyes, he still looked sinister.

I closed my eyes and focused on my other senses, trying to get a feel for whether Matias was alone or not. He seemed to be, but I wasn't sure I trusted Devin's potions enough to say with certainty.

"Oh, Genevieve?" he sang, looking deep into the trees. We had at least fifty witches and shifters on our side. Genevieve had called in more favors than I thought. I was confident we were hidden well enough that he couldn't see anyone. "Come out, come out, wherever you are."

Sondra gestured to Venn and me, and the three of us stepped out of the trees as we'd planned if he was alone.

Matias turned in our direction with a smirk on his face. "Well, well, well, I didn't expect to see you here. Have you come to join the cause?"

"We've come to make a deal," I said boldly as we stopped several paces from him.

"And Genevieve?" he asked curiously.

"Dead," Sondra stated flatly.

Matias placed a hand on his chest, like he actually cared. "Oh, bless her. I really had hoped she'd join me."

Keep dreaming!

He dropped his hand, and his demeanor quickly shifted. It was like he could only bear to spare a few seconds for the news. "So, what kind of offer are you proposing?"

Matias began to circle us, like he was some sort of animal and we were his prey.

Sondra held her head up confidently. "A trade for the Owl."

Matias paused his pacing and threw his head back in

maniacal laughter. "What could you possibly offer me that is of more worth than the Artifact?"

Venn shrugged. "Your life."

Matias's laughter quickly died, and he continued to circle us slowly. My gaze flickered downward, and I noticed he was tapping his leg rhythmically. He was trying to put some sort of binding spell on us without us noticing! I'd read about it in one of Genevieve's books.

I stepped out of the circle to break the spell before he could complete it. He looked over to me in dissatisfaction, but I kept innocence plastered to my face. He didn't seem to notice that I'd caught his intention.

"Are you threatening me?" Matias asked casually.

"Yes," Sondra said.

"We can do this the easy way or the hard way," I told him. "Either way, we'll be getting that Owl."

Matias stopped pacing and turned to look directly at us. "No. We do this my way. I'll be keeping the Owl, and you three will either join me or die. Besides, do you really think you can take me on by yourselves? In case you haven't noticed, I've taken your magic."

Matias held his palms up and began to levitate again. Lightning crackled out of his palms. "I am all powerful!"

And full of it.

"What will it be?" he challenged.

I looked to Sondra, then to Venn. They both gave me the same look, and I knew what I had to do.

I turned back to Matias. "It looks like we're playing this by your rules. Either way, one of us will die tonight. Time to find out who."

Anger built up inside of me, triggering the magic in the bracelet I wore. A blast shot out in front of me, sending

Matias reeling through the air. He flipped a few times, then landed in the ground on his ass.

"Now!" Venn shouted.

Witches and shifters came flooding out of the trees. Carla and Adrien led the charge, letting out matching battle cries as they sprinted forward.

I quickly slipped the dagger out of my boot, while Sondra and Venn cocked the guns they'd gotten from Genevieve's. Gunshots rang out around me, but Matias stood with confidence, unharmed. He stuck his fingers in his mouth and let out a high-pitched whistle.

Predictable.

Men came out of nowhere, raining down from the sky like supervillains. They all looked like clones of Matias in their dark suits. His men went toward the witches and shifters racing out of the trees.

All around us, the park broke out into the sounds of battle. I heard gunshots and the sound of magical weapons *whizzing* through the air. People screamed in agony. But I shut it all out as I focused on Matias and sprinted toward him alongside Venn and Sondra.

I gripped a vial of explosive potion in my palm and threw it at him as soon as I was close enough. He flicked his wrist, and it went flying off its trajectory. The vial burst against the ground and sent one of Matias's men off into oblivion.

Shit. I only had one of those potions left.

I smelled the scent of brimstone before fire shot out of his palms. It was enough of a warning for the three of us to jump out of the way. Three fireballs shot over our heads in quick succession. He held his hands up again and muttered something under his breath. Nothing happened. He looked down at his hands like there was something wrong.

That'd be the trinkets, jackass.

The momentary pause was just enough time for me to jump to my feet and aim my dagger at his chest. At the flick of his wrist, it went flying out of my hand. I didn't think. I just reacted. I drew back my arm and slammed my fist into his face. Matias stumbled back a few steps and wiped the blood from his nose. He looked at me in complete and utter shock.

And that'd be the cufflink.

Another gunshot sounded, but Matias remained unharmed. He must've been doing something to the bullets to protect himself.

Matias threw out his hand, and I went flying backward several feet, knocking Sondra to the ground on my way down. I gasped for breath that had been stolen from me.

Venn quickly realized his gun was no use against Matias. He raced forward so fast that he was a blur in my peripheral vision. His fist slammed into Matias's face faster than my eyes could process.

The superpower potion, I realized. It'd given Venn super-human speed.

I quickly got to my feet, as did Sondra. Her face twisted in rage as we raced toward him again. Matias slammed his fist against the side of Venn's head, casting him aside, then thrust his palm out at me. Lightning crackled from his palm and struck my shoulder. I was starting to realize it was one of his favorite spells. I went down where I stood, my muscles twitching.

As I tried to regain my strength, Matias shot a ball of red energy at Sondra's chest. She thrust her hands out on instinct and caught the magic in her hands, sustaining it as if she could still control magic.

She glanced down at the glowing ball with surprise, but it

quickly melted away as she realized it wasn't hurting her. Matias's face paled as she shot the magic back in his direction. He ducked, and the magic struck one of his men beyond us. The magic continued straight through him, like the thing that had killed Devin. I shuddered to think that had almost just killed Sondra. Her superhuman potion must've given her the ability to manipulate other people's magic.

"How did you—?" Matias started, but I'd already grabbed my knife from where it lay and gotten to my feet. I tackled him to the ground.

I didn't know how I got up so fast after the lightning strike. It should've stopped my heart, but my extra strength must've saved me. I didn't question it. I just fought.

My blade came down for his heart. He muttered a quick incantation, and my arm jerked to the side, like my blade had slammed into an invisible barrier above his chest. It sank into the grass at his side. A split-second later, it flew out of the ground and skidded across the grass, far out of reach, like Matias had used a telekinetic spell on it.

Fine. Whatever. I could fight without my blade.

Venn and Sondra were quickly at my side, coming to my aid. Their hands were inches from Matias when they both leapt back like they'd been shocked. I hadn't felt a thing.

Matias shoved me off of him, and my body rose into the air. My feet hung a meter off the ground, and a tight sensation squeezed my neck as if I were hanging from the gallows. I clawed at my throat but found nothing there. My heart hammered.

Matias chuckled as I hung there, gasping for breath. Venn and Sondra tried to reach him again, but they slammed into an invisible barrier. The sounds of fighting and death continued on around us. I couldn't look around to see who was still alive and who had fallen.

"Why aren't you… killing me?" I asked in the loudest voice I could manage. It sounded like only a whisper.

"Until your breath runs out, the offer's still on the table," Matias said, looking amused. "Join me."

He loosened his magical hold on me just enough to give me a chance to answer.

"I will—"

I was cut off as the sound of a throwing knife *whooshed* through the air. It sank into Matias's shoulder, and I fell to the ground. Matias's face contorted in anger as he ripped the knife from his flesh and turned on Fiona, who stood fifteen yards away from him, ready to throw another.

"Why don't you go to hell, asshole!?" she shouted.

In his anger, he flung a ball of black-colored magic at her. I gasped, but it never reached her. One second, she was standing in the line of fire. The next, she materialized three feet away.

Teleportation wasn't a usual witch gift. I'd only heard of two witches who were able to master it in all of history. Usually, witches avoided it because of how complicated it was. If you didn't do it right, you might leave a limb behind.

But Fiona was still in one piece. It must've been her superhuman potion. These potions were meant to be neat party tricks, not weapons, but they were serving us well tonight.

Matias stalked toward her. His eyebrows knitted in frustration while he shot magical energy at Fiona, only to miss every time. Venn and Sondra still hadn't broken through the magical wall he'd thrown up between them and were now trying to fight off some of his men.

I shot to my feet to help Fiona, but someone jumped in

front of me. I caught a glimpse of his face in the moonlight, and I realized it was Ellwood—the witch from Seattle we'd seen on TV with Matias. On instinct, I slammed my heel into his chest. He stumbled back a few feet but remained on high alert as a fireball flew out of his palm. It hissed as it rushed by me, catching the end of my hair and singeing it.

"Is that all you've got?" I taunted.

Ellwood stood between me and Matias, as if protecting his master. He smirked and formed another fireball in his hand. If that was his only party trick, this was going to be easy. I threw myself forward and clipped his jaw with my fist. I didn't give him a chance to recover before I punched him a second and third time.

On the fourth swing, he threw his hands out and caught me by the wrist. Red-hot heat rose to his palm to burn the skin beneath the bracelet I wore.

I let out a scream and shouted, "Jackass!"

Using all my strength, I shoved my fingers into his eye socket and yanked down. Warm blood rushed over my fingers as he let out a pained screech. I kicked him in the abdomen, and he went down, clutching his bleeding eye socket.

"That's right," I snarled. "I play dirty."

I quickly rushed over to where my dagger lay in the grass and dove for it. When I rolled over, Ellwood was almost on top of me. I held my dagger upright, and he landed straight on it. Shock crossed his features, and a disgusting gurgle bubbled up out of his throat. Then his body went limp.

His blood rushed over me and soaked into my clothes, but I didn't give myself time to think about it. He would've killed me if I hadn't killed him first.

I shoved his body off of myself and stood. I turned my gaze back toward Matias, but before I could spot him through the chaos, a heavy weight fell down on me from out of nowhere. Someone had jumped on my back and was pinning me to the ground. My dagger had flown out of my hand. Whoever it was, they were strong. He must've been a shifter. His hands clamped down around my throat. I tried to throw him off of me, but he just held down tighter. I didn't recognize the man, but there was so much rage in his eyes, like he had a personal vendetta against me. The sky above me started to blur as he squeezed harder and harder.

"How does it feel?" he growled.

I gasped for breath, but couldn't answer.

"Huh?" he demanded, lifting me by the neck and slamming my head down into the grass again. "You're about to die, raven shifter. Say hi to Valkas for me in the afterlife."

A Soulless, I realized.

I tried to reach for my dagger, but it was inches out of reach.

Come on, I begged. I wasn't about to let this asshole kill me. Not after everything I'd faced. The dagger wiggled in the grass, like it heard my command. It was like Matias's focus was waning, like we were gaining back some of our powers.

Come on! I shouted in my mind, willing the dagger to come to me.

But it didn't move before the man above me grunted and I felt his hands leave my neck. Air entered my lungs again, and I sucked in greedy breaths.

When I looked up, Zoey was standing over him, and a knife stuck out of his back. She ripped it out of his flesh as he fell to the ground in a lifeless heap. She stuck a hand out to me and helped me to my feet.

"Thank you!" I cried. I'd definitely been wrong about Zoey.

"Thank me later," she said as she grabbed my shoulders

and forced me to duck. An orange stream of magic flew over our heads and continued into the trees.

The sounds of fighting around me seemed to quiet as I focused on a figure in the trees. He ducked out of the way as the magic whizzed by him. The magic was bright enough to illuminate his features.

Cavanaugh? What was he doing here?

The answer was obvious. He was waiting to see if I'd fulfill my end of the bargain—a bargain I hadn't even taken yet.

Get your ass in here and fight if you want it so badly, I thought to myself.

"Down!" Zoey shouted.

Another stream of orange magic shot over us. This time, Cavanaugh didn't have time to jump out of the way. I threw my hands over my mouth as the magic slammed into his face. All I saw was burnt, bloody skin before his body crumpled to the ground. My guts ached as I witnessed him seizing in the trees.

It hit me that Cavanaugh was completely unprotected. I couldn't just let him perish this way. I abandoned Zoey and raced toward the trees.

"You idiot!" I shouted as I leaned down beside him.

He stared up at the canopy with glossed-over eyes as his body shook violently. His face was so distorted from whatever curse had hit him that it was barely recognizable. White foam had begun forming around his lips. I quickly reached into my pocket and pulled out the healing potion I had with me. I poured it into his open mouth. The potion was one of Devin's, so it would take a while to kick in. I hoped it was enough.

"You shouldn't have come! What were you thinking?" I

demanded. I could hardly hear myself over the sounds of battle all around me.

Cavanaugh continued shaking, but he found control over his hand and reached out toward me. I took his hand in mine and squeezed tightly.

"I… had to… know…" He could barely get the words out.

Damn him and his curiosity.

I shook him as his eyes began to close. "No! You didn't come here just to die."

Idiot, idiot, idiot! I wanted to scream, but I didn't.

"Stay with me," I demanded.

Cavanaugh moaned something, but I couldn't make it out.

"What?" I asked desperately. "What is it?"

He reached into his pocket with trembling fingers, then pulled out his phone. I was completely baffled. Now was not the time to make a phone call.

"Maggie… Grover," he managed to choke out.

I had no idea what he meant. Did he want me to call her, whoever she was? He pressed a button on his phone, then his whole body went limp.

"Cavanaugh?" I shook him, but there was no response. "Cavanaugh!"

It was no use. He was already gone.

Pushing past the bile rising to my throat, I reached down for his phone to see what was so important that he wanted to tell me. But I didn't touch it before a rogue stunning spell slammed into me.

It felt like someone had smashed a brick into the side of my head. I fell to the ground on my side, unable to move. The world swam around me, and all I could do was take it in. All around the park were unmoving bodies. Some were covered in blood. Others had been ripped apart by magic. Some looked unharmed but were clearly dead. They mostly seemed to be from our side, too.

Screams continued from both sides. I tried to move my eyes to find Matias in the crowd, but I couldn't. Directly in front of me, I caught sight of Venn and Sondra taking on a moose shifter alongside Clarita and Amalia.

Carla and Adrien worked as one as they fought a witch with glowing blue magic. Carla ducked out of the way of the witch's attack, then maneuvered around him. She grabbed his hair and dragged his head backward so that Adrien could shove a potion vial down his throat. The two quickly ducked out of the way as the vial exploded in his mouth, sending bits of flesh in every direction.

My eyes caught Fiona, who had just wasted her last throwing knife on a guy who was advancing on her. He flicked his wrist, and it went flying in the other direction. Purple magic sizzled in his palms as he stalked toward her. I wanted to run in and protect her, but the stunning spell hadn't worn off yet. Feeling was returning to my fingers, but I could hardly twitch them.

The guy threw the magic at Fiona, and she blinked out of existence only to appear several feet away a second later. She reached to the ground to grab her knife she'd thrown at him, then appeared at his back. She aimed the knife at him, but he whirled around at the last second and grabbed hold of her wrist. She cried out in agony, so loud that it cut through the other screams.

No! I wanted to scream, but it only came out a whimper. *Fiona!*

The man squeezed harder, and Fiona shrieked louder. He must've been crushing her wrist! She flickered in and out of existence, but it was like he had some magical hold on her that didn't let her abilities work.

Fiona let go of her knife, and it fell to her feet. He yanked on her arm, and her whole body whipped around and landed hard in the grass. He shifted into a huge, terrifying wolf and bared his teeth at her.

"That's my sister, you asshole!" Ryland voice came, and he raced into my line of vision. He aimed his gun at the guy, but when he pulled the trigger, nothing happened. He tossed the empty gun aside and snatched up Fiona's knife from the ground.

Watch out! I wanted to say.

The wolf turned on Ryland and lunged. It knocked him to the ground, but not before Ryland sank the knife into its chest. The wolf let out a howl, then snapped its jaw at Ryland's face.

The spell was starting to wear off. I pushed myself upward, but my legs still weren't working.

"Ryland!" I shrieked.

But it was too late. Blood spurted out of Ryland's throat as flesh went flying everywhere. The wolf didn't hold back. He ripped Ryland apart before I could even blink.

"No!" I shouted.

The world seemed to slow as I realized what had just happened. It all happened too fast.

Fiona looked a little disoriented, but she quickly focused when she caught sight of her brother's body lying in pieces on the ground. I'd never seen her look so angry in her life. She got to her feet, then aimed herself at the wolf, letting out a battle cry as she launched herself on top of him.

The wolf rolled over and snapped its jaws at Fiona, but she only held on to him tighter. Her arm wrapped around his neck, and her legs secured around his middle. She squeezed his neck tighter and tighter, giving everything she had into the rage. The wolf bucked and bit at her, trying to get her off of him, but she wouldn't give up so easily. A huge gash ran along her arm where the wolf's teeth had caught her, but it was like she didn't even feel it—didn't see the blood dripping down her arm and into the grass.

The wolf went limp, and still she held on. She wasn't taking any chances.

The feeling returned to my legs, and I pushed myself to my feet. I stumbled a little as the spell wore off, then found my footing and raced across the grass toward them.

But before I could get to them, hands swooped down out of the air and lifted me. I screamed as I flew higher and higher above the park. Venn looked upward at the sound of my voice, and sheer fear washed over his face.

"Rae!" he screamed.

"Venn!" I shouted back. He got smaller and smaller the higher I rose, until he looked like a mere ant beneath me. I caught sight of a white stream of magic knocking him to his side, then the park disappeared from view.

"What are you doing to me?" I demanded. I didn't try to struggle, because I knew if he let go, I'd surely fall to my death. But I sure as hell deserved an answer.

"Relax," Matias's voice sounded in my ear. "This will all be over soon."

26

Matias flew us over the countryside and into Nocton. He dropped me ten feet above a tall apartment build-ing. My ankles twisted under me when I landed on the rooftop, and I rolled across the concrete to slow my fall. He landed softly behind me.

I whirled toward him. "What is this!?"

"Isn't it obvious?" he asked, spreading his arms out wide. His brown hair was in disarray, and the buttons on his suit coat were ripped from the fight. He had a wild look in his eyes that made me uneasy. "I wanted to get you alone."

"Why don't you just kill me already?" I snapped. Seriously, what was the guy waiting for? Isn't that what he wanted?

Matias threw his head back and laughed. "Oh, Rachel. I don't want to kill you. You know what I want—what I've *always* wanted."

"You want me to join you. Why?"

He couldn't be that desperate. People had flooded in from all over the country to join him. What could I offer that the rest of them couldn't?

"Your power is unstoppable, Rachel, if only you knew how to use it."

"What makes you think I would *ever* take your side?" I demanded.

"Because it's your only option," he said like it was obvious.

"Why would you trust me?" I asked. "You could give me my magic back just to have me turn on you."

"I'd have no reason not to trust you once you saw the beauty of my plan," he said simply.

Pompous ass.

"I know what your plan is, and it goes against everything I believe in," I spat.

He raised an eyebrow. "Really, Rachel? You're against building a better world?"

"No," I stated firmly. "Just against your means. It won't work, Matias. Why can't you see that?"

"It will!" he roared, before quickly softening his voice. "It'd be a shame to kill you. It really would."

Why? I didn't get it. What was so much harder about killing me than all the other people he killed?

"You're one of the most powerful souls in all of history," Matias said. "You just need a little guidance. I could train you, Rachel. Together, we could unlock the magic that would allow us to live forever."

There it was. He'd trade a little training for immortality—because he knew he'd never figure that one out on his own. He wasn't powerful enough for it.

"And everyone else?" I asked. "Where do you stand on your followers?"

"Same place I always have," he said. "They will do as they are told or suffer the consequences."

"Then we have no deal," I snarled.

Matias and I struck at the same time. My bracelet blasted him backward as he shot blood-red magic at me. I dove behind an air-conditioning unit. The metal screeched and crumpled beneath the weight of his magic.

I quickly grabbed my last vial of magic. I tossed it over the air conditioning unit, then ducked down again. An explosion sounded, but it was at least twenty yards away from where I'd aimed. Matias must've deflected it.

My heart slammed against my rib cage. How was I possibly going to defeat him without magic to defend me? The only thing I *could* do was hope he wore out before I did. That, or surprise him.

I held my breath and listened to the sound of his light footsteps across the rooftop.

"Come on, Rachel," he taunted. "Let's not drag this out. We both know how this is going to end."

My whole body quivered. He was right. He was clearly holding the winning hand. But I'd beaten the odds before. I wasn't about to surrender.

He was only feet from me now. I leapt out from behind the safety of the air conditioner and grabbed him. I dragged him to the ground as my fingers tangled in the chain around his neck. It gave way, and the locket flew several yards away from us.

I shot another blast out of the bracelet. Matias reacted at the same time. He threw his palms out, and the blast reversed toward me. I went flying backward and flipped through the air. I almost landed on my feet, but my body kept moving over the lip around the edge of the roof. My feet slipped out from under me, and suddenly, I was falling.

Desperately, my hands reached out to grab anything. To my relief, I caught the edge of the roof with the tips of my fingers. I stole a glance beneath myself to see that my feet were dangling at least ten stories off the ground. My pulse quickened.

I quickly tried to pull myself up, which wasn't difficult with the extra strength the cufflink in my pocket gave me. But I barely made any headway before Matias's shiny shoe was pressing down on my fingers.

"Ah!" I screamed as the heavy pressure radiated across my right knuckles.

Matias pressed down on my fingers. He had that same wild look in his eyes I'd spotted earlier.

"I was going to kill you with magic," he taunted with a laugh, "but I think I like this idea better. Ironic that your wings won't save you now."

He leaned forward, and his suit coat opened. My eyes caught a bulge on the inside pocket.

"Please, Matias," I begged.

He smirked. "Ready to join me? Too late."

He pressed down harder on my hand and leaned even closer. "Rachel Collins hung from a wall. Rachel Collins had a great—"

As my last-ditch effort to survive, I reached up and tangled my fingers in Matias's inner pocket the moment he shoved me off the side of the building. The glorious sound of tearing fabric met my ears, and The Wise Owl tumbled out of his pocket and toward the ground with me.

It felt like I was falling in slow motion. My limbs reached out, as if I might catch something in the air that would stop my fall. I saw Matias's face go stark white as the Artifact fell out of his grasp. I knew the moment he lost his hold on it because I suddenly felt energized, like I could take on anything.

Shifter magic shot through me, and I spread my wings a moment before I was about to hit the ground. The jewelry I'd been carrying with me clinked to the pavement, but my enchanted clothing shifted with me.

A thrill swept through my body as I flapped my wings as fast as I could. I hadn't flown in what felt like ages, not since Valkas ripped my flight feathers out. I was glad to see they'd grown back, even when my magic was missing.

Behind me, magic slammed into a nearby building as it tried to knock me out of the air. It just barely missed my tail feathers as I dodged around it. I glanced down to the Owl in the alleyway below me to see it rising into the air.

I landed and shifted as fast as I could, then pointed my palms toward the Owl. It stopped around the third floor and wavered in the air as Matias and I fought against each other's magic.

I let out a cry of glee. I'd never done telekinesis before. I felt powerful. *Really* powerful.

I tugged harder with my magic, and the Owl went flying out of both of our magical holds. It smashed through a window in the building beside us and out of sight. Matias glanced over the edge of the building, his face paling.

I jumped and guided my body upward with my newfound power. Wind whipped my hair around, and lightning crackled out of my hands. I landed softly on the roof beside Matias.

He stepped back from the edge and smirked. "Two can play at that game, Rachel."

He held his palms upward. Lightning jumped out of them and connected with nearby buildings.

"*Quod dico facies,*" I muttered under my breath.

Matias stilled at my puppeteer spell, but the lightning continued to crackle out of his palms. In my hands, I gathered water from the air and formed it into sharp knife-like icicles, then aimed them at Matias's chest.

"Any last words?" I asked.

He chuckled. "Yeah. You think that's going to work on me?"

Rage entered Matias's features, and his face began to turn red, as if he were trying to move a brick wall.

I didn't waste another second. I shot my ice knives at his chest.

They never made it. Somehow, he broke through my hold on him. His palms shot out in front of him, and the icicles melted in mid-air.

Anger swept through me. I'd show him no mercy. This ended *now*.

I thought back to all the incantations I'd read in Genevieve's books and shot anything and everything I could think of at him.

Stunning spell.

Transfiguration curse.

Freezing spell.

Pain curse.

He deflected every one of my cursed with magic of his own, then started throwing magic back at me. I dodged out of the way and put up a shield. I could feel it weakening with each curse he threw at me.

Using my telekinesis, I tried to lift him up into the air, but his magic pushed against mine. His feet remained on the ground.

"Give it up," I warned him. "You said yourself I'm powerful."

Matias chuckled. "So am I. Looks like we're going to have to do this the old-fashioned way."

Matias came at me so fast he was a blur. His hands tangled in my shirt as he tried to take me down. I grabbed hold of his wrists and shot straight upward, using my telekinesis to fly through the dark sky.

Matias's face was only inches from mine. When he laughed, I could smell his breath. It smelled like rot. That crazy look in his eyes was even more apparent now. Matias shifted our course as we went higher and higher. I fought against him, and we jerked in the other direction.

"Just die already," he snarled.

Matias yanked his right hand from my hold and slammed his fist into the side of my face. Pain shot across my cheek, but I responded with a punch of my own. My knuckles slammed into his nose, and his head snapped backward. I'd lost the cufflink when I shifted—since it wasn't enchanted like my clothes were—so it didn't do as much damage as I wanted.

"Never," I snapped.

A ball of red magic formed in his palm. I was acutely aware of his hand heading toward my chest. I let go of him and kicked off his abdomen to distance myself from him.

Magic rained down on me from all angles as a primal scream ripped out of Matias's lungs above me. I dodged around it, then reoriented myself so I could see him. Magic shot out of my hands.

Fireball.

Boils curse.

Shrinking spell.

Matias moved around each attack. I turned my gaze forward again and quickly corrected my flight as I almost slammed into the side of a tall building.

We were blocks away from where we'd started, right at the center of Nocton. Tall hotel buildings and conference centers rose around us. People on the street below looked like ants beneath the street lamps.

I heard the flap of his suit coat in the wind and dropped several feet to avoid him. But he quickly followed and grabbed hold of the back of my shirt.

I screamed as Matias dragged me higher and higher. We landed on the rooftop of the hospital next to a helipad.

Matias flung my body around with all his strength. My head cracked into the brick safety wall at the edge of the roof. My vision blurred, and when I reached up to cradle the area of impact, my hand came away covered in blood.

Matias stalked toward me, but my eyes couldn't focus on him. Double vision assaulted me.

Matias clicked his tongue. "You were a worthy opponent, Rachel. I really am sorry."

He reached out for me, and I quickly shifted to avoid his hold. But he found my feathers anyway and slammed my body back to the ground.

I gasped for breath as his hands clamped down over my small neck. It felt like he was crushing bone. I shifted back to human form to give myself a fighting chance, but he only squeezed my throat harder. His eyes went wide in crazed satisfaction.

I grabbed his wrists and tried to burn them, but he only smirked, like he enjoyed the pain. I tried to blast him back with my magic, but all it did was send a strong wind through his hair. I was too drained.

Tears rose to my eyes.

Please, I begged no one in particular. *I'm not ready to die.*

At the thought, figures began to form around me out of nowhere. At first, they looked like shadows. Then they faded to white. Five see-through beings stared down at me. Matias didn't seem to notice the spirits.

Mom? Dad?

They nodded like they could hear my thoughts speaking to them. Tears began to fall down my face as I looked between each of the faces.

Genevieve, Ryland, and Amalia were there, too. My gut sank at the sight of them. Amalia hadn't made it, either?

How are you here? I asked in my head.

"The potion you drank," Amalia said. "It made you a medium—just for tonight."

I began to cry harder. *Why are you here? I'll be with you soon.*

Mom shook her head. I couldn't believe I was seeing her face again. "Not yet, Rachel."

She leaned down and placed a transparent hand to my head. It felt like a cool breeze across my skin.

I hesitated. If I waited it out just a few more seconds, I could be with them again. We didn't have to move on to a new life. They'd waited in the afterlife this long for me. We could just stay there forever.

"Rachel," Dad whispered. "You can't give up. You have more work to do here."

"Please, Rae," Ryland begged. "Everyone else needs you."

"Fight him, Rachel," Genevieve encouraged. "You're stronger than him. You have more than he does."

More than he does? I thought to myself. Clearly, our powers were matched. I might've had more strength inside of me, but I hadn't exercised it. I'd need more time. Time I didn't have.

As my eyes flickered between each of my family's faces, I realized what Genevieve meant. I had a family. Matias didn't.

And that was what made me stronger than him.

Gathering all my strength inside of me, I found just

enough for one last spell. I pointed my hand up toward the sky and closed my eyes.

This better work.

Red magic shot straight upward and into the clouds. It was so bright that it felt like the sun against my closed eyes.

Matias let out a frustrated scream and squeezed me harder. My airways were completely blocked off, and I could feel my consciousness slipping.

This is it.

I heard the sound of feet landing around me, then the low growl of a wolf—a familiar wolf.

Relief flooded through me. They'd seen my signal!

A primal growl ripped out across the night, then suddenly, Matias's hands vanished from my neck. I sucked in a deep breath, though my throat burned.

Yips, growls, and roars sounded across the rooftop. Shadows flashed by me. A fox, a raccoon, a lion...

The sound of an explosion burst across the roof the same time a bright green light lit up the night sky. The shadow of a wolf flew across my vision before I even had a chance to sit up.

My eyes followed Venn to see him roll across the rooftop and land beside the rest of the people who had come to my rescue. Jenna, Ronark, and Fiona had also been blasted back by Matias's magic. They got to their feet in their shifted form.

Everyone was here: Jenna, Venn, Fiona, Sondra, Clarita, Ronark, and Zoey. They all glared at Matias in rage.

I whipped my head around toward Matias and saw that he was on the ground. Three large gashes from Venn's claws marred his face, but he wore an expression of satisfaction.

I shot to my feet, cradling my neck with my hand. I faced Matias with my head held high.

Multiple pairs of footsteps approached, along with the sound of paws padding against the rooftop. I suddenly felt stronger—like just having my family here had restored my energy.

Sondra whispered just loud enough for me to hear. "Ready when you are."

"Perhaps I was wrong about you, Rachel," Matias chuckled, wiping the blood from his eyes. "I thought you were strong, but you're weak for relying on others."

"You're wrong," I said boldly. "I'm strong *because* of them."

He laughed. "You're nothing—"

"Now!" I shouted.

Matias lifted his palms, but we were faster. Sondra, Clarita, Zoey, and I used our magic to lift his body up in the air and bind his arms at his side. He struggled but couldn't get out of our hold.

"You're making... a big... mistake," Matias said through struggled breath.

"No," I said firmly. "I don't think I am."

Venn nudged my hand with his nose. I glanced down into his dark wolf eyes, and I was overcome with a sense of love—of belonging. Jenna came to my side in racoon form and sat at my feet. Warmth filled my chest.

My eyes swept over the others—the witches and shifters standing at my side and the spirits no one else could see. A magic I'd never felt before rose up within me. It felt strong, like electricity sizzling straight into my bones and across my skin. I knew what I had to do.

I walked forward until I was just feet from Matias's hovering form. "This is why your plan would never work. All you want is control."

He let out a chilling laugh. "How else do you get people to comply?"

"You treat them like *people*!" I shouted. "You listen. You compromise. You *love*!"

Matias's features hardened as he continued to struggle out of the witches' hold. "You can burn in hell, Rachel."

I smirked. "I'll meet you there."

I slammed my palm into his chest. Blinding white light shot out of my hand and into his body. He let out a scream so loud it echoed off the buildings around us. The white light built within him until his skin was lit up like the sun.

Boom!

Matias's body exploded in a dazzling array of tiny white stars. There was no blood. No flesh. Just a firework display of white light.

I dropped to my knees as all the energy drained out of me. The lights faded, and the city turned back to night.

I was vaguely aware of arms wrapping around me. It smelled like Jenna, then came Venn's scent as he knelt beside me. I looked up to Mom and Dad, who smiled back at me. A single tear streaked my face as the five spirits began to fade.

"I love you," I whispered out loud.

The five of them whispered back in unison. "We love you, too."

Then they were gone.

Jenna mistook my confession as directed at her. "I love you, too, Rugrat."

I dashed the tears from my cheeks. "How did you get here so fast?"

"We all felt our magic return, and it gave us the edge we needed," Jenna said. "We won the fight. But you were gone, so we came looking for you. We weren't far when we saw your signal."

Fiona knelt in front of me and drew me into a tight hug. "Did you get the Owl?"

My head snapped upward. "The Owl! We have to go back for—"

I was cut off by the sound of a helicopter coming in for a landing. I thought at first it belonged to the hospital, but then I noticed five other choppers hovering next to the building with guns trained on us.

Then came the sound of a voice over their speaker. "This is the DMR. Get down on the ground, and put your hands where we can see them."

27

W e were all covered in blood and bruises. None of us had any fight left in us. And so, we did as we were told.

Fear whipped through me. If the DMR arrested us, I may never see my family again. I had one last chance to say what I wanted to.

"I'm sorry!" I called over the sound of the chopper.

"It's not your fault!" Venn shouted back.

"No, I mean, I'm sorry for how I treated you." I glanced between him, Jenna, and Ronark. "I overreacted. I should've listened to you."

"Relax," Jenna told me. "It's ancient history."

"Cavanaugh offered me a deal," I told them.

"A deal?" Sondra asked.

"A pardon," I clarified. "The Owl for full immunity on our crimes."

"No!" Fiona cried. "You can't take it. The Owl has to be destroyed."

"I know—" I started, but I cut off as the helicopter landed and a woman in a red pantsuit stepped out onto the helipad.

"Don't take it," Venn insisted. "We'll serve our time. It's not worth stealing magic from everyone else."

"If anyone makes it out of here," I said quickly, "the Owl smashed through an apartment window on Fifth Avenue. Get it, and destroy it."

The sound of the helicopter blades quieted as they slowed. The woman stopped directly in front of me, with three guys bigger than Ryland behind her. I looked up and realized I recognized her. She was the vice president of the Department of Magical Regulation, the woman I'd recognized in the photo in Cavanaugh's waiting room.

"Rachel Collins," she said in a tone I couldn't read.

"I'm not taking the deal, so you might as well arrest us," I snapped.

She blinked a few times, then said, "I think you misunderstand my purpose here. I haven't come to arrest you. I've come to help."

My jaw dropped. "What?"

Vice Pres Lady glanced around the roof. "It seems, however, you didn't need our help after all."

I gaped at her. "Who... who are you?"

She reached out her hand and helped me to my feet. Slowly, my friends also stood.

"Don't you know who I am?" she asked.

"You're the VP of the DMR," I answered.

She held her head high. "President now. Mr. Robertson couldn't take the pressure of recent events and resigned. But that's not what I meant. We met two years ago, and I've been searching for the Ravenite ever since."

She didn't sound angry. She sounded... relieved.

And then it hit me. I knew exactly where I recognized her from. Her hair was different, and her features softer, but it was definitely the same woman.

"I saved you from Ivan Valerik," I realized.

She nodded. "I'm Maggie Grover."

"Cavanaugh called you for backup?" I asked.

"Yes," she said. "I'm aware of the deal he offered you, Rachel, but he didn't tell me about it until *after* he spoke to you. He was under no authority to make the offer in the first place."

I crossed my arms. "Doesn't matter. I wasn't going to sign the contract anyway."

Maggie smiled. "I think you'll like my offer more."

"Oh?" I asked curiously.

"You are free to destroy The Wise Owl, and I will wipe out all evidence Cavanaugh gathered against you. You'll walk free."

Venn took a step forward, like he was protecting me. "In exchange for what?"

"Nothing," Maggie said. "You've already done your part. You saved us. How could I possibly ask for more?"

I was so overcome with emotions that I couldn't speak. Jenna squealed and wrapped her arms around me. Everyone else followed suit and rejoiced, but I could barely process their voices.

"One more thing, Rachel," Maggie said. Everyone around me quieted. "The Department of Magical Regulation will be changing now that I'm President. I've been working for years to create better, fairer laws. Now, I actually have a chance to see those laws put into place. I'd like to offer you a job as a consultant."

Jenna and Fiona squealed again.

"What?" I asked breathlessly. "Why me?"

"I read through the files Cavanaugh sent me. You have always used your magic to serve and protect. We need someone like that on our team, someone who is willing to do the right thing for everyone. Plus, you know the magical community better than anyone else in our department. You can give them a voice for once."

"I-I…" I couldn't think straight. This was all too much. It was like a miracle.

No, not a miracle, I thought. *Synchrony.*

I'd said it before. We were alive for a reason. Synchrony wanted us to restore the balance. And here was my opportunity to do that.

But then there was my family. I couldn't leave them and move to another city to take the job.

"I'll have to think about it," I finally said.

"Of course," Maggie replied. "Take all the time you need."

The thing was, I didn't need more time to think it over. I knew I'd take the job.

After tonight, nothing would ever be the same.

EPILOGUE

THREE WEEKS LATER

"*Every day is beautiful when you're sitting next to me.*"

Venn strummed the last chords on his guitar, and my heart melted. We sat on the back porch at the lake house, looking over the sloping lawn and out toward the water. The sun was warm on my skin, and a pleasant breeze rustled through the trees around us.

I took a deep breath of fresh air. "Venn... that was so beautiful. You really wrote that?"

He nodded sheepishly. "For you."

I couldn't help the wide smile that spread across my face. I reached over and cupped his face in my hands, then brought my lips to his. He fell into the kiss, his lips melting gently into mine. My heart lifted in my chest. I'd never felt so relaxed in my life.

I drew away from him but kept my hands on his face. He ran his fingers up and down my arm, soaking in the beauty of the moment.

"It was beautiful," I whispered. "I'm glad you're enjoying the new guitar."

We'd lost everything when the Soulless captured the family. I was glad to see him so happy when we'd gone into town earlier to pick up a new one.

Venn sat up straighter and adjusted the capo, then began strumming again. "I am enjoying it. So much."

I looked out over the lawn. Teagan leaned back in the grass and rubbed her belly. Fiona sat beside her, trying to perform a simple cleansing spell on a pair of flip flops.

Further down the lawn, Jenna and Ronark were doing yoga beside the water. Ronark instructed Jenna to stand tall, stretching her hands high above her head in Mountain pose. But Jenna's arms didn't stop above her head. They kept moving until they were wrapped around Ronark's neck. Jenna dragged him closer to her, and their lips connected.

"Venn!" I pointed, and he looked up from his guitar to see Ronark hugging her back and deepening the kiss.

"Finally," he said with a chuckle.

I scoffed. "Come on. They shared a room at Genevieve's. Don't tell me they weren't fooling around then."

Venn shrugged. "Maybe they were. At least now they've made it public."

Jenna screamed as Ronark hoisted her up and threw her into the water. Her legs flailed, and she landed with a loud *splash*. I could hear Ronark chuckling from all the way up at the house. Jenna sucked in a deep breath of air when her head surfaced, then started for shore. Ronark reached out to help her out of the lake, but she pulled him in instead. The two laughed as they rolled around in the water and splashed each other.

I laughed while I watched them. "This is great."

"What is?" Venn asked curiously.

"*This.*" I gestured around me. "Being with all of you. It's just so… wonderful."

Venn smiled. He set his guitar aside, then took my hand in his. "*You're* wonderful."

He leaned over and pressed his lips to the side of my face. Warmth spread through my abdomen. I tilted my head his way and met his lips again. God, I'd never get sick of kissing this man.

"Where's Sondra?" I asked when he pulled away again. "It's too beautiful to be inside."

"She's probably working on house stuff," Venn said.

For all intents and purposes, the lake house was hers now, but she and Richard hadn't finished the official closing paperwork yet. Plus, she'd been having to deal with insurance claims on the old house, and I'd gotten the feeling that was a long and difficult process.

"I'm glad she's getting it all," I said.

"What do you mean?" He shot me a questioning look.

"Everything she dreamed of," I clarified. "Fiona told me all she ever wanted was to buy a house outside the city and lead a quiet life. This seems like the perfect place to do it."

After a beat, I spoke again. "What do you think she'll do now?"

Venn opened his mouth to answer, but before he could, Sondra stepped through the back door.

"I think I finally figured that out," she said.

I looked up at her curiously. "You sound excited."

"I am." She bounced on the balls of her feet and held her sketchbook in her hand. She took a seat beside us and gave us a wide smile. "Fiona and I talked about it last night. We're going to run retreats!"

"What kind of retreats?" Venn asked.

"Magical retreats!" Sondra exclaimed. "A place where witches can come to learn the basics of magic. We have to get approval from the Department of Magical Regulation, but I think with Maggie calling the shots, we have a good chance of this working."

"Yes!" I scooted to the edge of my chair, excited by her idea. "This is a great idea, Sondra. We could set this kind of thing up all over the place. No one would have to fear their magic if they're taught how to use it."

"We also thought of running classes for non-supernaturals," she said. "They could get a chance to interact with magic and learn more about it."

I sat back in my chair and chuckled. "Maybe *you* should be the one moving to D.C. to consult with the DMR."

She laughed and looked out over the water. "Nah, I'm good here."

She turned back to us. "What are you going to do in D.C., Venn?"

We exchanged a glance. We didn't tell anyone, as we only got the offer this morning.

He sat up straighter and rubbed his hands together. "Well… Rae talked to Maggie, and while she was discussing some of her reservations about working with the DMR, she mentioned the move out to D.C. and how it might be hard for me to find a job. So…"

Sondra's jaw dropped. "They offered you one?"

I nodded eagerly. "Yes! Along with a huge offer. They want Venn on their consultant committee as a shifter spokesperson. I'll be speaking for witches."

Sondra tossed her sketchbook aside and threw her arms around Venn. "Oh my God. That's great! You two are going to have so much fun."

"I think we will, too." Venn gazed at me with soft eyes.

"Hey," Sondra said quickly, changing the subject. "I have something I wanted to show you."

Sondra led us inside and told me to close my eyes. I covered my eyes with my hands, and Venn helped guide me over to the stairs. We stopped at the base of them.

"Okay. Open your eyes," Sondra instructed.

When I did, I saw my own face staring back at me. Sondra had completed the drawing she'd been working on and had framed it at the bottom of the stairs. My jaw dropped. I was speechless. It looked exactly like me, as if someone had snapped a black-and-white photograph of my face and printed it out. I couldn't believe her level of talent.

"Sondra…" I couldn't find the words.

"I'm starting up the wall again," she said proudly. "And I wanted your portrait to be the first."

Tears rose to my eyes, and I welcomed them. I turned to her and drew her into a hug. "Thank you. It's beautiful."

"Guys!" Fiona's excited voice came from the back door.

We turned to see her rushing into the house, waving her flip flops. She hurried over and shoved them into Sondra's hands.

"I did it!" she exclaimed. "I performed the cleansing spell."

Sondra looked over the flip flops. They looked brand new, not a spec of dirt on them. Her eyebrows shot up. "Wow. Fiona, this is great."

"I know! This means I'm officially a low witch, right?" She bounced on her toes.

"Yes," Sondra said, sounding impressed. "You performed magic, Fiona. You're officially a witch."

"Booya!" Fiona did a little dance in front of us, then turned to Teagan as she stepped inside.

Teagan smiled, looking amused at Fiona's dance.

"Told you!" Fiona hurried over to Teagan, then bent to her belly. "Hear that, little niece or nephew? I'm a witch!"

Teagan chuckled, then checked her watch. "Relax, Auntie Fiona. It looks like it's time to go."

"Oh, crap," Sondra said, checking the time. "You're right. Everyone in the van."

Sondra's brand-new minivan sat in the driveway, and we all piled in—after she performed a quick drying spell for Jenna and Ronark.

The drive only took about a half hour, but Clarita and Zoey were already there when we arrived at the Nocton Cemetery. We met them beside a fresh grave.

I bent down and placed my flowers below the headstone. We'd already said our goodbyes at the funeral, but it didn't feel any easier facing his grave again.

"We miss you already, Ryland," I said, already feeling myself choke up.

Venn placed a comforting hand on my shoulder. "We'll never stop missing you, bro. We'll always love you, in this life and the next."

Fiona knelt down next. She placed a kiss to the tips of her fingers, then pressed it against his name on the marble stone. "I'll never forget what you did for me, Ryland. But the crazy thing is, I know you'll be back. You told me when Mom and Dad died that I'd never have to live without you, and even though you're gone in this form, I know you won't be gone long. I love you, big brother."

Sondra knelt beside her and wrapped an arm around her shoulder. "Fiona's right, cousin. I can already feel you with us."

Teagan knelt beside the two of them. Silent tears streamed down her face. She placed a large wreath beside his grave. "You were always there when I needed you, and I know you won't let me down now. I finally decided on names for our baby."

Teagan glanced down and ran her hand over her belly. Everyone was completely silent as she spoke to Ryland like he was here with us. "Ryland, if it's a boy, and Genevieve, if it's a girl."

"Teagan," Fiona said, leaning into her. "Those names are beautiful."

Teagan dashed the tears away. We stayed at Ryland's grave for another few minutes in respectful silence.

Finally, Clarita spoke up. "Shall we?"

We followed her to another corner of the cemetery, where two other figures stood.

"Carla. Adrien," Sondra greeted, shaking their hands. "We're so glad you could join us."

"Anything to help," Adrien said.

We stopped beside Genevieve's grave. Clarita sat over Genevieve's body and gestured for the rest of the witches to join her. Carla, Adrien, Sondra, Zoey, Clarita, and I formed a circle in the grass, while the others stood off to the side.

Sondra waved to Fiona. "Come on. You're a low witch, aren't you?"

Fiona's eyes lit up, and she joined us around the circle. "I am now."

Clarita smiled, then turned to me. "The Owl?"

I pulled it out of my bag and placed it in the center between the seven of us. We'd retrieved it—along with my trinket, bracelet, cufflink, and the Leora Locket—the night of the fight, but with the funerals and everything that followed, we needed to take time to recover before we could perform the spell.

"Do you think we have enough witches to do it?" I asked.

Clarita cocked an eyebrow at me. "The question is not about our numbers. It is about our power. Do you believe we have the power to do this?"

It sounded like a trick question, but I answered honestly. "Yes."

She nodded. "Then there's your answer. Everyone, please join hands."

I took Clarita's hand on my left and Sondra's hand on my right. My eyes connected with Venn's momentarily, and I was filled with a sense of peace. This would work.

"Where did you find the spell to destroy something like this?" Fiona asked Clarita curiously.

Clarita gave a knowing smile. "I didn't."

Fiona shot her a questioning glance.

"Magic comes not from incantations, but from inside ourselves," Clarita explained.

"Which means we can write our own," Sondra said in realization.

Clarita nodded. "Precisely. I'd like everyone to repeat after me. *The Owl's power is too much to contain. Send it back to hence it came.*"

The spell began as a murmur at first, but as we all began to hear the words, we fell into a harmonious chant.

"*The Owl's power is too much to contain. Send it back to hence it came. The Owl's power is too much to contain. Send it back to hence it came.*"

I could feel the magic pulsing through my arms, in through my left and out through my right, around and around the circle.

"The Owl's power is too much to contain. Send it back to hence it came."

The sky began to darken above us, and the air cooled around us.

"The Owl's power is too much to contain. Send it back to hence it came."

Wind whipped by my hair as we continued the incantation. I pushed away the chill and focused solely on the magic inside of me, calling it to the surface and sending it out to share with the other witches around me. Their magic mixed with my own, until I couldn't distinguish mine from theirs. The pulsing of magic through my body transformed into a powerful, constant hum.

"The Owl's power is too much to contain. Send it back to hence it came."

The owl skull began to rise into the air. All eyes followed it as it rose higher and higher above our heads. Our incantation grew more intense the more we repeated it.

"The Owl's power is too much to contain. Send it back to hence it came. The Owl's power is too much to contain! Send it back to hence it came!"

The incantation grew so loud that it seemed to echo in my ears. I raised my voice, and the others around me followed suit.

"The Owl's power is too much to contain! Send it back to hence it came!"

The Owl continued to spin above our heads, but that was it. We needed more power!

As everyone else continued speaking the incantation, I sent another message out. *Genevieve, we're here because we need you. Your soul is still here with us. You still have power. Complete our circle, and help us finally defeat this magic.*

The earth rumbled beneath our feet, and thunder cracked above our heads. Suddenly, bone shattered, sending bits of dust all around us. All that remained was a broken portion of the eye socket. It fell to the ground as the sky lightened once again and the wind let up. The earth stilled.

Nobody moved. Nobody spoke.

The dirt rose to consume the last piece of bone, then swallowed the rest of the Owl whole.

Genevieve?

We'd destroyed the Owl! It was hard to believe that after all the effort we went through to retrieve it, it was finally gone. No one would ever be able to use it again.

A soft breeze brushed across my cheek, and in that moment, I knew. Genevieve had helped us from beyond the grave. And somehow—I could feel it deep down in my gut—that had brought her the peace she'd been looking for all these years.

"We did it!" Fiona exclaimed.

Teagan, Venn, Jenna, and Ronark all looked at us in awe.

Clarita took a deep breath, then broke the circle. "It is done."

"Wow!" I threw my arms around Sondra beside me, and she hugged me back. "I can't believe it!"

Sondra laughed and drew away. "I can. We all make an amazing team!"

Fiona leaned over to hug Sondra, too. "That, we do."

Venn came up behind me, and I rose to my feet to pull him into a hug. He squeezed me tightly. "Are you okay?"

"Yes!" I exclaimed as Jenna stepped up beside us. "Better than okay."

I kept one arm around him while I drew away, then placed the other around Jenna's neck. She beamed at me.

"Nothing has ever been better," I said, pulling them both close to me. "I have my family at my side, and that's what matters."

My gaze flickered over to Ryland's grave across the cemetery. "Though we didn't all make it."

Jenna's face fell, and she dropped her gaze. I could tell by the look in her eyes that she was thinking of Mom and Dad. I never stopped thinking of them either, but now, the memories that came to mind were warm and happy—as they should be.

"No, we didn't all make it," Venn said in agreement. His eye flickered with a hint of sorrow. He got that look on his face that he always got when he thought about Tyson.

"But you know what?" he said, perking up.

"What?" I asked curiously.

Venn rubbed his hand over my shoulder, then placed a kiss on the top of my head. "I think we're all finally at peace."

My heart warmed at the thought, and I smiled. Venn was right. My family may not all be with me in the physical sense of the word, but they were still here with me—in spirit and in memory. And that made all the difference.

As long as I had my family by my side, nothing could ever stop me.

THE END

ABOUT THE AUTHOR

Alicia Rades is a USA Today bestselling author of young adult and new adult paranormal fiction. When she's not dreaming up magical stories, she's either binge-watching paranormal TV shows, meditating, or spending time with her family. She has an unhealthy obsession with psychic characters and writes with a deck of tarot cards next to her computer.

www.ingramcontent.com/pod-product-compliance
Lightning Source LLC
Chambersburg PA
CBHW061122310726
48974CB00002B/647